GHOST MARINES

BOOK 1

INTEGRATION

Colonel Jonathan P. Brazee
USMC (Ret)

Copyright © 2018 Jonathan Brazee

Semper Fi Press

A Semper Fi Press Book

Copyright © 2018 Jonathan Brazee

ISBN-10: 1-945743-23-9
ISBN-13: 978-1-945743-23-8 (Semper Fi Press)

Printed in the United States of America

All rights reserved. No part of this book may be used or reproduced by any means, graphic, electronic, or mechanical, including photocopying, recording, taping or by any information storage retrieval system without the written permission of the publisher except in the case of brief quotations embodied in critical articles and reviews.

This is a work of fiction. All of the characters, names, incidents, organizations, and dialogue in this novel are either the products of the author's imagination or are used fictitiously.

Acknowledgements:

I want to thank all those who took the time to offer advice as I wrote this book. Thanks first goes to Micky Cocker, James Caplan, and Kelly O'Donnell for their editing. And thanks to my friend, retired Marine Craig Martelle, who besides being a valuable sounding board, helped me with the Imperial Marine Corps collar device as well as the book's blurb. A special thanks goes to fellow writers Lauren Jankowski and Karen Herkes for exposing me to more of the many facets of the human condition. Finally, I want to thank Melton A. McLaurin for his book, *The Marines of Montford Point: America's First Black Marines* and Henry Badgett for his book, *White Man's Tears Conquer My Pains*. Without these books, *Ghost Marines* would not have been possible for me to write.

A few hours after I wrote the above acknowledgments, I found out that Mr. Badgett passed away a week ago on April 24, 2018. RIP, sir!

Cover by Jude Beers

DEDICATION

This book is dedicated to the Montford Point Marines.
1942-1949

BOOK 1

Jonathan P. Brazee

HOME

Chapter 1

Kollu stood alone, twenty meters in front of the jury, spear held out at a 45-degree angle, the butt resting on the ground. He looked relaxed, as if this was any other day, but Leefe knew him well enough to recognize the tension in the corded muscles across his shoulders and back.

Leefe was beside himself with excitement, though. At eight years old, this was the first time he'd been allowed to accompany the jury on an *a'aden* hunt. Granddad Qinnun, who was Leefe's maternal grandfather, had a firm hand on his shoulder, as if he were about to break free and join his cousin.

Not hardly, Leefe told himself. He was half the size of Kollu, barely old enough to hunt grazpin in the fields and far, far too small to take on a lion. Some day, though . . .

Leefe idolized Kollu. Leefe's own brother, Opor, had died on his a'aden hunt when Leefe was a baby, and Kollu had taken over the big brother role, teaching him what it took to be a provider for the people. He'd made Leefe his very first *lustig*, the small javelin with which young *ada* hunted grazpin for the family pot, then spent hours with him until Leefe was skilled enough to actually use it. More than that, his cousin always had a moment for him.

And now, standing ahead of the jury, Kollu was about to face his test. Out in front of him, the beaters could be heard as they approached, singing traditional songs praising the lion and imploring that he tear apart the impudent youth who stood alone in its path.

Leefe shifted his feet, and Granddad Qinnun tightened his hold on his shoulder, whispering, "Easy, young one. You are safe."

Leefe wanted to protest. He wasn't afraid. He had the utmost confidence in Kollu and was simply excited. But he'd promised to remain quiet if allowed to be part of the jury, and he wasn't an oath-breaker.

The singing got louder as the beaters approached. Closer and closer they came, and that meant a lion was getting closer as well. Kollu took a casual glance back at the jury. He caught Leefe's eye, then gave him a slow wink before turning back around.

Leefe caught his breath, just about ready to ask Granddad Qinnun if he saw that, only just remembering his vow of silence in the nick of time.

"The *wasilla* is close, and he's a big one. I can feel it," Granddad Qinnun said, taking a deep draught of air into his lungs.

Granddad was a traditionalist. Most of the young had taken to calling the wasilla a "lion," after the Earth animal. There was enough of a similarity between the two animals, if you could ignore the resplendent scales that covered the wasilla's throat pouch and the mane on the lion. The two were about the same size, and both were apex predators. Leefe knew that Granddad Qinnun hated the term "lion," considering it one more appropriation of the humans. He felt it was a crime against the ancestors that the People let one tradition fall after another.

During the old man's lifetime, the People warred against each other, and the rumor among the young was that he'd killed a person for his a'aden. Leefe didn't know if that was true—but he didn't know if it was untrue. It gave him the shivers sometimes, though, when he thought of it.

Most of the People, decimated by millenniums of warfare, had given up fighting centuries ago, but everyone knew that out here in the Silver Range, ritualized combat and raiding had been kept alive until the arrival of the humans. Now, while a'aden hunts were still conducted in the nethers, back in the cities, the act of transitioning from ada to aden was based on age alone.

Not with us, Leefe thought proudly. *When I'm old enough, I'm going to get a lion, the biggest one out there.*

As if answering his thoughts, the lion stepped out of the brush, standing there for a moment as it surveyed those who faced him. Leefe couldn't hold back a gasp. He'd had one or two fleeting glimpses of lions in the past, but this was the first time he'd seen one like this. He was huge! For the first time, Leefe felt a twinge of fear for his cousin.

"Ah, it's One-Ear. A good omen," Granddad Qinnun said.

The lion swept his gaze over the jury first, then focused on Kollu. Behind him, the beaters came closer, their songs getting louder and louder, imploring the lion to kill anyone standing in his way.

The lion ignored the singing of the beaters, and Leefe realized that the lion didn't need the beaters—he knew what waited for him, and he was willing—no, eager—to meet his opponent. He trotted forward a few steps, tail held high, the red tuft a signal for all sane creatures to run.

Kollu wasn't sane.

He picked up his spear, which now looked like a toothpick, and leaned into his azari stance, the butt under his left foot as he leaned over his left leg, right leg cocked to drive forward.

As if waiting for him to get set, the lion let out a roar and bolted into a full-out charge, covering the intervening distance in a flash. Kollu raised the tip of his spear slightly, and Leefe could see his muscles bunch as he waited for the impact.

Except that the lion didn't cooperate by running himself up the spear—with amazing agility for something so big, it pivoted five meters from Kollu, dodged to the right, then left again, jumping to sink his 10 cm claws into Kollu's bare chest.

Kollu had already started to lean into the spear and was now caught off-balance. Leefe's heart jumped into his throat as his cousin kept moving forward, but with nothing to stop him, fell to the ground. The lion leaped through the space where Kollu had been standing an instant before, reaching out with one clawed paw to try and snag his opponent as he passed over.

Leefe started to step forward—to do what, he didn't know, but Granddad Qinnun's iron grip on his shoulder held him fast.

The lion hit the ground on the other side, and with a back-breaking maneuver, spun around to close with the grounded Kollu. With one more roar, it pounced . . . and met the tip of the spear that Kollu just managed to raise. The roar turned from powerful to angry as the lion batted at the spear, which had barely penetrated his scaly throat.

Kollu was holding the spear in his hands, the butt free and not kept in place by his foot, so he couldn't use the lion's weight to drive him up the spear. He stumbled to his knees, then to his feet, struggling to keep the tip of the spearhead buried inside the burnt-orange beast's throat, a creature that was doing everything he could to knock the spear out of the way. Blood coursed down his throat and onto his broad chest.

Kollu started moving forward, shouting with each step as he pushed the spear deeper and deeper. The lion's struggles grew weaker and weaker, the snarls fading to gasping grunts, as Kollu managed to drive the spear all the way to the stop, a crossbar designed to keep a lion from running itself up a spear and getting the hunter into his jaws. With one last heave, Kollu twisted and threw the lion on his side. He stepped back and wordlessly shouted a victory cry into the heavens.

Leefe let out the breath he hadn't realized he was holding. Promise or not, he let out a screech of his own.

"Go ahead, son. Congratulate your cousin," Granddad Qinnun said, giving him a little push.

Leefe didn't need any encouragement. He ran at Kollu—no, Kollun, now—almost tackling the *man* as he wrapped his arms around him.

"That was amazing! I knew you could do it!" he shouted, face buried in Kollun's stomach.

"Well, you should have told me, Leefe, because I didn't know! When he pulled that fake, I thought I was a goner!"

Leefe had thought the same thing, and tears started to flow as he realized how close he'd come to losing his cousin. He held Kollun tighter, ashamed of his tears and not wanting anyone to see.

And then the rest of the jury was around them, offering their congratulations. Leefe pulled back to give Kollun room, and he was surprised to see his arm covered in blood.

"Kollu . . . I mean Kollun, you're bleeding!"

Kollun was having his back pounded by some others in his tri-year, but he bent to look over his shoulder and said, "I guess I am. That sneaky wasilla got me after all."

He didn't seem too concerned about it, and his tri-year seemed impressed, so Leefe stepped back.

He walked around the milling group and approached the lion, which was laying on his side, the spear moving with each breath he took. He looked at Leefe with malevolent eyes, and the young boy stopped well clear of the powerful claws.

Dorken, Kollun's older brother, stepped past Leefe and grabbed the spear, pulling it free with some effort. The lion grunted but didn't move. Blood pooled in the dirt, bright red against the dusty-tan.

"One-Ear's getting better, and he's going to get an aden-hopeful one of these days. Maybe he'll get you," Granddad Qinnun said as he walked up to stand beside Leefe. "Look at those scars, there." He pointed to the scars marring the lion's throat scales and chest. "He's been through hunts six other times before this."

"Is he going to die?" Leefe asked.

"Like I said, this is his seventh time, and he's a tough bastard. He'll pull through for an eighth try, I'd be guessing."

Leefe stared at the lion's eyes, which glared hate back. He shivered.

"Why don't we just kill it? Before it learns too much about fighting us?"

"Why? Because if we killed this one, and the next, then the next, we won't have any wasilla left. Then what would we do when our ada want to become aden? Do we want to be like the city folk who don't have to prove their worth?

"Bah, no thanks. We're weakening our blood, that's what we're doing. Letting the weak breed. No wonder the humans have taken over us."

Leefe had heard the old man go off on rants in this vein, and he wasn't alone in his ideas. Hope Hollow and other villages in the Silver Range might seem backwards to much of the rest of the People, but that was only because they embraced the traditions, traditions that made them strong as a race.

The old man reached between the lion's giant paws and dipped his finger in the beast's blood. The lion didn't move as the man lifted the finger to the sky, an offering and prayer for a speedy recovery.

"Well, lad, it's time we be getting back. I promised your ma that I'd have you back early. Tomorrow's going to be a big day, you know."

Kollun's a'aden hunt fell on the day before Spice Day, one of the most important holidays of the People. His stomach growled in anticipation at the thought. He looked over to where Kollun was still being congratulated. He'd planned on walking back to the village with him, but he was with his tri-year friends. Most of the older members of the jury were already starting to walk back.

Granddad Qinnun's mind was sharp, even if his body was breaking down. Leefe knew he could use a shoulder to lean upon.

"Well, if you don't mind, then, I'll walk back with you."

"That's mighty kind of you, lad."

"Not kind, Granddad. If we're late, I can blame you!" Leefe said with a laugh.

"Hah! I always knew you were a smart one."

Leefe took one last glance at the lion as the two started on the hour-long walk back. The creature's breathing had calmed down, but the hate was still bright in his eyes.

I'll come back for you in six years, One Ear. I'm going to make sure the People remain strong.

Chapter 2

Leefe had been riding high yesterday after being allowed to attend Kollun's a'aden hunt, but today was Spice Day, the absolute best day of the year. The entire village had gathered, with family coming from as far as Crooked Gorge, a three days' journey by boscart. Normally, Leefe would be pestering S'ven or Greetn for stories of plying the river all the way down to Diamondtown on the shores of the Green Sea, but this was Spice Day! There was simply too much excitement for one small boy to contain.

Already, the smells wafting out of the communal house were filling the village, and Leefe's mouth was watering. This was only in anticipation, though. This year's spice wouldn't be finished for another six hours. He couldn't imagine how this year's could possibly beat the spice mix from last year—but then, every spice mix seemed more delicious, more stupendous than any other he remembered during his short life so far.

"Let's go look," Sora said, pointing to the communal house.

"We're supposed to leave the grannies alone," Leefe said.

"How can we bother them just looking through the window?" Sora asked, hands on her hips.

A week younger than Leefe, Sora was a bad influence, as his mother kept reminding him. It wasn't that Sora was a bad girl. Everyone loved her. But the blood-kiss that ran from her throat and down her chest was the mark of an independent will. Mischief was her shadow, following her everywhere, and she usually dragged Leefe into trouble with her.

He knew better, but he couldn't imagine how simply looking in the window would bother the grannies. The granddads were keeping station at the entrance, ceremoniously pipe-smoking the last of the shoat, the mixture of spice mix and runyard leaf that they favored.

The spice mix was not only the core of the People's culinary efforts for the next year, but Spice Day was also a social highlight, second only to Equinox Day. Everyone who could came home for Spice Day, and the entire planet ground to a halt. Courier companies, both interplanetary and on Home, had long been fully-booked to bring the mix to every child of the Mother, no matter where they were.

"In the back, so the granddads don't see us," Leefe said, as the two tried to saunter casually around the communal house.

Leefe knew they were walking awkwardly, but no matter how hard he tried, it got even worse. He was sure everyone in the village knew what they were up to. He shouldn't have worried. There were eight windows on the back wall of the communal house, and it looked like half of the village was clustered around them, chatting while they looked in to watch the progress.

Not everyone was peering in the windows. A group of eight Tri-Year Fours, his sister Harra among them, was standing under the big poska tree, smoking their shoat in hand-rolled runyard leaves and drinking aleese. Harra was too young to be smoking, and she glared daggers at Leefe when she spotted him, but he ignored her. No one else seemed to care about the tri-fours, so why should he? Besides, he wanted to see inside the building.

He and Sora managed to worm their way between several of the larger adults and tried to look in, but they couldn't see much. Some of the spice dust had coated the inside of the window, and neither of the two children was tall enough to get a better view. Leefe jumped up, banging into one of the adults behind him.

"Take it easy, young Leefe," Kollun, said, the big white bandage covering his back his souvenir of yesterday. "Let me help."

His cousin lifted him up so Leefe could see the entire breadth of the building. All of the chairs had been pushed to the side, and the huge copper mixing kettle had been trundled out to the middle. As Leefe watched, Granny Oriano tipped a bag of something that Leefe couldn't identify into the kettle.

"How many ingredients have they used, Kollu . . . I mean, Kollun?" he asked.

If his cousin noticed the slip-up, he didn't react. With Kollun only being aden since yesterday, Leefe knew it would take him a while to get used to his cousin's adult name.

"This is the fifth, I think," Kollun said. "Now watch this."

"Hey, I can't see," Sora said as she tried to jump up to get a better view.

"I've got you, little Sora," Palano said, lifting her up alongside Leefe.

Nine of the grannies took their positions around the mixing kettle, spice whisks ready, then as Granny Oriano started chanting the ancient stanzas, the nine lowered the whisks, and a moment later, a cloud of spice dust rose into the air. Some of it reached the back windows, coating them even more.

"How many more ingredients are they going to use this year?" Leefe asked as Kollun lowered him back to the ground. "Are they going to make it hot, like the year-before-last's, do you think?"

"Ha! Only the grannies know that. Now, you two let someone else see."

Leefe wanted to protest, but Kollun was now an adult, and technically he could tell the two of them what to do, even if only yesterday, he was a ada just like he and Sora were. He pushed clear. Harra was still under the tree, taking a drag on her shoat. Leefe mimicked taking a drag as well, then dropping a shoat and stepping on it, grinding the imaginary shoat out. Harra's eyes widened, and she took a step towards him, but he grabbed Sora's hand and ran off. He wasn't going to tell their parents, but it wouldn't hurt to remind his big sister that he could.

"That was total-one," Sora said excitedly. "I can't wait."

"Yeah, total-one. Better than last year's mix, I know."

"One day, I'm taking Granny Oriano's place," she said as they wandered over to the square.

The People didn't differentiate between male and female for most things, but the spice mix was done as it had been for millennia. The grannies made the mix according to their rituals while the granddads stood guard. Legend was that early People did this to protect the special mix from raiders or wild animals, but this was modern times, and Leefe felt it wasn't fair. Sora could join the grannies someday, Mother-be-willing, but that was something forever out of his reach.

"Come on, I'm hungry. Let's see if we can get something," Sora said.

About a third of the village's adults were working at the cooking station set up before the House of Hope. Most of what was being done was prep work. The majority of the cooking couldn't be started, after all, before this year's spice mix was presented. Only a single dish with last year's mix was simmering away in a large, wood-fired pot. The aroma of the kabash stew made his mouth water and stomach grumble.

Leefe felt a pang of loss. This would be the last time that he tasted last year's mix, something he'd eaten in various dishes every day for the year. He loved the Puripo's Mix, named after the grannie who honchoed its making, just two weeks before she died. Suddenly, he wished he'd squirreled some away, even just a little bit so that he could pull it out and smell the woody, slightly pungent mix with a quiet kick that could sneak on on people.

Keeping a previous year's mix, though, was considered bad luck. Some of the older kids passed rumors of caches of mix going back centuries, but Leefe didn't believe it. No one would risk the bad luck. When Low Rock had been swept away in the floods last spring, Granny Oriano had said it was because the people of the town didn't follow the old traditions, and the Mother was punishing them. Leefe was sure that meant they had eaten food prepared with old mix.

Sora grabbed a piece of cut momo root from a pile on one of the outside tables. That took Leefe by surprise, but he grabbed a piece, too, ducking the swing of a wooden spoon as he darted after his friend. He didn't like the taste of raw momo root, even if he loved the pudding-like dessert his mother made from it, but he ate it anyway. It was going to be a long time before dinner.

They joined another group of their tri-year friends who were playing jump-on-it. Leefe considered himself the king of jump-on-it. A few others disagreed with him, but they hadn't beat a bunch of tri-fours last week, had they? No, he had, so he was the king. Simple logic.

He waited for his turn, feeling the competitive blood starting to well within him. It was a familiar feeling. As early as he could remember, back when he was a tri-one, he'd always wanted to win. Whether playing babies' games like where's-the-bird? or running races, he had to beat everyone else. Of course, most of the others wanted to beat him just as much, and that was what made it all fun.

Finally, it was his turn, and he quickly sent Rumme to the nana square with a double hop. Forty minutes later, he was still playing. He'd been sent to the nana square several times, but he'd sent far more of the others. Breathing hard and sweaty, he'd forgotten how hungry he'd been when the first bell chimed.

Everyone stopped dead, then erupted into a cheer. The grannies were done with the mix. Now, they'd be putting it into the molds and pressing them. In another hour or so, the adults could start cooking. His forgotten stomach reminded him that except for the filched piece of momo root, he'd eaten nothing since the ceremony just before midnight the night before.

"Oh, my gosh, this is going to be good," he told Renne and Sora, patting his stomach.

Sora punched his hand, driving it into his stomach, then shrieked as he started to chase her. With Rene and the rest of their tri-year following, he chased her through a complicated and tortuous route under tables, up and over tree branches, and even over the front steps of the communal house where the granddads sat and scolded their displeasure.

Leefe could have skipped over the obstacles to catch her, but there were forms to be followed, even for Tri-Year Threes.

Leefe was closing in on her when she decided to take the little army around the communal building, and she was just keeping out of his reach when she started around the corner, stopped dead, and pointed up in the air. Hondo was not going to fall for that trick, so he kept his eyes focused and slammed into her, ready to go into a tickle attack, when he followed her finger.

And he stopped, chase and revenge forgotten.

"Look," he said as the rest of his tri-year creche came to a stop beside them.

"A ship," Renne said, excitedly.

The People didn't have space-faring ships. They'd had lighter-than-air ships when the Empire first came, but nothing beyond that. Even now, while one of the People could charter a ship, no one could own one. Chartering a ship, however, was well beyond the people of Hope Hollow. Ships might come and go from the Imperial spaceport at the capital, but that was on the other side of the planet. Out here, in the Silver Range, seeing a spaceship, was extremely rare. Leefe had spotted some high in the sky before, but never like this.

"It's landing!" one of the Tri-Year Four boys shouted.

"It is!" Sora said, grabbing Leefe's arm. "Let's go see!"

Leefe's heart raced. Spice Day and a human ship? And yesterday, being part of a a'aden hunt jury? What could possibly be better?

As one, people started merging in a single mass, streaming from where they'd been standing, sitting, and just waiting for the grannies, then heading for the halfball pitch, a virtual river of People. Two of the granddads started to join them before being pulled back by the others.

"Total-ten to be you," Leefe said as he ran past the granddads, glad he wasn't guarding the mix and eager to see the humans.

The ship was huge, bigger than anything Leefe had ever seen, bigger than the barges that plied the river. He couldn't imagine how it could stay up in the air as it did a slow pass over the village. He raced to the field, anxious to get there before the ship came in to land.

"Give it room!" someone shouted as the first of those to reach the field made a wall, arms outstretched.

Leefe pushed his way through, followed by Sora, to get to the front just as the ship made a graceful turn, coming in to land with nary a bump as it settled on the ground, smashing the goalbox. Leefe didn't care about that. He couldn't play halfball until the next tri-year anyway, and by that time, they'd put up another one.

There were sounds of air rushing out as the ship seemed to power down. Leefe waited with the rest for the humans to make their appearance. He'd never seen a real human before, and he was a little nervous. They looked so powerful in the ubiquitous holovids they'd seeded throughout the planet. Everyone, including the grannies and granddads, who'd resented the technology when it had first arrived, now happily watched them along with the rest of the village. Even Granddad Qinnun, who complained about the tech, but watched anyway.

A low moan of expectation rose from the people when the main hatch hissed open. Leefe took another step forward before a strong arm grabbed the back of his harness and pulled him to a stop. He barely noticed, so focused was he on the hatch.

And then, as if a demon emerging from the Prime Swamp, the first human appeared. She stopped for a moment at the hatch, surveying the crowd.

She looked, well, a little ratty to Leefe, if quite colorful. On an intellectual level, Leefe knew that humans were not all Marines, Explorer Corps, Bright Company, or the rich and powerful who lived in crystal cities, but the female human was still a slight disappointment. A moment later, a male human joined her, and if anything, he seemed even scruffier. The People wore very little clothing out in the nethers. Even in the capital, where more clothing was worn in deference to the humans, the People liked to feel the air and sun on their skin. Leefe's harness was enough for him, something with which to carry things and not much else. Still, the uniforms of the Bright Company were dazzling, and Leefe had-expected something similar.

"They're short," Sora said beside him.

Leefe wasn't sure they were really that short. They were not as slender as the People, being broader across the chest and with thicker legs, and that could be skewing their perspective. He made a promise to himself to stand next to one as soon as he could and measure himself against them.

Several more made their appearance before they started to march down the ramp. The people of the village started to edge forward before a few voices called out, "Don't crowd them. Let them come."

More and more humans appeared, up to 40 or 50, all following the female as they approached them. The female, who seemed to be their leader, stopped about three meters from the people, hand on one hip, the other holding an assault rifle, and she scanned the gathered people.

Leefe waited anxiously to hear one of them speak.

She turned to the male next to her and, in the guttural Standard of humans, said, "That one," pointing at Palano, who was standing just to Leefe's right.

The male raised his weapon and fired, a blue light hitting and surrounding Palano in a blue corona. Leefe stared in shock as Palano's body tensed up, rigid with corded muscles, before he fell face first to the ground and lay still. An acrid scent burned Leefe's nose.

What? he wondered stupidly, staring at his second cousin.

The other humans started to fire their weapons as everyone around him began to scream in panic. He was vaguely aware of hands pulling at him as he stared in shock at Palano, confused.

Is he dead?

And then reality sunk in. Sora was still pulling at him, and he wheeled to run away. The two started to bolt back to the village, surrounded by others as they tried to put distance between themselves and the humans. Wallon, Sora's cousin, was hit right in front of them, his body going rigid as Palano's had. Leefe had to jump over the body to keep going. He was ashamed that he didn't stop to help, but panic filled his mind. He had to get away.

"Why are they doing this?" Sora asked through tears that ran down her face.

Leefe didn't know why—the only thing that mattered was to find safety. There was a boom to his right as the runyard drying shed exploded, sending shards of wood flying. A piece hit Leefe just under his right eye, and blood started to flow down over his mouth. He could taste the coppery tang. Another boom reached the two youths, then a third.

The humans were destroying Hope Hollow, and Leefe didn't understand why. This was utterly foreign to him, something too terrible to even grasp. He shoved the why out of his mind. The why didn't matter now. Saving themselves did.

The square was in chaos. People were screaming, running in all directions. Someone slammed into Leefe from behind, and he lost his grip on Sora's hand as she was knocked off her feet. She looked up at him, her blood-seal a bright red.

"Come on!" he shouted, reaching past another panicking ada, grabbing her hand and hauling her to him.

Crouched on the ground, people knocked into them. He knew they could get crushed. They were near the food tables, so Leefe dragged Sara over to the nearest one, scooting under it for protection.

Out in the square, most of the people were in panic mode. Blue lights reflected on the front of the communal house as the humans fired, dropping people into rigid statues. The granddads formed a united front, their ceremonial *flaaks*, held at the ready.

Most of the long-handled clubs were not even real, manufactured in mass for the tourist trade at the Purple Sea resorts. Granddad Qinnun had his cherished *flaak*, passed down over the generations, but the granddads were old men, past their prime. Protecting the spice mix was only a tradition. Leefe wanted to shout out for them to run, but he could see the granddads steel themselves, *flaaks* at the ready.

And the humans entered the square, firing their blue beams that dropped everyone they touched. The granddads took a step forward as one, shouting "Ayah!" the ancient war cry of the People of the Silver Range.

One of the humans turned and fired, and Granddad Malomun spasmed into rigidity before falling over.

Through the noise and commotion, Leefe clearly heard the female human shout, "Harris! Not the old farts. No one's going to pay us for them. Waste the fuckers."

The human male shrugged and pulled out another weapon, something sleeker that reeked of evil. He lowered the barrel and fired, a stream of something immediately tearing into the granddads. Granddad Quinnun, Granddad Sosperan, Granddad Orifin—all 16 of the grand elders—came apart before Leefe's eyes. Blood exploded into a mist finer than the spice mix dust as parts of what had been the elders of the village flew in every direction. Something red, something he couldn't recognize, bounced in front of him, leaving a crimson trail in the dirt. Up on the communal house porch, nothing was left but a spray of red on the walls and chunks of meat and guts on the floor.

"No!" Leefe shouted, anger coming over him.

He started to scramble out from under the table, but Sora grabbed his leg.

"Stay here, Leefe!"

He kicked once, hearing her grunt as she let go. He knew he'd hit her hard, and somewhere in the deep recesses of his mind, he regretted that. But one thought overwhelmed him. He had to extract revenge.

"Ayah!" he shouted, his voice high and shrill, nothing like the warrior cry of the granddads.

His target was this Harris, the human who'd killed the elders. He wasn't the only one, he saw as he ran across the square. Kollun was rushing forward, a rake held high as he charged the human. Leefe wasn't OK with that. Granddad Quinnun was his grandfather, not Kollun's. The revenge should be his!

"Kollun!" he shouted out.

Despite the shouting, Kollun heard him. He faltered a moment and shouted, "Leefe, get back!"

The Harris-human heard Kollun, turned, and in a fluid motion, fired. The top half of Kollun simply ceased to exist, turned into a few scraps of grisly tissue as the rest of his body fell into the dirt.

"Harris, that's coming out of your share!" the human woman yelled as Leefe skidded to a stop, mind blank as one of Kollun's legs, which had fallen under the rest of what was left of him, slowly slid out as if he was still alive and trying to find a more comfortable position.

"We can't sell meat, and he was a good 'un."

The rage came back, at the man who'd just killed the granddads, who just killed his cousin, at the woman who called Kollun "meat!"

"Ayah!" he screamed once again, charging across the square. The Harris-human turned just as Leefe slammed into him with every ounce of his Tri-Year Three body.

He bounced off the human, barely making him even shift his feet. The Harris-human turned to look at him in surprise, his momentary shock turning into a smile. Leefe would not accept that. He could not accept that. He scrambled back up to his feet, intent on tearing the Harris-human into tiny pieces. He charged, a wordless yell piercing the chaos of the square. Everything around him disappeared, only the human's throat filling his senses. He held out his hands, ready to tear it apart when the Harris-human's fist hit him in the chin, dropping him like a sack of runyard leaves.

Leefe barely clung to consciousness, dazed and confused. The Harris-human smiled again as he leaned over to look at Leefe.

He pointed the weapon at him and said, "Stupid move, ghost-boy. Last stupid move you'll make."

Leefe lay in the dirt, his anger replaced by fear. He was powerless. He was nothing.

"Harris, do I have to goddamned babysit you? You're on half-share now, and if you kill one more of the ghosts, you get nothing."

The Harris-human looked as if he was going to argue, but he shrugged, unslung the blue-light weapon, and lowered the rifle until the muzzle filled Leefe's field of vision, big and ominous.

Leefe never saw the blue light. Everything just went black.

****

Leefe struggled to reach the surface. His mind was trapped in a sticky morass, and he knew he had to escape, but it was so damned hard. He couldn't see, he couldn't move. Only a low moan filled his senses, the moan of someone in despair.

Finally, with an effort worthy of the Five Giants, he pried his eyes open . . . and realized he was back in Hope Hollow, laying on his side on the ground. The moaning he'd heard was his. He tried to raise a hand to his pounding head, but he couldn't. For a moment, he thought he'd been paralyzed, but the cord digging into his arms told the story. He was trussed up like a *orrak* ready for the spit.

He wasn't the only one. Someone's back was right in front of him, arms pulled behind him and tied, elbow to elbow and wrist to wrist.

"Who's that?" he managed to croak out, his tongue numb. "I'm Leefe."

There was no answer. He tried to remember who had on a yellow crop-vest. Toratun? Maybe Massanen? His mind was working at quarter-speed.

I'm not dead, I know that. At least, I don't think I am.

He lifted his head a few centimeters, which brought a stab of pain centered behind his eyes. He ignored it. Beyond whoever was in front of him, he could see more trussed-up bodies, at least a hundred of them, laid out in the halfball pitch. Moving among them were about a dozen of the humans. They were picking up people, two humans to one body, and carrying them into their ship.

Leefe's heart sunk. Even with a muddy mind, he knew what was happening.

Slavers!

He hadn't thought slavers were real, not within the empire, at least. Sure, he'd seen them in the holovids, but he'd seen humans battle 50-meter-tall tentacled monsters on the holovids as well. Slavers were a thing of the past, and if they still existed, they were out on the far fringes of the galaxy, well beyond the limits of controlled space.

But his eyes were not deceiving him. There was nothing else they could be. And that meant that Leefe, along with all of his people, was about to be stolen off of Home, never to come back.

Momma? Dad? Harra?

Leefe tried to turn around, to see if he could spot them. He knew that Granddad Qinnun was dead, murdered by the Harris-human, and he choked up at the thought. He knew Kollun was dead—killed because he'd gotten in the way and distracted his cousin.

He closed his eyes again as a wave of remorse swept over him, but the image of Kollun turning to him before he was killed was burned into his brain.

I killed him. Me!

He tried to push back the depression that threatened to overwhelm him, and he let out a moan.

"Hey, Harris, your trophy ghost-boy is awake."

Leefe opened his eyes and froze.

"Little fucker tried to tackle me. My elbow still hurts."

Leefe didn't have to see the human who was speaking from behind him somewhere. He could never forget that voice.

"What a pussy. He's half your size and naked."

"Hey, I took his ass down, Fukido. He just hit my elbow at the wrong angle."

"Big, bad merc, Harris. 'Ow, the little ghost hurt my elbow,'" the second voice said, the last part pitched much higher.

"Fuck you, Fukido. I still get my share, just like you," the Harris-human said, coming closer to Leefe.

"Half-share, is what the captain said."

The Harris-human muttered something, then Leefe felt a blow to his kidneys that almost took his breath away. Hands gripped him and turned him over to his back.

"You awake, little ghost?" the human asked. "Don't see how you're worth anything, as small as you are," he muttered to himself before Leefe could answer. "Lucky for you, though, or I would have zipped you but good." The human looked around, then said, "Don't need no help none with this little thing."

He grabbed the front of Leefe's harness, then with a smooth lift, hefted Leefe to his shoulders and started walking through the other bodies and towards the ship. Panic swept through Leefe. In a few moments, he'd be in the slavers' ship, and it would be too late. He'd be taken off Home, taken away from everything he'd ever known.

Slung over the Harris-human's shoulder, all he could see was the ground. A few people where moaning, and someone was crying out for help. A small body caught his eye, and before he could help himself, he called out, "Sora!"

"Hey, quit your ghost talking. No one can help you," the Harris-human said, giving him a smack on the ass. "Doesn't even sound like no fucking civilized language nohow."

"Sora, wake up!" Leefe said, ignoring the human.

"I said shut up," the human said, swinging Leefe around and holding him up, face-to-face. "I don't like the sound of your slithering and hissing. I got to get you alive on the ship, but nobody says you gotta be in good shape. Understand me? You ghosts understand regular talk, right? You'd better, or you're gonna regret the trip to the market."

Leefe stared at the Harris human's face, afraid in his core. He was at the mercy of this monster.

"Yes, I can speak Standard," he managed to get out past his numb tongue.

"Hmph. Maybe, but you sound like shit. I can barely understand you," the human said.

And a red flower blossomed from between his eyes, blood spraying to cover Leefe's face as both fell to the ground. Leefe landed awkwardly in a sitting position, which he barely managed to maintain. The Harris-human had fallen back over his bent legs. A hole between his eyes spouted blood in a stream a meter high before it petered out to a steady flow.

"Harris, quit fucking around. We've got to get the product loaded and out of here," a human shouted.

Sitting, Leefe could look around. Ten meters behind and to his left, a female human was looking at them.

"Harris? What's . . ." she started before shifting her gaze to Leefe. "What did you do to him?" she asked, unslinging the rifle on her back.

Something zipped past his ear with a buzz like a vivifly and hit the human with a wet-sounding thunk. She collapsed on the spot.

Leefe stared wildly around. Something was happening, and he didn't know if it was good or bad. He feared bad. The People had hunting rifles, but he'd heard no report. This wasn't Painted Rock coming to the rescue. Even among the humans, there was fighting, he knew. The Corporates were not above land-grabbing or diverting valuables, and when that happened, rumor—rumor not much believed—had it that they didn't like to leave witnesses. Leefe hadn't believed that, but he would have never believed that slavers existed, either.

There was a human shout, then the sound of the slavers' rifles as first one, then more joined in. Two humans rushed past Leefe sitting on the ground, running for the open hatch of the ship not 30 metes away. One looked like he tripped, and then as the female turned to help, she spun and went down clutching her chest. Her legs kicked twice, then went still.

Leefe tried to get to his feet, but his legs didn't want to cooperate. A burst of fire from behind him quelled his desire to stand up in the middle of a firefight. He sunk back down to a sitting position, knowing he should go prone, but unwilling to be blind. He wanted to be able to see what was happening.

Two more humans darted inside the spaceship as the door started to close.

"Captain!" someone else shouted, along with a "Fuck you, Captain!" from someone else.

Leefe looked around trying to count the People's bodies on the ground outside the ship. There had to be about 150, the best he could tell. Hope Hollow had a population of 412, and there were at least another 200 relatives from other villages there with them. Leefe didn't know how many had been killed in the fighting nor how many had managed to hide or escape into the woods. Whatever that number, there were almost assuredly more than a hundred on the ship, a hundred of his friends and relatives who were about to be pirated off Home, ripped from the protection of the Mother.

A body crashed to the ground, sliding to a stop a meter from him, blood spreading across the human's lilac shirt. Leefe ignored it, his eyes locked onto the ship. The door closed, and a whirring sound, almost something he could feel more than hear, filled the pitch. The ship rose a meter, then started to swing around when a trail of white smoke shot out of the trees and hit the front of the ship, which immediately crashed back to the ground, tail first, before the front slammed down, a 3-meter portion breaking free.

"I surrender," a voice cried out.

Leefe turned to see one, then another two humans stand, hands in the air. The three stood there for a moment, looking around nervously, when all three were hit almost as one, and down they went.

"Total-one," Leefe said aloud in awe.

In the holovids, when humans surrendered, they were taken prisoner. Whoever was out there evidently didn't play by those rules. Even if that meant they would be "cleaning up" the scene, to include the surviving People, he couldn't help feeling a thrill course through him as the three slavers were killed.

Three didn't seem like many, even with the other five he'd seen killed. That was only eight. The firing had stopped, so Leefe managed to struggle to his feet and look around. There weren't only eight dead humans. He counted 18 within his sight. He couldn't see any who were even wounded, positive that those 18 were all were dead.

Motion caught his eye, and he spun around to face a figure coming out of the treeline. It was a nightmare, a creature of myth from when the People told stories around the campfire about the dangers of the dark. Black and green, it was all angles and hardness. It walked on two legs like a person, or a human for that matter, but it screamed death. It was the embodiment of Brother Wontun, the purveyor of death, but even more terrifying than any person had ever imagined.

And it wasn't alone. Another, then two more emerged. Four of the demons walked into the pitch.

Leefe pissed himself.

They ignored the People. Leefe recognized Aunt Sallion, tied up as she was, but struggling to worm herself out of the way of the advancing demons. She knew what they were, too.

One of them pointed a hardened arm, not made of flesh, at the door of the ship. Immediately, two of the others sprinted ahead and took positions on either side of it. One placed an object alongside the frame of the door, barely visible. A moment later, the light of a thousand suns flared and started eating away. Humans believed in a hell full of fire, unlike the People's hell of ice and bitter cold, but maybe the humans were right. The demons might have brought the fire of hell with them.

The door to the ship slipped to the side, and with a couple of kicks by one of the demons, it fell off. Like wraiths in the night, all four demons flowed inside.

A hundred, probably more of the People were inside the ship, and Leefe's heart turned to ice. They would be helpless.

"What's going on," Toratun asked, squirming around with a confused look on his face. "Leefe, is that you?"

Leefe ignored him, his eyes locked on the ship. He half expected it to explode in a fireball.

"I can't move," Toratun said, sounding frustrated.

"Quiet," Leefe told him. "Don't attract the demons."

"Demons?" the aden said, then shut up.

Five minutes, ten minutes, a day—Leefe didn't know, but suddenly, one of the demons was standing in the doorway, looking out over the pitch. Leefe didn't remember all the grannies' tales from the past, but he hoped the demons had drunk enough blood inside the ship to be satisfied and leave.

Blood of the humans, that was, not of the People.

He'd never believed the ancient tales. He still didn't— almost. But there was something standing in the door, something real.

The demon stepped out, then turned toward him. Leefe knew he'd been spotted, and he immediately dropped to the ground. It was too late, but he couldn't think of anything else. He stared ahead, hoping against hope that the demon would ignore him. Even that was too much to hope for. Feet appeared in his vision, striding right at him. He held his breath and tried to still the heart threatening to beat out of his chest.

Hard hands grabbed him and pulled him to his feet. The demon was towering over him, and Leefe whimpered in fear. A blade shot out of the demon's arm, looking so sharp that it could cut time.

Leefe was done, like a towar fawn, too exhausted to run. He didn't resist as the blade came down . . . and cut the bindings on Leefe's arms.

The demon's face came apart, sliding into itself, and a human face looked out in its place.

"You're OK, little man. Don't be afraid. You're safe now, all of you are," the human said, waving an armored arm to encompass all of the People. "I'm Sergeant Washburn Gonzales, Imperial Marines."

Chapter 3
Three tri-years later

The dirigible sunk toward the capital. Leefen kept his face pressed up against the window, marveling at the size of the city. It was hard to imagine that so many people were crowded together down there, crammed like jostons in a hive.

Leefen had been traveling for six days now: three days to Crooked Gorge, then another three to the capital. He could have taken the twice-a-week plane, but he didn't have nearly the funds for that, so the slow airship it was. Not that it had been a bad trip. Leefen had spent hours looking at the window, fascinated by the Big Dry, filled with craggy peaks and swirls of browns and tans, and then the dark and brooding Green Sea.

"Over there's the spaceport," Jordun said, leaning over him, pointing off into the hazy distance.

Leefen couldn't see anything, no ship breaking free of the Home's grasp to ply the stars.

Jordun was from Hottento, a village in the headwaters of the Cold Muddy. He'd boarded the airship at Crooked Gorge as well, and the two had bonded during the trip, telling stories and playing five-up with some of the other passengers. They were both Tri-Year Sixes, and both had their a'aden hunts the same day. Being Silver Range folk, both had faced lions. That enough would create a bond, but Leefen simply liked him.

The airship gracefully came in for a landing, the nose cone catching the mast with hardly a bump. Within moments, the ramps extended, and the passengers began to debark. The two waited while the others filed out, then, with packs slung over their shoulders, followed in trace.

Crooked Gorge had been enough of a culture shock to him, but the crowds at the capital caught him by surprise. There were more people in the terminal alone than in all of Hope Hollow. Leefen paused for a moment, suddenly out of his comfort zone.

Jordun evidently mistook the cause of the hesitation, because he grabbed Leefen's arm and started pulling him through the crowd, pointing and saying, "There. I see the sign."

Leefen had doubted they could make it through the mass of people, but the others somehow stayed just out of reach in an intricate dance, never bumping into him. A few moments, and the two were standing before a bored-looking woman holding a sign that said, "IMR."

"You're the last," she said, not even asking for their names. "The other airship came in an hour ago, and the rest are in the van. No luggage?"

"Just this," Leefen said, pointing at his pack.

The two followed her out of the terminal, through a sea of hovers. A few taximen looked up with eager eyes as they approached, then quickly went back to their scanscreens once they realized the three were not potential fares. Leefen was fascinated by the array of hovers. He'd seen the commercial lorries, of course, as they picked up and delivered goods to and from Hope Hollow, and he'd seen the police cruisers that made their checks each month, but he'd never seen the private models in real life. He recognized a red Sunburst, one of his favorite models, and if their guide weren't hurrying them along, he'd have liked to stop and look at it.

Someday, I'll have one just like that.

The woman bundled them into a van parked at the end of the lot. Three more people were inside. All five made their introductions as the woman spoke a destination and the van rose on its skirts.

"Woah, smooth," Leefen said, blurting it out.

Like all ada of Hope Hollow, he'd clambered onto the sides of the lorries that came to the village, holding on while the big trucks maneuvered around. Those had been big, clunky things, and the ada shrieked and laughed as they jerked and jolted. This van was in a different class. It rose as if on the gentlest breeze and started forward as if on a track. Leefen didn't want to sound like an uncivilized nethers boy, but he couldn't help it.

No one else said a word, though. They looked like they were surprised, too, if the smiles that became fixed on their faces were any indication.

For the next twenty minutes, the van shot through traffic, too quickly for Leefen to feel comfortable. He kept flinching, sure a collision was imminent, but somehow, the hovers avoided each other. Small talk started and stopped in spurts as one near-collision was followed by another. Leefen had hoped to enjoy his first real ride, but he was glad when it came to a stop outside a large, three-story building. It looked strange, what with the right-angled corners and smooth walls. Leefen knew that many of the buildings in the capital reflected human sensibilities, and he'd seen these and real human buildings on the holovids, but standing in front of one was both exciting and disconcerting at the same time. They stood there gawking until their still unnamed guide shepherded the group up the stairs and through the broad doors.

The walls inside were soothing pastels, the same colors as inside the communal hall and homes back in Hope Hollow. The place seemed "off," however, with too-hard angles that insulted his eyes. The people walking back and forth didn't seem to mind, though.

Their guide led them down a hall to the end, pausing in front of a door. "One at a time, you'll report to the staff sergeant to get registered. You all have your receipts, right?" she asked as if suddenly remembering it. When they all nodded, she continued, "Give the staff sergeant your name and your receipt. He'll give you a scan-bracelet. Keep that on throughout the entire process. If you lose it, you're out. Understand?"

"When do we leave Home?" Tuten, one of the other three asked.

"Leave? You aren't going anywhere unless you're accepted," she said with the sharp nasal snort of disdain that capital people affected. "Don't know why any of you are stupid enough to want this, anyway."

Leefen stared at her in shock. This was approved by the Council of Elders. They'd sent representatives to every village on the planet to explain what was happening, why this was good for the People. He didn't understand her attitude.

"Don't just stand here keeping him waiting. You," she said, pointing at Leefen, "go in now."

That was fine with him. He'd taken a sudden distaste for the woman. He turned and pushed on the door, but it wouldn't budge. He stepped back, confused, then stepped up and pushed again. It still remained closed.

"Oh, for the Mother," their guide said as she reached forward and pressed a small depression alongside the edge of the door.

Leefen reddened. He knew that in the bigger cities, doors had releases, even locks. Houses in Hope Hollow had latches, too, on outside doors, to keep them closed in the wind and rain, but they were obvious, not tiny depressions in the wall.

Who closes interior doors, anyway? he wondered as he stepped into the room.

The Marine was sitting behind a human desk. This was the first Marine he'd seen since they'd rescued Hope Hollow three tris ago, but Leefen had devoured everything about the Imperial Marines since then. He recognized the chevrons on the human's sleeve, depicting his rank. He could count up the service stripes and know how long the human had served. He could see from the ribbons on his chest that the staff sergeant had served in five combat campaigns, and he'd been awarded a Double Star for valor. Leefen felt flushed, even a little giddy as he tried to march up to the Marine in his best military manner.

He was about to announce himself just as they did in the holovids when the staff sergeant held out a hand, palm up. Humans liked to shake hands, but they did it with the hand held vertically. He hesitated, then reached out and placed his hand on top of the staff sergeant's.

The Marine jerked his hand back as if burned, scowling at him. "What the fuck? I'm not here to play pattycake with you. Your receipt. Give me your receipt."

His face burning with embarrassment, Leefen pulled the receipt out of his harness pocket and gave it to the human.

The Marine rolled his eyes, then shouted out, "Diana, here's another one. Not a word of fucking Standard!"

The door hissed open, and Leefen turned to see their guide come in.

Diana? That's not a proper name for one of us.

She took the receipt from the Marines hand, glanced at it, and gave it back.

"He's from the Silver Range. They still follow the old ways over there. No Standard. But he's authorized. There's his number on the top of the receipt."

"Shit, a hick. That's all we need," he muttered before looking up at Leefen, then asking in a loud voice, "DO YOU SPEAK STANDARD?"

"Yes, sir. I speak Standard."

"Shit, Diana, he speaks Standard. Why isn't this in something I can read, then?"

"Standard is cast out to the entire planet. But some of the local elder councils stick to the old ways. Too much so, to my mind."

"OK, son, what's your name, then," the Marine said, staring at the receipt. "I'm just going to have to enter you manually."

"Leefen a' Hope Hollow," Leefen said, using the Standard translation for his village.

"Leefe Home Holloo?"

"Leefen a' Hope Hollow."

"Leefe Hope Hollow. OK, I've got it."

Leefen wanted to correct the Marine. He was an aden, so he was no longer Leefe, but Leefen. The "n" honorific was barely enunciated, true, but certainly the human could hear the difference. He started to speak, but the human's fingers were flying across the screen.

"OK, I've got you," he said as a strip of plastic emerged from the printer. "Keep this on you at all times. This will give you access to the testing areas. Lose it, and you're out. Understand?"

"Yes, sir," Leefen said as the Marine pressed the scan-bracelet around his wrist where it immediately sealed upon itself.

"Yes, Staff Sergeant, not yes, sir," the Marine said. "That's your first lesson.

"Diana, send in the next one."

Leefen knew he was dismissed, and he followed this "Diana" out of the office. She told Jordun to go next.

"Am I a Marine now?" Leefen asked.

She snorted again. "No, and you probably won't be. You've got two weeks of testing, and only then, they'll decide if they want to give you a chance at their boot camp. Now, you sit back down and wait for the rest. I'll take you to your hotel where you'll stay until morning and your testing begins.

Leefen took a seat, and Tuten leaned over to look at the scan-bracelet.

"Leif?" he asked as he looked at it.

Leefen hadn't bothered to look at it himself, so he pulled back his arm to see. There were scan codes, barely visible, but printed above them was a number, and under that, "his" name: "Leif H. Hollow, IMC Candidate."

****

"So, what do you think?" Jordan asked as they sat in the theater.

"Who knows?" Leif answered.

"What good are you, then, *Leif*," Jordan said, emphasizing his human name.

Leif blew a puff of air out through his lips, the go-to gesture of disdain among the people. All of the candidates had a humanized version of their names, and they were expected to use them. Leif, was short for Leefen, losing the aden "n." Jordan—and Min, Stalin, Ann Nathan, and a handful of the others lucked out. Jordun became *Jordan*, and he kept his "n."

Leif or Leefen, he hadn't really known what to expect, but ranking the candidates, or "poolees," as the staff sergeant referred to them, on their physical scores would have been a logical assumption. Staff Sergeant Wysoki had only paid attention to that aspect of their evaluation. He was at every test, and he led the candidates at what he called "the daily seven" each morning. The exercises were not difficult, at least for most of them. A few of the poolees, had problems, and the staff sergeant could be relentless on them, screaming and calling them names that none of the poolees understood. They didn't have to—they knew the names weren't exactly compliments. After the second day, the staff sergeant started dropping poolees until everyone left could keep up with him.

Only a few of the physical tests had pushed Leif. The eight-juto run (ten kilometers in human distances) with a 22-slag pack (60 kilos) had him breathing hard. The water test had been frightening. They'd been taken in the middle of the night to a swimming pool in the human enclave and told to jump in the water. Leif didn't know how to swim. The nearest body of water was the Cold Muddy, and its currents were too strong to challenge. Without Jordan surreptitiously helping him keep his head above the water, Leif probably would have failed. Even while he was in near panic during the test, he still noticed three humans, staring through the fence at them. The look of disgust on their faces as People dared to dirty their pool drove Leif to push through his fear.

Despite those two tests, if it was solely up to physical abilities, Leif knew he would make the cut. But there was more to the evaluations than that. All of them had been given psychological tests by a human doctor, assisted by three of the People as assistants. The tests were . . . well, odd, would be putting it lightly.

"What would you do if a fellow Marine was stealing government property?"

"If you could save only one of two animals, a puppy or a kitten, which one would you save?"

"Would you lie to your mother and tell her the dinner was delicious when it was not?"

Leif didn't know what those questions, and many more just like them, had to do with serving as a Marine.

Marines steal? Not in the holovids, they didn't.

Why not save both animals, if they had some intrinsic value? He knew what the Earth animals were, and both were small enough to hold together in one hand.

His mother was an excellent cook, and everything she prepared was delicious. If she somehow made a mistake, she would want to know so she would not make the same mistake again.

Leif realized that there had to be correct answers for each question, answers that would ensure he was selected. He just couldn't figure out what those answers were. None of the questions made sense to him.

He might not have understood what the human doctor was trying to determine, but he sure understood the battery of interviews he had with the government officials. He spent more time being prodded and tested by fellow People. He was asked his opinion on the People's place in the universe, their relationship with humans, the moral implications of taking a sentient life as a member of the military, and much more, enough to make his head ache, enough to make him want to scream out in frustration.

Leif knew his people were testing him as well. What he didn't know was what did they want to hear. What was the "right" answer? He tried to game them at first, but the questions piled on, and he finally just let go and responded with the first thing that came to his mind.

And now, waiting to see who had been selected, he feared he'd made a mistake. He knew that no matter who Staff Sergeant Wysoki and those above him chose, if the Elders did not approve of a candidate, then they would not be leaving Home.

The door opened, and 93 sets of eyes swiveled as one. But it wasn't the staff sergeant or the mysterious major they'd barely seen. It was an elder with the flash of the prime council on the shoulder of his harness. Ninety-three poolees straightened up, their attention focused on the elder as he walked to the podium, stopping beside it and leaning his elbow on it as if he needed the support. He slowly swung his gaze across the candidates, and as he caught Leif's eyes for a split-second, Leif felt as if his very soul had been pulled out, evaluated, and shoved back inside. His heart pounded.

"So, why are all you here?" the elder asked. "No, you don't have to tell me. You all are here to forge bonds between humans and the People, right?"

That's what I said in the interviews, Leif thought.

"That's wasilla shit."

Oh, hell. Did I blow it?

"We are under the thumb of the humans. You can choose to believe in the propaganda that they protect us. I ask you, protect us from whom? The sassares? What do you think would be the situation if the sarrares had reached us before the humans? Well, we'd be in the Hegemony, with the sassares *protecting* us from the *humans*. The simple matter is that the humans came first, and we could not stand up to them. And of all the humans, the empire was here first, laying claim to Home.

Leif stared at the elder in shock. The empire protected them. He'd seen that with his own two eyes when the Marines had saved Hope Hollow from the slavers.

Human slavers, he suddenly realized.

"I'll be blunt with you. You 93 are here as part of a grand social experiment. The humans of the empire preach equality, that all within their embrace are as good as anyone else. Yet, while they use their slaves. . . yes, I said slaves," he said as he saw the reaction of the poolees. "They use slaves to serve them in factories, on farms, as servants, everywhere except for the military. Their own history, going back to Spartacus, taught them never to arm the slaves."

Leif didn't know who this Spartacus was, but the logic was sound.

"Until now. The Empire is in decay, and other humans are rising in power. They have Forsythe III on the Granite Throne, an ada, not even aden, a child controlled by shadowy figures. So, in an effort to gather more into their sphere, they look to us, to prove that all the beings controlled by the Empire are equal citizens."

He snorted at that, unable to restrain himself.

Leif didn't know much about galactic politics. They were under the thumb of the humans he knew, as the elder had just put it, and there were sassares, leera, and noxes who jockeyed for power in this corner of space, but none of that had affected him back at Hope Hollow. He had the feeling now, though, that he'd better learn more if he was going to become a pawn in the great game.

"And why us? Why the People? Is it because we are stronger than most? Is it because of our stamina?"

"Sure," whispered Jordan.

"Yes, we can carry a pack, but the real reason is that we are *peaceful*," the elder said, almost spitting out the word. "They think we are not a threat, and we can be controlled. They think they are getting *gorring*, pack animals to carry their weapons, but without a brain to think."

"Peaceful?" Leif muttered, surprised.

Sure, the People had managed to mostly control themselves for over 130 tri-years, since before the humans came. They'd had to for simple survival. Peace had become a mantra, a religion, continually emphasized—yet all the People knew that the veneer between peace and war was thin. It wouldn't take much for the dam to break, and their true natures would be revealed once again.

"So, the strong, dumb, peaceful People were selected as an offering of good intent to all of us, humans and non-humans alike. We were a good, safe choice.

"And we can do nothing about it, because, frankly, we *have* become peaceful. We don't have the capability to say no to the humans. We are sending you because the humans demanded it. You are the chattel price we, in the Prime Council, paid to to our masters.

"I will tell you this, however. This was not a unanimous decision. Some feared us getting drawn into a war where the only outcome would be our destruction, and with the Empire in decay, we fear that war is coming. Home would eventually become a soft target, punished for fighting on the side of the Empire, but unable to defend ourselves.

"Some fear that it would awaken our dark past, when People warred with People. We almost killed ourselves off in the past, and many fear the evil that still resides within us.

"I, on the other hand, agreed with the majority, although perhaps for different reasons. I did not agree merely to appease the humans. I agreed for the good of the People."

Leif and Jordan exchanged looks, wondering what that meant.

"If we are to be drawn into a war not of our making, we will need to be integrated into the human sphere. We need to become too valuable to them to risk our destruction. We don't have the technology, and our resources are limited, but we do have the most valuable commodity: the People.

"You 93, or the 50 who will make the first Marine recruits, you will be the first of us to integrate into the Empire. You will prove the value of our People, and you will pave the way for more of us to follow in your footsteps. And as you serve, you will absorb all you can about human warfare, knowledge that you can bring back to Home. If your efforts are not enough to make the humans value us, then we must have the means to bite back, if necessary, either against them or whoever thinks we are weak enough to subjugate."

This was too much for Leif. He wanted adventure, he wanted to prove himself. He wanted to be the Marine standing over a small boy he'd saved from the slavers. He didn't want to be part of some political maneuvering.

"So, why am I telling you this? Because you must realize the gravity of your task. You will be dancing between the knives, each blade capable of cutting your throat. You must excel in the tasks they give you, but not so much as to become a threat. You cannot make the humans fear you, that you might rise against them. You must not antagonize them, to give reasons for those who are against this social experiment, and there are many of those."

"They don't want us?" Jordan whispered.

"Many in the Empire want you to fail. They want to keep their military pure. You cannot fail, but not for the Empire's reasons. You cannot fail because the day will come when the People need you, you and those who must be allowed to follow you. Keep that foremost in your hearts. You will swallow your pride when necessary. You will take abuse without complaint."

He looked out over the group once again as if marshaling his thoughts, then said, "Here on Home, we have separate areas for humans and the People. We are second-class citizens on our own world. It will be worse out there, among them. We are *ghosts*, *caspers*, and even worse. We do not deserve to be among them. We are a drain on their resources to protect us. So, when a human comes up to you and demeans you, what will you do?"

"Demean him back," Jordan whispered.

"You will accept it. You will apologize and leave."

The hell I will, Leif immediately thought.

"This may be the hardest thing for you to do. To accept injustice. But that is the only way for us to be accepted. This *onus* I place on you, in the name of the Mother."

An onus? This is real.

There was nothing so binding on a person as an onus. To disobey meant to be expelled from the People, to be one of the anchorless. Leif couldn't imagine that half-existence.

"Think back on this afternoon when you are challenged, when you are insulted. You . . . will . . . accept . . . *everything!*"

He paused, looking at each one of them as if he could read their minds, to see who accepted this and who didn't.

"I can go into more, how you cannot show cowardice, how you cannot quit, how you fight for the empire, but I have no doubt as to all of you succeeding in that.

"But there is one more thing I should mention," he said, almost as if an afterthought. "The Mother gave life to the universe, so all of us, human, People, sassares, leera, all life, came from the same seed. The humans call the Mother the "Progenitors," the noxes, the "Primes," but the science is clear. Our DNA has only a slight genetic drift. More than that, with the sentient life, there are "reconvergences" that could only mean that the Mother made adjustments to bring our lines back toward each other. Humans and the People are cousins, maybe closer. We can eat the same food, and in some cases, even interbreed."

There were a few gasps from the people, to hear an elder say what had only been rumors.

"When you leave Home for the Empire, you will be discriminated against, true. But there is an ongoing rumor as to the sexual prowess of the People, and a certain portion of the human population finds the idea of sexual relations with one of us exciting. The majority will not, and they will find *miscegenation* abhorrent."

From his emphasis on the word, Leif knew that it wasn't only the humans who would find miscegenation abhorrent.

"Some of you may be approached by humans, male or female. You will not act on those suggestions. There may be little else that can cause such a problem as this, if we look at ancient human history. This is a second onus I place on you today."

Leif didn't know what to make of that. It hadn't even crossed his mind. His tri-year sisters would not enter their first estrous for another three years, and that was when the males entered musth. He's had casual sex, of course, since becoming an aden, but that was for pleasure only, without the mind-numbing emotions and desire that came with procreation.

The females among them who became recruits would wear inhibitor patches, developed by humans, that would delay estrous. The males would take monthly injections that when combined with the lack of the estrous trigger, they would never enter musth. Leif did not think this would be a difficult onus to follow.

"Know that the future of Home could rest on how you perform."

That was a heavy load for Leif to bear, far more than he'd expected.

"Or not. I could be wrong," the elder said in a suddenly lighter tone.

"But you won't be alone. Let me introduce you to Ferron a'Silverton," he said, pointing to one of the people who'd followed him into the room. "Ferron will be with you through your training. Officially, he is a liaison. In reality, he has the Voice of the Prime Council. When he speaks, he speaks for the council."

Ferron nodded his head but said nothing. Leif doubted the man would stay silent long. He started wondering what he'd gotten himself into, and for the first time, thought that not being selected wouldn't be so terrible of an outcome.

"With that, I will leave you. Rest assured, though, that I will be following everything you do and don't do among the humans with extreme attention."

The elder turned and left, followed by his small retinue. As soon at the door closed, 93 voices erupted in conversation, the noise level rising to a dull roar, a roar that was cut instantly as the door opened once again, and Staff Sergeant Wysoki and the major came in. The major stood to the side as the staff sergeant walked to the podium, opened his tab, and without preamble, started naming the 50 who's been selected for the first recruit class of the People.

The third name he said was "Leif H. Hollow."

IWO JIMA

Chapter 4

"Get on the footsteps, get on the footsteps!" the Marine DI shouted as the recruits piled out of the bus . . . and into a media frenzy.

Leif, blinded by the cam-lights, stopped for a moment, blinking, when a DI grabbed him by the arm and almost threw him forward. He stumbled ahead, finding a pair of yellow footprints and positioning himself over them.

Ferron a'Silverton had warned of them that there was significant media attention on the 50 of them, but Leif hadn't expected this much. There were more media-types than recruits, their lights turning the night into day.

All of them had received hours of classes on human culture, history, and the current political environment. There were already non-humans in the Navy, mainly tokits and hissers who served in limited and specialized billets, but this was the Marine Corps, the Emperor's Own, so the media attention was intense.

Leif let his eyes wander over the mass of reporters, just beginning to realize what he'd gotten himself into. There could be a billion eyes on him now, a simple Silver Range boy from Hope Hollow.

"Quit eye-fucking them media slicks, ghost-boy," a DI quietly snarled, pushing his chin up against Leif's chest--he hadn't realized it was possible to snarl and be quiet at the same time, but the DI managed it. "Get your eyeballs locked to the front."

Leif came to the position of attention, something at which they'd all drilled before leaving Home, and the DI moved to the next recruit. He didn't even know who was standing beside him now, and he wasn't going to risk a glance to find out. More DI's were screaming as others fell into place on the yellow footprints.

A short—most humans were short compared to the People—woman in reporter orange centered herself right in the middle of Leif's view, a camdrone hovering over her shoulder, and yelled out, "What does it feel like to be a Marine?"

Leif ignored her. First, he'd already been told that none of them were Marines, and they wouldn't be until and if they made it through boot camp. Second, and more importantly to his well-being, he knew that the DIs would come down on him like a ton of bricks if he spoke out.

"*Aden,*" she said, using *Uzboss*, the language of the People, "what does it feel like?"

Leif flinched, hearing her use his native tongue, and immediately another DI wheeled to him, yelling, "Freeze, worm!"

The top of this DI's head reached Leif's eye level, and a horrible stench washed over him. It took a moment for him to realize that the source of the stench was the DI—her breath reeked of rotten runyard stems. Leif couldn't help it; he recoiled.

"I said freeze, you piece of shit!"

At least I don't smell like shit, Leif thought.

The DI went on a litany of Leif's past, his unworthiness of even hoping to become a Marine someday, and how the DI gave him a day before he'd quit and run home to the backwater ball of shit that had unfortunately given him birth. At least that was what Leif assumed she was saying. Leif spoke Standard, of course, but the DI used a slew of slang Leif didn't understand. He understood the general tone of it, however.

The yelling died as if turned off with a switch. One moment, the DIs were on full display; the next, they were silent until a single voice from somewhere to Leif's right cut through the night air.

"I am Senior Drill Instructor Larry Richardson. For the next sixteen weeks, I own you. Your souls may belong to whatever gods you worship, but your ass belongs to me."

Leif kept his eyes locked to the front, but the "sixteen weeks" caught his attention. They'd been told that boot camp was twelve weeks long, not sixteen.

"If you prove worthy of the title, something I very much doubt as I look over you, after those sixteen weeks, you will become Marines. Until that time, you are nothing. Never forget that, and you might have a chance. Start to think otherwise, and you will be crushed.

"With deference to our guests, Captain Khan is going to swear you all in here on the grinder for the galaxy to see. If any of you have doubts, even the slightest, do yourselves a favor and leave now. No one will stop you."

There was a long pause, then the senior DI said, "OK, then, it's your funeral.

"Detail, atten . . . HUT!"

They were already at a position of attention, but Leif pulled himself even more erect. Directly in front of him, just behind the first row of reporters, he caught sight of a civilian with a one-star general beside him. The general was not hiding her look of disdain, but Leif didn't know whether that was because of the circus this had become or because the People were being enlisted in her Marines. The civilian, though, a dark-skinned, short, slender man, stared at the soon-to-be recruits. The intensity of his gaze unnerved Leif, and he felt it in his bones that this small man, standing next to the broad-shouldered Marine general, had power.

"Raise your right hand and repeat after me," a new voice reached out across them.

Leif dutifully raised his right hand, but he couldn't keep his eyes off the dark man. And then, the man's eyes caught his, eyes so dark and foreboding that they sucked at his very soul. A small smile creased the edge of the man's mouth, and he gave the slightest of nods. Leif almost sighed in relief when the man shifted his gaze toward his left.

"I, state your name . . ."

"I, *Leefen a'Hope Hollow*," he repeated, his heart fluttering at his act of defiance, using his real name, spoken in his real tongue.

". . . do solemnly swear that I will give fealty to Emperor Forsythe the Third, mind, heart, and soul, as the embodiment of the Empire of Man; I will bear true faith and allegiance to the same; I will obey the orders of the Emperor and the officers appointed over me; and I will uphold the traditions and honor of the Imperial Marine Corps to my dying breath. So help me God."

There was a brief moment of silence after the now-Marine Corps recruits finished the last word before both cheers and what sounded like boos erupted from the gathered observers. Leif risked another look at the dark man, and there was no doubting the look of satisfaction on his face.

"Right FACE!" someone shouted, sounding like the senior drill instructor to Leif's still unused-to-human-voices-yet ears. "Column of files, MARCH!"

Someone must have missed teaching them what that command entailed, but with the DIs' "assistance," the meaning became clear. Leif filed after the rest, leaving the staging area and entering through the gate into Camp Navarro proper. Above the gate was a sign with the words *Sic Transit Gloria Stellae*. That wasn't Standard, and Leif wondered briefly what they meant.

That curiosity disappeared as soon as they were inside the gates, when Senior Drill Instructor Richardson set his DIs on them. "Now that we're out of sight of the media slicks, we can get down to business," he said with an evil-sounding laugh.

Leif knew it was going to be a long—and thoroughly unpleasant—night.

Chapter 5

It took only one day for the first casualty. It wasn't Leif, but he was involved, and that type of attention was what he'd wanted to avoid at all costs.

They'd just returned from breakfast and were in formation, going through an initial wearing-of-the-uniform inspection. Five DIs were noting every discrepancy they could find—and in Leif's opinion, some discrepancies that didn't exist. He stood at the position of attention in Second Squad, listening to the yelling that was going on, just waiting his turn to be the object of a DI's attention.

He wasn't sure why the DIs were being so blusterous. It wasn't as if anyone was frightened of them. They knew that the DIs couldn't physically harm them, so there was no fear of danger, no matter how loudly they screamed. Leif thought the hubbub was ridiculous, but it was easy enough to take.

When it was his turn in the breech, Drill Instructor Wasyk-Templeton stepped in front of him, then turned his head and said, "Hell, recruit, you smell like shit!"

Leif said nothing, keeping his eyes focused on a point beyond the DI's head as they'd been told to do.

"I mean, all of you smell, given that shit you put on your food, but you, you smell like something crawled up your ass last week and died in there."

That's a strange thing to say, Leif thought, keeping his face emotionless.

Leif was fluent in Standard, but it had become apparent that they all had a lot to learn about human expressions. Since no animal had somehow crawled up his ass, and the Navy doctor who had examined them all after being sworn in the night before hadn't noticed any such creature, the DI must have known that was impossible.

"Well, Recruit Hollow," he said, looking at the name tape sewn over Leif's breast pocket, "did something crawl up your ass and die?"

"No, Drill Instructor," Leif said, keeping his voice calm.

For some unknown reason, that seemed to make the DI angrier, spittle flying out of his mouth as he screamed, "Well, then your momma didn't raise you right, for you to stink like that. What about it, did your momma teach you how to keep clean?"

"She did teach me, Drill Instructor," Leif said, wondering what the DI wanted him to say.

The DI was large for a human, almost as tall as Leif, but out-massing him by at least 30 kg. He leaned closer, mouth at Leif's chin-level, and said in a quieter voice, "Well, then, I guess it's true what they say. You fucking ghosts must live in huts with dirt-fucking floors, shitting wherever you want. I bet you sleep with the animals keeping you warm at night."

Leif didn't answer because he didn't know how to respond to that.

The DI got even quieter and said, "Hell, I bet your momma *slept* with the animals. I bet she fucked a dog, and you're the sorry result."

Leif finally broke his stoic expression, totally confused.

My mother fucked a dog? That's ridiculous. How could one of the People mate with a dog and have a child, an ada? It's biologically impossible. Even if it was possible, a dog was an Earth creature, not a Home animal.

Leif looked down into the DI's eyes, trying to see if the human was deranged.

"Don't you eye-fuck me, Recruit!"

Leif snapped his head up, staring at nothing again.

"That's a good little recruit, doing what you're told. It don't matter none that I just said your momma fucks dogs, you just sit there and take it," he said, almost sounding disappointed.

Leif was totally confused. First, the DI goes on some fantasy trip which he was sure was meant as an insult, and now the human seemed disappointed that Leif didn't argue or object. All of them had been lectured ad nauseum that they would be pushed, but they had to keep calm and not react. All human recruits who enlisted were pushed to see who would break, but if one of them did, they were simply discharged.

For the 50 of them, it was different—they represented their entire race. They had to maintain proper decorum.

In this case, it wasn't even difficult for Leif to restrain himself. How could he get upset by a fairy tale? It didn't make any sense to him.

"And here they told us you ghosts are tough hombres, that you even take on ghost lions with a spear," he said, almost to himself. "Is that true, Recruit Hollow? Did you go out there and face down one of your lions?"

Out of the 50 recruits, Leif was one of eight who'd done his a'aden hunt. Seven were Silver Rangers, and one had gone to a preserve on the main continent. He felt relieved—at least this was a logical question, and one he could answer.

"Yes, Drill Instructor, I did."

The DI, who'd looked like he was about to move to the next recruit, stopped, and swung back to him.

"What? That shit's true? And you say you did this?"

"Yes, Drill Instructor."

"Bull-pucky, Recruit. I'm calling bull-pucky. Unless your ghost-lions are the size of gerbils, there's no way you ever did that. You've got no backbone to do something like that."

Leif felt the blood leave his face. He didn't know exactly what "bull-pucky" meant, but he did know what "bullshit" meant, and from connotation, he thought they were about one in the same. This human was calling him a liar, and over something of honor. The People had curbed most of their violent tendencies with a strict adherence to social intercourse, and one thing that wasn't done was to accuse someone of lying.

The People did lie on occasion, but not about something like this.

Leif lowered his gaze to meet the DI's eyes again, anger flooding through him. He wanted nothing more than to smash in the human's face, but the need to slough off the insult fought to keep him restrained. It was possible, but not likely, that he didn't understand exactly what the DI was saying.

"Are you calling me a liar about my a'aden passage?" he said, struggling to keep his voice calm.

"I don't know this aden thing from shit, but yeah, I'm calling you a liar, and we don't keep liars in the Corps."

Leif felt the rage overtaking him, his fist clenching as he fought to hold back . . . and with a lunge, Kelli, who'd been next to him in the line, pushed him aside to level a punch at the unsuspecting DI's chin that dropped him like a sack of spice.

"You don't insult someone who's completed an a'aden hunt," she screamed, leaning over the prone human.

The fire left Leif instantly, and he put his arms around Kelli, afraid she'd attack the human again. Almost as quickly, the other four DIs pushed their way through the formation to tackle the two of them, screaming at the other recruits to back away.

Kelli was struggling, flinging out a stream of invectives in the *hanna* dialect of *Uzboss*, as Leif held her tight. The DIs were all over the two, and Leif didn't want Kelli to inflict any damage on them as well. He absorbed her blows as well as more than a few given by the DIs.

More humans rushed to the formation, and they pulled the two apart and to their feet.

Senior Drill Instructor Richardson, breathing heavily and with his uniform twisted out-of-place, shouted, "Get those two to the skipper's office, and call the MPs."

"It wasn't him," Drill Instructor Dream Bear said, pointing at Leif. A trickle of blood dripped down from his lip. "It was her."

The senior hesitated a moment, then said, "OK, get her there. Hartson, get the rest into whatever classroom is free, and Pauama, I want that ghost liaison rounded up and brought to the skipper—no, to the CO. And get a corpsman for Tempy, the dumb fuck. How the hell did he let this happen? Shit!" he yelled, picking up his cover, the brim broken and barely barely still attached. "Shit fucking shit!

The recruits were hustled off the grinder and into a classroom where they waited in silence for almost 40 minutes before Ferron a'Silverton arrived, breathless and flustered. For the next two hours, he harangued, pleaded, and threatened them, all the time stressing that no matter what happened, no matter how they were treated by the DIs or any other humans, they were to simply take it. There was far more at stake than personal pride.

Leif was ashamed of himself. This was bigger than any single one of them, and he'd come close to assaulting the DI over mere words. No matter how insulting they were, they were still only words, words that the human had been using as a tool to invoke a reaction that would prove the People were not worthy. If Kelli, who had never done the traditional a'aden hunt, had not interceded, Leif might have assaulted the human himself. He might have let himself be manipulated.

Finally, they were turned back over to the DIs, all who looked at them warily, as if they were all about to explode in an orgy of violence. Drill Instructor Wasyk-Templeton was gone, a replacement already called up.

Later that afternoon, Jorge Blue, who'd been one of the five alternates who had accompanied them to Iwo Jima, joined the platoon. As for Kelli, they never saw her again.

Chapter 6

"My fucking great grandmother can move faster than that," Gunny—Senior Drill Instructor--Richardson screamed out. "And she's been dead for ten years now!"

Rumor had it that he'd done three tours on the drill field, and he'd had his orders extended—involuntarily—to run herd on the *wyntonan*—the Standard alliteration the humans used for the People's name for themselves—recruit platoon. He didn't seem overly happy about his new job, and over the last two days, he let the recruits know his feelings and opinions of them in a variety of unpleasant ways. He never directly mentioned Kelli's attack on Drill Instructor Wasyk-Templeton, but he continually harped on the recruits' lack of discipline. Leif tried to hurry as the mass of recruits rushed to get in formation on the parade deck. They'd just been pulled from a class on Marine Corps etiquette—which looked to be the exact same class they'd had back on Home—when the senior drill instructor came barging into the classroom, ordering them to run, not walk, to the parade deck and fall in. The mere fact that they were in a cluster fuck was indication enough that something was up. Before this, the recruits marched everywhere in formation.

Getting into a semblance of a formation on the parade deck took even longer than running over from the classroom, even with the entire DI team on their asses. Once in formation, the DIs starting inspecting them, adjusting their uniforms. Leif was inspected three times: Sergeant Dream Bear pulling Leif's gig line to the left, then Staff Sergeant Frehm pulling it back to the right less than a minute later.

At last, the platoon presented an acceptable front, and the senior took his position in front of the platoon while the other DIs disappeared somewhere to the rear. Standing at parade rest, they waited . . . and waited. After all the rush and commotion to get there, nothing was happening.

"What do you think is going on?" Ossie whispered out of the corner of his mouth.

Leif stiffened, waiting for the inevitable backlash, but nothing happened. The junior hats were not hovering just behind them, waiting to pounce on any transgression.

"Don't know," Leif whispered back.

He was curious, though. The first two days had been . . . *interesting*, to say the least. Not much had gone according to their briefs back on Home before embarking for Iwo Jima. Instead of going through a receiving phase first, they'd been introduced to their permanent DIs that first night while getting off the bus. Instead of a 12-week boot camp, they'd been given an extra month of "evaluation." All 50 of them had made the cut back on Home, but it was made very clear that meant nothing, and over the next month, recruits would be evaluated for suitability before moving on to T-1, the first day of official recruit training. They weren't even in a recruit series, but rather a stand-alone platoon, but with double the normal number of DIs.

Whatever was happening now, however, seemed like something out of the ordinary. The DIs had been too hyped for this to be routine.

Sweat started forming on his brow and flowing into his eyes. Camp Navarro was far dustier than Hope Hollow, and his eyes were having a hard time getting used to the irritation. His sweat was doing nothing to improve that. He blinked a few times, but he resisted the urge to raise a hand to wipe the sweat away. After only two days, he knew better than to do that.

After at least 20 minutes, movement caught his peripheral vision. He couldn't help but turn his head slightly to see, and a squad of the Imperial Guard double-timed into view, resplendent in their bright red hussar tunics, white jodpurs, and silver helmets. Over the years, the Imperial Guard had gone from being the emperor's personal secret police, with a long history of civil abuse, to the crack unit protecting the emperor that it was today. On Home, the less-savory history of the Guard tended to be emphasized, but still, their almost mechanical precision almost took Leif's breath away.

"Steady, eyes front," the senior growled over his shoulder at the platoon.

Wait, if that's the Imperial Guard, then . . .

Leif was a citizen of the empire, and he'd sworn allegiance to the emperor two nights ago, but the young emperor was some abstract figure back on the human's homeworld of Earth. He had no real impact on Leif in thought or deed. But if the Imperial Guard was taking positions around the reviewing stands, that could only mean one thing.

"Oh, shit," Ossie whispered, coming to the same conclusion.

"Oh, shit" indeed.

A series of scandrones flew up and down the lines of recruits. Leif imagined he could feel whatever processes they used to make sure none of the recruits were armed or posed a threat. A plainclothes human with the air of a military man stepped forward and into the ranks of privates, moving to Fourth Squad, and hence, out of sight of Leif. He could hear some murmuring, then the man appeared again, clutching something in his hand. Whatever he'd found must not have been deemed a threat, and none of the Fourth Squad recruits were taken away.

The media platform started filling up, then the stands. Within another 15 minutes, both were full. The whine of engines reached them from the direction of the landing pad, and heads of those in the stands turned in unison, straining to see.

Eight minutes later, a full hour since they'd been hustled out of the classroom, the senior shouted, "Present, HARMS!" as the imperial party arrived, walking past the assembled recruits and to the reviewing platform. Keeping his head locked in place, hand raised in a salute, Leif strained to see the emperor, barely getting a glimpse of a head that might have been his among the other worthies as they approached the platform.

"Order . . . HARMS!" the senior shouted out again.

At least the reviewing platform was right in front of the formation, and as the imperial party climbed the steps into it, they were in full view of the recruits. Leif got his first full view of Emperor Forsythe the Third, the titular leader of the largest and most visible faction of humans in the galaxy.

The emperor looked much younger in real life than in his holos, a rather slight man when compared with the four-star general . . .

That's the commandant! Leif realized.

The emperor might not have an imposing physical appearance, and Leif had never really felt a strong sense of loyalty to the man, but still, a trill ran up his spine as he watched him exchange pleasantries with the others in the stands. This man was the latest member of the family that had shepherded humans to become one of the prime forces in the galaxy. The empire might be in what some charged was a death spiral of decay, but there was a lot of history riding on the young man's shoulders.

It took another minute for all the hands to be shaken and waves made to the spectators before the commandant stepped forward and said, "Ladies and gentlemen, Marines, and recruits of Platoon 5001, it is truly my honor and pleasure to welcome His Imperial Majesty, Forsythe the Third, Protector of the Empire and Servant of the People, to Iwo Jima, and more specifically Camp Navarro."

He turned to the emperor, leading the spectators in a round of applause.

"Thank you, General Jelani," the emperor said as he stepped forward, his voice amplified to resonate across the parade deck. "I appreciate the hospitality you have shown the empress-in-waiting and me."

Leif had been focused on both the emperor and the commandant, missing the broad-shouldered young lady who nodded back, a smile on her face. Jenifer Roseanne Chen was only 14 years old, a daughter of the powerful Jin Long family, a rich industrial clan that was often at odds with the imperial line. As part of their classes on humans in general and the empire in particular, they were introduced to the convoluted politics of the Granite Throne. The empress-in-waiting had lived in the imperial household for eight years, promised to the then-prince. Now, with him as emperor, she was promoted to empress-in-waiting, and would become empress, co-ruler of the empire, the day after she reached her 18th birthday and she married the emperor.

A little sleuthing on the omniweb had revealed that there had already been two attempts on her life, but whether from rival clans or supporters of the Granite Line was unknown. A strong-willed young woman, some people thought she would simply overwhelm the emperor by force of personality and scheming alone, imposing her own will on the empire. It was no secret that the Advisory Council considered Forsyth III more "manageable" by the powers behind the throne.

The emperor stepped off the reviewing stand and onto the parade deck, striding forward towards the formation. Four of the Imperial Guard started to flank him until he waved them back. He walked up to Senior Drill Instructor Richardson, shook the flustered senior's hand, and spoke quietly to him for a moment.

The senior nodded, did and about-face, then shouted out, "Platoon . . . parade . . . REST!"

None of the recruits were expecting the command, and they rather raggedly took the position, legs spread, arms clasped behind their backs. This wasn't a shining example of Marine Corps close order drill.

With the senior one step behind and one to the emperor's left, the leader of the Empire casually walked forward until he was just a few paces from First Squad.

"*Edyatil wyntonan*," he said in the language of the People, welcoming them. His accent was flawless, even adding the "n" after "wyntonan" that most humans seemed unable to pronounce.

If he wanted to catch the interest the recruits, this was a good way to do it.

"I'm sorry if that is about my limit of *Uzboss*," he said with a slight chuckle. "I hope you'll forgive me if I continue in Standard.

"I wanted to come here from Earth and personally thank you for volunteering to join the Imperial Marines. I fully realize that this hasn't been an easy transition, but I want to stress just how important this is for not just the Empire, but for humanity *and* wyntonans. The Empire is only as strong as its citizens, and that means all citizens, no matter their race. I am the emperor of not just humans, but for everyone within the Empire.

"In our mutual pasts, there were some unfortunate clashes. My great-grandfather, Castiogne II, issued a formal apology for that over a hundred years ago, but that has not erased all of the ill-will."

The emperor did not mention the Wars of Subjugation, where humanity conquered first the tokits, then the alindamirs and the hissers, and treated them like chattel until the Proclamation of Sentient Rights when all races were declared equal citizens. The People came into the sway of the empire after the proclamation, but they all knew to what he was referring—and they all knew, proclamation or not, that prejudice still existed not just within the Empire, but was even worse within some of the outlying human governments.

"It is my fervent hope that all citizens within the Empire will enjoy the full inalienable rights accorded anyone else, and I am dedicating my life to achieving this cause."

That was all well and good, Leif thought, but it was probably out of reach. As Leif had learned, the emperor was merely a figurehead, a pawn of the clan powers that really ruled the empire. Still, he appreciated the sentiment.

As if realizing that he wasn't an all-powerful monarch, he said, "One of the many titles attached to my name is 'Supreme Commander of the Armed Forces.' That means I don't have to get approval from the Advisory Council or Civil Commission to enact changes that don't affect the budget. Right General Jelani?" he said, turning back to the reviewing stand.

The commandant gave him a thumbs-up to the laughter of the spectators.

Despite a class on the organization of the empire, Leif still wasn't completely sure how it worked. The Advisory Council, made up of representatives from all of the major clans, "advised" the emperor, which meant they told the emperor what to say and do. However, the Civil Commission, made up of bureaucrats, controlled the purse strings. How all three worked together, and who really had the power, was lost on Leif.

"So, since it doesn't cost anything, they let me shape the military to my vision. and that is how you are here. You might wonder, however, as to the *why* you are here.

"As I just mentioned, the Empire is not just an empire of humans. There are eight races within imperial space, eight races of full citizens, citizens who deserve not only all of the benefits of the Empire, but who also owe a duty to serve. The military is the pinnacle of duty, and it is important that all races are represented in it. It is the bulwark between the citizens and oppression, and it should reflect the society that it serves.

"Your service is vital, both from a practical as well as a philosophical standpoint, to the vitality and equity of the Empire, but it is also important to you, the *wyntonans*. By serving, you are taking your place as the equal of all citizens, human and non-human alike."

"This program is near and dear to my heart because I believe in it, and I believe in you. I wish I could spend more time here, but the needs of my position will not allow that. However, I am leaving my *pinkernes*, Sept-Minister Constantine Iaxi," he said, turning and holding out a hand to indicate the dark-skinned civilian who'd been observing the training over the last couple of days. "If you have any problems, any at all, you may go to the sept-minster for assistance."

Leif had no idea what a "*pinkernes*," was, but he knew without a shadow of a doubt that he couldn't just decide one day to go look the man up to complain about Senior Drill Instructor Richardson yelling at them a little too hard. The emperor might be serious, but the Marine Corps didn't work that way.

"I may not be here on Iwo Jima, but I will be monitoring your progress. I charge your DIs to push you to your limits, but I charge each of you to meet the challenge, and in another sixteen weeks, I expect to see fifty new Marines, the first of many from *Kandelhan*.

"So, before I leave you, I want to express my utmost gratitude for your sacrifice in the name of the Empire. Semper fi, Marines!" he said, shouting out the last.

Leif almost winced at being called "Marines." They weren't yet, and he hoped the DIs would not punish them for the emperor's mistake.

The emperor looked back up to the reviewing platform, and after a moment of jostling, the entire party, led by the commandant, rushed to join him on the parade deck.

"Platoon, atten . . . HUT!" the senior shouted as the group milled about for a moment.

The commandant quickly took charge and escorted the emperor off the parade deck, followed by most of the others, and with the imperial guard flanking him. Most ignored the recruits, but the empress-in-waiting stopped for a moment, staring at them with frank interest. An older man gave her a gentle nudge on the elbow, but before she joined the rest, she raised a hand and blew them all a kiss. The recruits stood stock still until the group was off the deck and into some waiting vehicles. For the first time, the senior broke his position, looking up to where Captain Khan had been behind the reviewing party.

The captain held up a hand for him to wait as the sept-minister and the commanding general climbed back onto the reviewing platform. The sept-minister accepted a lapel mic from a Marine, said, "Can you hear me?" nodding as his voice reverberated across the parade deck.

"OK, good. As his imperial majesty told you, I am Sept-Minister Constantine Iaxi. I was a member of the previous imperial court, and I've been his imperial majesty's *pinkernes* since he ascended to the Granite Throne."

His pride was evident when he said the word "pinkernes," and Leif made a mental note to look the word up when he had a chance.

"As such, I am the emperor's direct representative here on Iwo Jima with regards to all of you *wyntonans*," he said, stumbling over the Uzboss word for the People, unlike the smooth, accentless delivery of the emperor, who'd even used the *Uzboss* word for "Home." "My door is always open to you, and your drill instructors and officers have been explicitly directed to allow any of you to see me at any time."

The CG, Brigadier General Tannenbau, who was standing just off the sept-minister's shoulder, stiffened slightly at that, the corners of her mouth turning down. That just cemented Leif's opinion on whether there really was an open-door policy in practice.

"I am here for you, Marines. It is very important to his imperial majesty that all races eventually join the military in service of the empire, and you are the first vanguard of this endeavor."

He paused for a moment, then said, "I helped make the decision that you wyntonans would be the first non-human Marines. You may be pacifist at heart, but you are stronger, faster, and can handle a wider range of environmental conditions than humans can. In short, you can be better Marines than any human, and with the current deteriorating situation, we are going to need those extra capabilities."

If the CG had shown her displeasure about the open-door-policy before, now she stared daggers at the back of the sept-minister's head. She very obviously did not like hearing that the wyntonans would make better Marines than humans. There was a low exhalation of 50 pairs of lungs as all of the recruits came to the same conclusion—such comments were going to make their lives just that much harder.

Leif wasn't sure the sept-minister was even correct. The wyntonan might be stronger, they might have better endurance—he didn't know what the man was saying about "environmental" advantages—but the humans could put on bursts of speed and effort when required. More than that, while wyntonan militaristic tendencies had been suppressed over the years, the humans thrived on it. Leif didn't know many humans, but from what he'd observed, they were a quarrelsome, aggressive race. They couldn't have taken over seven other races without a proclivity to warfare. They could not have beaten back the sassares in several confrontations without being a warrior race.

The sept-minister continued for almost 20 minutes in that vein. Very little of it registered with him. He simply zoned out while the sept-minster droned on. All the time, the commanding general seemed to be getting more disgusted with the man. At last, the man finally quit. He left the reviewing platform, then came down to the platoon, bypassing the senior, and went up to Martin, the recruit squad leader for First Squad, and shook his hand. He went down the line, shaking hands before moving back a rank and starting in with Second Squad.

The general didn't follow, instead stopping beside the senior. She said something to Gunny Richardson, but too quietly for Leif to hear.

If there was some protocol for shaking hands while in formation, the recruits hadn't been taught that. Coupled with the fact that wyntonans didn't shake hands as a practice, the entire evolution was awkward. Once the sept-minister had shaken his hand and passed on, Leif kept watching the general and senior, knowing those two had far more control over his life than the emperor's *pinkernes*.

When the sept-minister had shaken the hand of the last recruit in Fourth Squad, the general's visage changed to a pleasant smile as the man approached her.

"Shall we join the reception?" she said, loud enough for Leif to hear.

"Yes, yes, yes," the sept-minister said. "His imperial majesty will be leaving within the hour, but I think we have time for me to introduce you to him. Have you met him before?"

The general said something, putting an arm around the man's shoulder and escorting him away. The senior turned around, ever so slowly, then stood there for along moment, saying nothing, until he broke the silence with a quick, "DIs, rejoin the platoon."

There was a rush of feet from behind the formation, and within a moment, there was a DI at the head and tail end of each squad.

"The honored sept-minister seems to think that you ghosts are supermen, better than us mere humans."

Oh, hell. Here is comes.

"Far be it from me to *ever* question such a worthy, so we're going to take a little jog right now to the Stick and back."

Leif had never heard of the "Stick," but whatever it was, he was pretty sure he wasn't going to like it.

Chapter 7

Seven days after their first trip to the Stick and back, Leif's lungs were burning despite the thick air of Iwo Jima. As he'd discovered after the emperor's visit, the "Stick" was the remains of some transplanted Earth tree that had not managed to survive the planet's temperature fluctuations. The Stick was exactly 2.7 klicks (Leif was still having problems converting distances to the human system) from the back gate, and at least twice a day over the first week of Phase 1, some transgression resulted in a "Stick call." This time, not one, not two, but three of his fellow recruits had dropped their dummy rifles during drill. That had been too much for Drill Instructor Dream Bear, one of the calmer DI's, and he'd exploded, sending the platoon out on the punishment run.

Leif didn't mind it. He *hated* drill with a passion. Why a modern Marine had to put up with the mind-numbing marching torture was beyond him. Running, now, that was different. Pushing his body to the limits was something he understood.

Some 20 meters ahead, the lead pack of four had remained out of reach for the last klick to the Stick, but there was still a lot of ground over which he could catch up. He focused on the small of Ann's back as if he could lock on with his eyes and have her pull him along.

A sharp pain on the back of his thigh broke him from his reverie, causing him to stumble.

"Get your ass up there, Hollow. You going to let them beat you back?" Sergeant Dream Bear said as he passed him, casually swinging the baton he'd used to smack him.

A small growl escaped from his lips before he could clamp down. The People were made for long distances, not sprints like this, but the humans, at least the DI's, were ungodly quick. It didn't make sense. With longer legs and slimmer frames, he and his fellow recruits should be faster, but the stocky humans, with their short legs, could fly.

Leif reached down deep inside him and pushed to speed up. His breath became even more labored, his lungs burned, but he started to close the gap to the lead four. Sergeant Dream Bear rounded them and headed back.

"Don't let me pass you, Hollow!" he shouted as he ran to the stragglers in the rear of the pack.

Leif immediately started to relax just a bit with the DI facing away from him, but he thought, *No, Leefen, just push through it!*

He doubled down and kept up the pace, closing in centimeter by centimeter. Halfway back to camp, the lead four were only ten meters ahead.

"I'm coming, don't let me pass you," the sergeant shouted from somewhere behind. "Lester, I mean you. Get your ass in gear."

For the Mother, shut up!

He didn't have to turn around—he could hear the sergeant's progress as he moved up the pack. Closer and closer he came, and a wave of fury washed over him. He wasn't going to let that . . . that *human* beat him, even if it killed him. From somewhere, he found an extra gear, an extra milligram of energy.

"I'm on you, Recruit Hollow. Do not let me pass you," the sergeant said in an infuriatingly calm voice.

Worse than that, he started poking Leif in the ass with the baton. Not hard enough to make him stumble, but tap, tap, tap, tap, enough to enrage him. He lunged ahead, getting just out of reach of the baton, but a moment later, the sergeant was back: tap, tap, tap, tap.

I don't care what a'Silverton says, I'm going to kill the sergeant!

He pushed ahead, past the pain, somehow reaching the front four, and gloriously, the double-damned tapping ceased—for a few moments. Sergeant Dream Bear took turns, tapping each of the five in the butt as he wove his way through them, all the time his ogre voice making fun of them, demeaning them. Each time Leif was the sergeant's target, his entire body tensed up, but he managed to fall into the rhythm, ignoring the humiliation while he sped up, putting another target between the DI and him. Anger fueled him.

And then they were inside the gate and back on the parade deck. The five came to a stop and bent over, hands on their knees. Leif could barely see straight, and it was probably good that he was so spent—he didn't have the energy to confront the sergeant.

"See, it doesn't hurt any more finishing first than if you'd lagged back twenty meters," the sergeant said to him, hand on his shoulder. "Remember that."

And in a flash he was gone, going to round up the stragglers, yelling, "Don't let me pass you!" as he ran.

What the hell? Leif started before he realized what the sergeant had said. Not just the words, but the lesson there.

Sergeant Dream Bear was right. His lungs were on fire, his guts were aching, and he was ready to puke up the human chow he'd eaten for breakfast—not that puking would be a new experience—even with their meds, none of them were yet used to human food. Despite his pain, he knew that it would be just as intense as if he'd finished the run 20 meters back.

If he was going to hurt anyway, then why settle for second? He might as well push himself and come out on top.

More and more of his fellow recruits reached the parade deck. Jordan, stopping alongside of him, did puke, some of the oatmeal splashing on Leif's boots. And he didn't care. He'd learned something today. That short, *radli*-legged human had taught him a life lesson, and those kinds of lessons needed to be treasured.

That didn't mean he was happy, though, when a barely-breathing-hard sergeant said, "OK, back in formation. Let's see if we can't get through the next hour without anyone dropping their weapons."

He might have learned something today, but close-order drill still sucked hind tit.

Chapter 8

"What is this stuff?" Jordan asked, sitting down next to Leif, then poking at the mass of yellow-covered tubes on his tray.

"They call it Mac 'n Cheese," Leif told him.

Jordan leaned in and took a sniff, then recoiled, disgust on his face. Leif understood the feeling. Food—if what the humans ate could be called that—was the worst thing about "the Pit," the nickname for Camp Navarro. Along with the supplements and meds they took each morning, they could tolerate the food and got their needed nutrients, but that didn't take into account taste.

Well, "tolerate" was a generous term. Most of the platoon spent a good portion of the first few days in the head, shitting their guts out, but most of them had adjusted by now. They just didn't like the taste of most of the food being served to them. Leif would give anything for just a taste of hunter's stew or a fresh pokkyfruit.

"Just put your spice on it and eat. We've got a 15-klick hump this afternoon, and we don't need anyone falling out," Leif said.

Every single recruit had brought a supply of spice with them—something the officious Ferron a'Silverton had demanded they be allowed to bring—and frankly, the only good thing the council rep had done for them. Without the spice, Leif doubted that he'd have been able to swallow half of what had been served to him. The problem was that with such bad food, the recruits were going through their stashes quicker than expected. There was no way their spice was going to last until the next Spice Day.

Jordan shrugged and pulled out a packet of spice from his pocket, sprinkling it liberally over the mac 'n cheese.

Not that your weak Hottento mix is going to do much good, Leif thought. *You need some good Hope Hollow spice mix.*

He didn't voice that aloud. The People took great pride in their village or neighborhood mix, and criticizing another mix was a good way to start a fight.

"At least the bread is good," Leif remarked, taking another bite of the slice in his hand, the third slice he'd begun.

The humans loved their bread, with several varieties offered at each meal. They slathered the pieces with butter—a rather disgusting concoction made from animal milk, of all things—fruit preserves, and a brown paste called Vegemite, which wasn't bad, but Leif liked the "sandwich" bread, on which he put a dark, Greunhild mustard. There was always bread and mustard available, so no matter what vile mess the humans served, there was always something he could eat, and something on which he didn't need to use his spice mix.

"It's OK, but I need meat! A good ibent steak, so rare it hoots when I stick my knife in it."

"Shut up, Jordan," Crissy said from across the table, throwing a wadded-up napkin at him. "I don't need you reminding me."

Jordan mimed using a knife and fork to cut his mac 'n cheese, then hooted his best ibent hoot.

The wyntonan recruits were kept separated from the humans, but there was only the one chow hall at the Pit, so there were always humans eating at the same time as them. There had been lots of staring and more than a few comments meant to be overheard, but so far, there had been no direct contact between human and wyntonan recruits.

When Jordan hooted, however, a group of human recruits at the next table turned around, one of them saying, "Fucking animals."

"Jordan, cut it," Crissy said quietly.

Jordan looked around, caught the eyes of the humans, then raised his fork with a piece of mac 'n cheese impaled on the tines and said, "Hoot, hoot!"

One of the recruits, a pale—for a human—stocky guy stood up, shaking off the arms of his buddies who tried to pull him down, and walked over to them.

"So, you *ghosts* really think you can become Marines?" he said, sneering down at the sitting recruits.

Leif kicked Jordan's legs under the table.

"I heard you're all just here to be politically correct. You'll never be real Marines."

"Knut, that's enough. You know what the senior told us," one of the other humans said.

"I'm not messing with them. I just want to get to know our *brother* recruits," he said.

Leif was becoming better at understanding the humans, but even before, he could not have missed the human's sarcasm.

"So, what is that shit you keep putting on our good Marine Corps chow, anyway? Is it some drug, you know, to keep you high?"

"It's our spice," Leif said in a calm tone, hoping a simple answer would make the recruit go back to his table. "We use it on all our food back on Home."

"Well, you ain't back home now, so you should be eating what we eat if you want to grow up big and strong," he said, pulling up his arm and flexing an admittedly impressive bicep. "Not your spice, and not, what is that, just bread and mustard? Who the hell eats that?"

"Knut!" the same human who'd spoken before said with a note of urgency.

"Don't get your panties in a twist. The senior said we're going to have to get used to having ghosts around, so, I'm just trying to get to know our good buddies."

He turned back to the wyntonan recruits, leaned over Jordan and picked up his plate of food. Leif grabbed Jordan's thigh in a death grip, keeping him from standing. One thing no one did, especially in the Silver Range, was touch another's food once it had been served.

Knut took a deep sniff of the mac 'n cheese, then erupted in a sneezing fit, the plate falling out of his hand and splattering both Jordan and Leif.

"Holy crap! They're eating shit!" he wheezed out. "Oh, my God! You guys should smell it."

"Nilson, what the hell are you doing!" an authoritative voice rang out, silencing the murmur of conversation that filled the chow hall as a couple of hundred sets of eyes swerved to see who was the voice's target.

"Nothing, Drill Instructor Tannery!"

"It sure doesn't look like it's nothing to me," the voice cut like steel.

"I'm . . . I just wanted to welcome our guests, Drill Instructor!"

The recruit was now standing at attention, and Leif could see him wrinkle his nose before erupting in a huge sneeze that sprayed his fellow human recruits.

"What did the senior tell you about lying? On T-1?"

"Marines don't lie to each other, never, Drill Instructor Tannery."

"So, why are you lying to me now?"

The entire chow hall was deathly silent, 200 recruits afraid to breathe.

"I'm not—"

"Can it, Recruit! You and me, right now, to the Stick and back. You can explain it to me while we run."

The recruit visibly wilted, and for a moment, Leif felt a twinge of sympathy . . . but only for a moment.

"Yes, Drill Instructor Tannery," he said, then under his breath, "Don't think I'll forget this, ghosts. I'll pay you back."

"Now, Nilson. Oh, and bring the rest of the platoon with you."

There were groans as the entire platoon stood up and started making their way to the still unseen drill instructor somewhere behind Leif. The recruit who'd started it all gave Jordan a bump on the back as he ran to meet the drill instructor. Leif didn't watch, but kept his eyes locked on Crissy sitting across from him. A few moments later, the chow erupted into noise as everyone tried to talk at once.

"Tannery's going to run them into the ground," one of the remaining humans said, loud enough for the wyntonan to hear. "And it's all because of those fucking ghosts."

Leif wiped the mac 'n cheese off his shoulder the best he could, then offered Jordan his last piece of bread. "Better eat up. We've still got that hump this afternoon."

Chapter 9

All 50 recruits waited in the classroom, excited that they were finally going into T-1, the first day of recruit training. The last four weeks had been hectic, a constant physical and mental push. Despite dire threats, despite half-a-dozen recruits being continually called out for extra training, every one of them (excepting Kelli) had passed the evaluation phase. They'd have the same DIs, so in reality, nothing much had changed, but to simply get to the official training was a huge psychological boost.

"Platoon, atten . . . HUT!" Sergeant Dream Bear shouted as the 50 recruits jumped to attention.

Captain Kahn and Senior Drill Instructor Richardson walked in, followed by Ferron a'Silverton and Sept-Minister Iaxi. Leif had never seen the two civilians together, but it made sense that they were working with each other.

Captain Kahn stood by his seat in the front of the classroom and shouted out, "Platoon 5001, you have completed your evaluation phase of training and are now ready for T-1."

A chorus of "ooh-rahs" echoed throughout the room. He held up a hand to quiet them down, and Senior Richardson shouted out, "At ease!"

"There have been some changes, though, and I'll turn this over to Sept-Minister Iaxi."

The sept-minister nodded, then walked up to the podium. "Is this thing on?

"OK, then. As you know, the plan was that the wyntonan platoon," he started, almost getting in a reasonable "n" at the end of the word, "would go through training as a separate platoon, apart from human recruit platoons."

Whatever the sept-minister was going to say next, Ferron a'Silverton didn't look too happy about it.

"However, his imperial highness has taken it upon himself to interject into your training. You are here to initiate the integration of your people into the Imperial Marines, so, it doesn't make sense to segregate you during training. He was direct in his orders that from T-1 on, all of you will be integrated into the general recruit population."

Leif had not seen that coming, and he wasn't quite sure what he felt about it. He'd gotten comfortable in the wyntonan platoon, all of them of the People. His perception of how the human recruits felt about them was wary at best, antagonistic at worst. Sure, there were some that had reached out to them, to ask questions or to say they were glad the wyntonans were entering the Corps, but those were in the minority.

Integrating the wyntonan recruits with the humans, though, made sense. If they were going to be integrated into the fleet upon graduation, then they might as well start now. The emperor was right in that.

The sept-minster was droning on, stressing how well this reflected upon the concept, taking what seemed to be an inordinate amount of credit for the fact that they were there in the first place and now integrated. Leif wondered just how much of that was true.

Ferron a'Silverton frowned during the sept-minister's speech. That made sense as well. Splitting up the platoon was going to make it that much more difficult to ride herd on them.

And they were going to be split up. Captain Kahn took the podium, explaining that First and Second Squads were going to the incoming lead series, one to each platoon, and Third and Fourth were going to the trail series. The end result was that each recruit platoon would start with close to 90 recruits, a dozen being of the People.

Captain Khan was going to be the Lead Series commander, and Senior Drill Instructor Richardson was to be Platoon 4013's lead hat. The other DI's were to be spread-loaded among the four platoons.

The 50 recruits had been excited to be finally advancing to T-1. Leif was still excited, but now that was shaded with just a bit of uncertainty. Recruit training was about to get real.

Chapter 10

"What do you think?" Tessa asked. "Should we try?"

Leif didn't respond, more than willing to let the others make a decision. The twelve wyntonan recruits in the platoon were huddled in the back of the squadbay. They had just returned from their weekly meeting with Ferron a'Silverton, the first since they'd joined the integrated platoon.

Without the human sept-minister at the meeting, their minder had been blunt. Eyes, both human and wyntonan, were on them, and how things proceeded would have a major impact on the future of the program, which had not yet fully recovered from Kelli's assault on a DI.

Several of them had mentioned the outright racism some of the humans exhibited, and a'Silverton told them to try and enlist allies from the other humans. Peer pressure, he explained, could go a long way in achieving social engineering.

Leif wasn't sure that would be effective, or even if it was needed. Sure, there were some racist assholes, and even some of the DIs seemed to resent them in the two series. Leif hated that to no end, but there was nothing overt, no physical harassment. Most of the recruits seemed oblivious to the People in their presence—boot camp was stressful enough to worry about things out of their control. Some recruits even seemed to welcome them, going out of their way to say hello or decry racism. Leif was of the mind that it was better to leave things alone. Let them prove their worth, and the humans would accept them well enough.

It seemed as if he was in the minority, though. Most of the others seemed to want to implement a'Silverton's direction. The question was who to "enlist." Two humans had already dropped, so there were 87 of them left in the platoon. They came from a wide array of planets and social classes and were from a handful of subgroups. Tessa and Keijo seemed to think that the subgroups were the answer, specifically the trolls.

"Trolls" were heavy-worlders, humans who'd been genetically modified in the womb to live on heavy-G planets. Shorter than most human subgroups, they had huge shoulders, no necks to speak of, and pylon-like legs. Immensely strong, they were sometimes teased by other humans as being dumb, an assumption for which Leif saw no evidence. They were still 100% human, but they seemed to be the butt of jokes among other humans, the "regs," as in "regulars." That is why they seemed to be a logical ally. As being on the receiving end of discrimination, they would know what it was like.

"I guess they'd be a reasonable choice," Jordan said, not sounding too sure of himself.

"But who?" Johari asked. "There are nine trolls in the platoon."

Leif had to keep from shaking his head. "Troll" might be a commonly-used term, but he didn't think the heavy-worlders appreciated it. Here they were, gathering to discuss how to combat racism, and Johari casually used a term for a subgroup that almost certainly had negative connotations.

After a few more moments of discussion, the group decided on approaching Krys and Manu. Krys had seemed pleasant enough with his ever-present smile and easy-going nature. Manu, whose nickname was "Tank," was quieter, but he seemed to be a leader among the heavy-worlders.

"No time like the present," Keijo said, pointing with his chin in wyntonan fashion to Manu, who was sitting on the deck beside his rack, head buried in a scanscreen.

Almost as one, the group started to move across the squadbay to the other recruit.

This is not how to do it, Leif thought, even if he stayed with the others.

The People liked to flock together in groups, but that sometimes stifled individual initiative. If the group was doing something, then it was the right thing to do—at least that was the psychology. This groupthink seemed to serve them well at bootcamp, but that didn't mean it was the best way to proceed in every situation.

With most of the platoon at one of the three chapels, not many recruits were there to watch the 12 wyntonan as they reached Manu and stood in a loose semi-circle around him. He ignored them for a long moment, still reading, but at last he looked up.

"What do you freaks want?" he asked.

"Recruit Savea, we would like to talk with you," Tessa said, taking the lead.

"About what?"

"We would like to extend our hand in friendship to you and the other trolls."

The slight twitch of Manu's eyebrows confirmed Leif's belief that the term was not appreciated.

"And why are you doing that? I see others in the squadbay. Why am I blessed by your attention?"

"Why, because we understand that the other humans discriminate against you, so by logic—"

Manu stood up, all 1.7 meters of him, but exuding an almost malevolent power. "And you fucking ghosts think that I want anything to do with you mohawk-headed freaks? Get the fuck out of here. I'm *human*, not some skinny-ass, pale mother-fucker."

"But, doesn't it make—"

Manu stepped forward and gave Tessa a shot in the chest, knocking her back. The heavy-worlder might be short, but he was probably stronger than any of the wyntonans.

"I said, get the fuck away from me. I don't want anything to do with you."

The moment he'd shoved Tessa, the other eleven of them took a step forward, but the human didn't follow through with anything more.

"Let's go," Leif said, grabbing Tessa by the arm.

"Smart fucking ghost," Manu said with a sneer on his face. "That's right, go and don't ever come up to me again."

As Leif pulled Tessa away, the rest followed.

Leif hadn't been confident that the direct approach would work, but he hadn't thought Recruit Savea would react aggressively. It was obvious, that even after five weeks on Iwo

Jima, they knew next to nothing about what made humans tick.

And that did not bode well for the future.

Chapter 11

"Here we go," Tessa said as they ran up to the wall.

This was going to kill Leif, but he knew it was the right thing to do. The attempt to befriend Savea had resulted in the recruit becoming a leader of those who were opposed to the wyntonans' presence. Their fearless minder, safe in his apartment out in the ville, had not been deterred, and he'd told them to try a new tack. This one might even work, however.

During their first run of the O-course—a torturous, 31-obstacle run, the wyntonan recruits had fared very well, with Keijo finishing in 22 minutes, fourteen seconds. Leif was eight seconds behind, and all twelve finished among the top 25. Leif was sorry he hadn't finished with the quickest time, but if someone had to beat him, he was glad it was a fellow wyntonan. The twelve gathered together to the side as the rest of the humans straggled in—and had to join in the punishment run when the last 16 recruits finished after the 40-minute cut-off.

Leif hadn't been happy at that, and for once, he agreed with Recruit Tolbert, the human with the fastest time, coming in ten seconds behind him. As they ran to the Stick and back, Tolbert muttered that it wasn't fair. This was an individual evolution, and if someone had to be punished, it should be the "limp dicks" who couldn't hack it.

That made sense to Leif as well. In drill or other platoon events, it was reasonable that they were all graded together. The O-Course, however, was an individual event.

During their weekly meeting with a'Silverton, the discussion centered on how to best gain allies, and Tessa suggested they help some of the slower recruits. If they did that, surely those recruits would see their value?

Leif had never been onboard with simply going up to the heavy-worlders and asking for some sort of alliance, but this made more sense to him. Show the humans their worth, and they'd be accepted. As much as he wanted to push the pace and come in first, he could accept the plan's potential viability.

The problem with the O-Course (and what made it so alluring to Leif) was that unlike a simple run, it tested all aspects of a recruit's fitness. Tolbert was faster than any of the wyntonans, but as he was shorter than most humans, he had a harder time climbing the Stairway to Heaven or the Reversed Pyramid. Some of the larger humans had problems with the Gopher Run or the Habitat. By the grace of the Mother, the wyntonan were tall enough to reach the climbing obstacles but without the mass the heavy-worlders had to haul up and down. They could almost match the smaller recruits crawling on their bellies. It was as if the course was designed specifically for them to kick human ass.

The first of the difficult obstacles for some of the humans was the Berlin Wall. Three meters tall and with a reverse tilt, it was quite a reach for the shorter recruits. Just ahead of the wyntonans, running as a group, Tolbert and the rest of the lead pack were already on the wall, some pulling themselves easily over, while others struggled a bit.

Eight of the wyntonan recruits were up and over. Four—Tessa, Leif, Ulysses, and Mark—stopped on the near side, ready to assist the others. Tolbert was struggling, just missing his grab for the top.

"Use me," Leif said, cupping his hands down around his knees. The recruit looked at him suspiciously, then took a couple of steps and used Leif's boost to reach the top.

"Hey, thanks!" he said as he disappeared over the other side.

They weren't the only ones staying back. As during last time, a couple of other human recruits stayed to help, and with the four wyntonans' assistance, all of the recruits made it over—some barely, but at least over.

That didn't stop the DIs, though. They kept a screaming tirade going on, including at those who stopped to help as well as those having problems. Evidently, they weren't as happy with the strategy. Their fellow recruits were, though.

With the last recruit over the Berlin Wall, those assisting went over as well. Four obstacles further was the

Reverse Pyramid, an ascending series of platforms, each one larger than the one below. Jordan, Eva, Keijo, and Moria were there with two humans, helping anyone having problems. Jordan and Moria were on the ground with the two humans, Eva and Keijo on top of the first platform. This had proven to be a killer obstacle for the heavy-worlders. It took jumping to catch the edge of the higher platform, then upper-body strength to pull themselves up, all with legs dangling in the air.

Recruit Savea was at the obstacle, and he was not happy. Leif didn't know whether that was because he needed help or that it was Jordan and Moria who were boosting his heavy body up to the first platform.

The four wyntonans didn't stop to help at this obstacle. Leif easily jumped up, pushing past the panting Savea with a trite, "You've got it, Manu." He turned before the big recruit could see his smile. They had promised each other to help the humans, but that didn't mean Leif couldn't interject a little dig.

Not just human recruits, though, had problems with the Reverse Pyramid. Mark had come in as the last of the wyntonans on the first O-Course. This obstacle, along with the Stairway to Heaven, had proven difficult for him. Leif reached down, offering a hand, and with a small boost from Jordan, he pulled Mark up. With three more platforms, it still took Leif and Mark another 45 seconds to get to the top. Up ahead, he could see recruits half-way through the course. Shouts of the DIs rose from the dust below.

"Let's go, *Merkan*," he said, using Mark's real name.

Lark, Azure, Dubois, and Johari were at the Snake Bridge, but now joined with six humans who were helping as well. All were shouting encouragement, steadying the recruits as they attempted to low-crawl across one of the ropes.

Leif and Mark stuck together, attacking each obstacle. Leif knew he'd given up finishing in first place, but he still wanted to give it his all. It just wasn't in him to take it easy.

Up ahead, recruits were already going over the Stairway to Heaven, a 30-meter tall platform with cargo nets on either side. The cargo nets were loose, so they gave with each step, making them difficult to climb. On the last run, six recruits had frozen on the net, refusing to climb farther. Another ten took too long and were not able to finish the course before the cut-off.

There were still many recruits behind the two wyntonans, and Leif tried to estimate how much time was left. There was nothing he could do about it, so he pushed on.

A few minutes later, Leif and Mark flew over the Wicked Z, the second-to-last obstacle. Standing tall, as if guarding the last run to the finish line, the Stairway to Heaven stood, looking imposing. Leif had managed to finish second, but the Stairway had kicked his ass. He'd been so beat that he'd almost let Tolbert catch him on the sprint to the finish. If the finish line had been another 20 meters farther, the human *would* have passed him.

And now, here he was, instead of climbing it now, waiting. That made him nervous. Depending on when the last few recruits reached this far, he wasn't sure he'd have enough time and energy to finish in time himself—and the thought of failure was almost too horrible to bear.

Two human recruits stopped with them, breathing heavily, but turning to face the rest. A minute later, Tessa and Ulysses reached them.

"You ready to get these recruits over this thing?" Tessa asked.

The two humans gave a loud ooh-rah.

Tessa had been asking Mark and him, and she looked up in surprise before a huge smile broke out over her face and she raised her hand to give them a human high-five. "Let's do it!"

Hell, maybe this is bringing us together.

The recruits reaching them were among the fitter ones, and they didn't need help other than a bit of encouragement. It wasn't until ten or twelve fellow recruits hit the net that there was a problem. With the DIs screaming, Recruit Angus Zhen stopped, five meters from the top, arms clasped through the net.

"You've better get moving, Zhen," Drill Instructor Petrov shouted. "If I have to come up there, that will be two failures, and this isn't even in full battle rattle. Three failures, and you get dropped."

Leif was moving before he realized it. He clambered up the net, struggling to get a rhythm. It was impossible, though. His upper body hung out, and there was too much give in the ropes. He wasn't sure how the heavier recruits managed it.

Below him, Petrov kept up his tirade, but Leif kept his eyes locked on Zhen, afraid he'd fall. There was spongemat under each obstacle in case of falls, but this was 25 meters up, and he wasn't sure mats would be enough to protect him.

Finally, Leif was beside the trembling recruit.

"Come on, Zhen-man," he said. "You've got it."

"No, I don't. I'm going to fall," he whispered.

Zhen-man was one of the more popular recruits, a squadbay leader, and one who seemed to accept the wyntonans. Even the DIs liked him. But this was one of the five pass-fail events at boot camp. If he failed this three times, he was out, no matter how well he performed everywhere else.

"No, you're not going to fall. You're almost at the top. Just look up."

"I can't," he said, his eyes screwed shut.

Yes, you can. Look, I'm going to put my hand on yours and guide you up another step," Leif said, reaching out to grab Zhen's hand.

"No!" screamed the recruit, jerking back so violently that Leif almost lost his grip.

Recruit Urban, one of the heavy-worlders the 12 wyntonans had hoped to approach, came up beside them, Tessa alongside, giving him encouragement. Each step made the net shake, which caused Zhen to hug it tighter.

Urban gave Leif a sad shake of the head and said, "You might have to leave him."

"Come on, Krys," Tessa said. "Leif will take care of him. Let's get you over."

With a grunt of effort, the recruit pushed forward, not stopping until he had his hand on the top.

"Thanks. I've got it from here," he told Tessa, who nodded and started to climb back down.

"You need any help?" she asked Leif as she drew level with them.

"No, we've got it. Right, Zhen-man?"

The recruit said nothing, and his arms were trembling more. Leif knew something had to happen before Zhen's arms gave out.

He shifted his body, moving behind Zhen, until he was straddling the human, almost pinning him in place.

"What are you doing?" Zhen asked in a panic. "Stop!"

"Well, if all you're going to do is hang here until you do fall, I thought I'd help myself to your sweet ass," he said, trying to put the same tone into his voice as he heard when the human recruits trashed-talked each other.

"What?" Zhen asked, grabbing the next rope and pulling himself in closer to the wall to get some distance between them.

"See, you can still climb," Leif said. "Just keep doing it."

"But—"

"But nothing. You can't fall. I'm in the way. Look at me."

Slowly, Zhen turned his head, looking out of the corner of his eyes until he could see Leif perched there behind him.

"If you fall, I've got you. You've got four more rungs, and you're home free."

Zhen's head started to tilt down when Leif yelled, "No! Head up. Always up."

"My arms are too tired," Zhen said in a defeated voice.

"They sure had enough left in the tank when you thought I was going to rape you up here in front of the entire platoon."

Zhen gave a brief chuckle, then said, "Well, I guess that's true enough. You took me by surprise."

"You guys OK?" another recruit asked, coming alongside of them. "Zhen-man?"

"We're OK. You keep going."

"You've got it Zhen," the recruit said.

"We are OK, right?" Leif asked Zhen. "We're about to climb to the top, right?"

"You won't let me fall?"

"I won't let you fall."

I hope.

One key to the Stairway to Heaven was to keep vertical and let the legs support the weight. With Zhen between him and the net, he was hanging back at an angle, and that was rough on his arms. He couldn't hang there forever.

"Now, Zhen. We're running out of time. Right hand, reach up."

Amazingly, Zhen reached up, grabbed the next horizontal rope, and pulled up while pushing with his legs before bringing up his left hand.

"Again!"

Zhen responded . . . and again.

"Keep going. You've got this."

Somehow, Zhen reached the top, where a bar made for an easy grip on the beam. Zhen quickly slid over, then hung on the other side, looking through the nets at Leif, face-to-face.

"I've got it now. I . . . thanks."

"You sure? You're OK?"

"Yeah. I'm OK. Hey, what's your name, anyway?"

"Leif," he answered, somehow hurt that Zhen didn't know it.

"No, your real name. I heard you all got human names assigned to you."

"Uh . . . Leefen," he said, taken aback by the question.

"Thanks, Leefen," Zhen said, almost managing the final "n." "You're good people."

And with that, he started down—not quickly, but without stopping. Leif watched him for a moment, a warm feeling in his heart, before he started back down himself.

"You coming back down, Hollow?" Drill Instructor Petrov yelled up at him. "You don't have much time."

Leif ignored him, passing others on their way up. Down on the ground, five more were starting.

"Is this all?"

"Porterhouse is still coming. She's the last one," one of the recruits shouted down from five meters up the net.

"I've got her. You go," Mark said.

"No, I'm quicker on the net. You go."

Mark hesitated only a moment before nodding and starting to climb.

What Leif had said was true, but he was also beat. His arms were burning, and he needed a few moments of rest. Within a minute, he was the only one left on the ground—except for Drill Instructor Petrov, of course.

"You fucked up, Hollow. No way you're going to make it in time."

"I can fail three times, Drill Instructor. I can afford it," he snapped before his brain could stop his mouth.

He froze, waiting for the inevitable, but Petrov only laughed, saying, "Risky, Recruit, risky."

Where is she? he wondered, turning his attention away from the drill instructor.

He jogged back to the Wicked Z and spotted her, edging her way along the raised rail.

"Come on, Porterhouse!" he shouted. "Move it!"

She startled, looking up and almost losing her balance. If she fell, she'd have to go back to the beginning of the obstacle.

"I hurt my ankle. You go on."

He looked back at the Stairway where the last of the platoon had reached the top and were climbing over. He was pretty sure that no matter what he did, it was too late, so he decided to stay.

"Just get through it. Take your time."

Stupid thing to say, he thought as he paced, waiting for her.

Four DIs slowly walked alongside the course, even with her, watching and saying nothing.

She reached the end and jumped off, almost collapsing as her leg buckled.

"Recruit Porterhouse, do you need a corpsman?" Drill Instructor Dream Bear asked.

She looked up at Leif, who shook his head, and she said, "No, Drill Instructor."

Leif stepped up beside her, and with her limping, they jogged to the Stairway. He didn't know how she would manage that, but whatever she'd done to her ankle, it didn't stop her from climbing. It was Leif, as tired as he was, who held her back.

At the top, he looked toward the finish line, some 500 meters distant. He could hear cheers as the last of the other recruits reach the finish. Leif couldn't hear their times, but he hoped they made it before the cut-off.

"Just down, then a little jog," he told Porterhouse. "Easy."

His arms were burning and his thighs trembling by the time his feet touched good old Iwo Jima again. The cheering was getting louder, and he looked up. It looked like the entire platoon was charging them.

"Can you run?" he asked.

"I can try."

The two started jogging, Porterhouse's face contorted in pain as the platoon got closer.

The first Marine to reach them was Tolbert, and as he reached to help Porterhouse, Senior Drill Instructor Richardson yelled out, "No touching. You're already off the course!"

Tolbert froze, confused.

"You're off the course, Tolbert. All of you," the senior shouted, his voice piercing the hubbub. "All of you are off the course. You will *not* intervene."

There was dead quiet for a moment, and in the silence, Leif heard a voice shouting out, "Thirty-eight, twenty-five, thirty-eight, twenty-six . . ."

"Come on, Porterhouse! We can make it," he said, bolting forward.

"Ahg!" Porterhouse shouted, falling to the ground. "I can't," she said, sobbing in frustration while holding her ankle.

Leif looked back to the finish line. He could make it, he knew. Porterhouse was a lost cause and staying back with her would do no good. He wasn't abandoning her—he was just making a rational decision.

You can't.

In one of their first classes on Marine Corps history, they'd been taught that a Marine never leaves another behind. He wasn't a Marine yet; Porterhouse wasn't a Marine yet. But if he wanted to become one, he had to embrace the ideals that made the Corps what it is.

He ran back to her and picked her up, putting her arm around his shoulders.

"Walk it off. It'll get numb."

That worked for wyntonans, and he hoped it worked for humans, too.

He started running as the platoon started cheering. Tolbert and . . . and Zhen-man came alongside, yelling their encouragement. Porterhouse limped heavily, but her stride evened out a bit. Each step elicited a grunt, but she kept going.

As they got closer, he could see one of the Physical Fitness DIs standing at the finish line, holding a stopwatch. Leif strained to pull Porterhouse along, breathing heavily, but unable to hear the count.

"We've got this," he kept saying, over and over.

"Thirty-nine, fifteen," he finally heard over the noise of the platoon.

"Shit!"

They were still too far way and moving too slowly.

"Porterhouse, I want you to grab my belt, and whatever you do, don't let go!" he yelled into her ear.

A look of . . . fear? . . . came over her, but she nodded, and Leif slipped her arm off of his neck. As soon as he felt her hand clamp on his belt, he sped up, pulling Porterhouse with him. She cried out in pain, but she didn't let go.

He could run faster, but she'd lose her grip. He was skirting a fine line.

Everything else faded. He no longer heard the platoon as they ran beside them. He didn't even see them. His entire universe was the DI up ahead, the path to him, and Porterhouse who was still holding on. At 100 meters, he felt a thrill as he knew they would make it. He pushed hard, trying to will themselves over the finish.

He was so excited that he almost missed the DI shouting out, "forty-oh-nine" as the two lunged over the line and fell to the ground, Porterhouse on top of him.

Forty-oh-nine? It can't be!

But it was. Recruits were cheering, but they must not have heard. They'd failed. Eighty-seven recruits had passed the O-Course—and two had failed.

The adrenaline that had fueled that last sprint faded as if it had never been there. He had expected to fail when he waited for Porterhouse, but then his hopes had been raised. That was somehow worse, to come so close and not make it.

"Thank you for trying, Hollow," Porterhouse said, leaning into to his ear.

The senior strode over and stood over to them for a moment, his expression unreadable. He turned to the DI with the stopwatch and took it from him, looking at it for a moment.

"Thirty-nine, fifty-nine," he said. "Well, everyone passed, Captain," he added, looking up to where Captain Khan had been watching.

What?

Leif knew what he'd heard when they crossed the line. They'd failed.

Evidently the senior didn't think so. Neither did the others. Even Petrov had a shit-eating grin on his face.

"You've got 30 minutes to get showered and be ready for evening meal formation. I'd suggest you get moving."

The recruits did move . . . but to Leif and Porterhouse, pounding their backs and cheering.

For the first time since he'd arrived on Iwo Jima, Leif had a tiny inkling of what it might mean to be a Marine.

Chapter 12

Leif hummed as he scrubbed the urinals. The People had music like all sentient beings, of course, but humming was something that wasn't normally done. After being around the humans for five weeks, however, Leif had picked up the habit.'

Besides, he was happy. Ever since the O-Course two weeks ago, he was on at least neutral terms with most of his fellow recruits. Not everyone, though. A few of the haters seemed to take it as an insult that it took the wyntonans in general, and Leif, in particular, to figure out that the DIs treated the platoon as a living entity, not as a mob of individuals. Of course, that contention ignored the fact that there had been human recruits helping out others on the O-Course as well.

That didn't mean that haters aside, everyone was best of friends. Zhen-man, Tolbert, "Hawk" Porterhouse, Hernandez, and a few others welcomed the wyntonans. Once the euphoria of the O-Course ended (right about the next morning when the platoon failed an inspection), however, it was mostly back to normal with the wyntonan recruits being outsiders. Not necessarily hated, but outsiders, not brought into casual conversations.

And now, he was doing his favorite duty. His fellow human recruits shied away from the heads. These were old-fashioned heads, with white plasticero urinals and crappers and no automatic disinfectant spray, something most humans just weren't used to—the accepted reason for them was that the DIs wanted something with which they could demean recruits as well as punish them by assigning their cleaning as "special duty."

The head might be primitive to most humans, but not to all, and certainly not to the People. He'd had much worse back in Hope Hollow, and cleaning them was a chore often left to the ada. When Leif volunteered to clean the heads, the rest of his squad were more than happy to let him do it.

It wasn't the actual cleaning that he liked. The best thing about the duty was that it was a chance to be alone. He could hear the rest of the platoon out in the squad bay, but inside the head itself, he was alone. One of the most annoying things about humans was that they talked incessantly, even when they had nothing to say. Jordan said it was because they just enjoyed the sound of their voices, while Lark thought it was because they had some deep-rooted fear of being alone. Leif didn't know the reason—he just wished they'd shut up for a few minutes.

Leif looked down the line of urinals. He had seven more left. He wondered if he could stretch out the time to clean them. If he played it right, he could finish just as everyone else finished up the squadbay. Then they'd have 15 minutes of blessed free time before marching to chow.

The hatch to the head swung open, and Leif expected to see Jordan, in his billet of recruit squad leader. Jordan was the first wyntonan to be assigned as a squad leader, and he'd managed to keep the billet for two days now. Leif knew he wanted to keep it for longer before the inevitable screw-up that would cost him the position.

Leif wished him well, but he wasn't too keen on being assigned the billet himself. He knew most of the human recruits strived for positions of authority. He, along with most of the rest of the wyntonan recruits, just didn't feel the need. When the senior told them a wyntonan had to step up, Jordan had volunteered. Jordan might like the position, but Leif's boot camp was more self-centered. He wanted to prove to himself that he not only had what it takes to succeed, but that he could outdo all the rest. Having a little plastic stripe of a squad leader on his collar didn't do much for him. Still, he'd support Jordan and help him keep that plastic stripe for as long as possible.

Only it wasn't Jordan coming in to check up on him. It was Knut Nilson. Leif turned back around and focused on the urinal. "Viking," as the others called him, was an ass, and he still blamed Jordan for the incident at the chow hall nine weeks ago. He'd pulled a hammy on the Stick-call that day and had been recycled for several weeks, falling into their platoon on T-6 to complete his training. Somehow, in an amazing leap of logic, that was Jordan's fault, too, and by proxy, the fault of all the wyntonans. The O-Course hadn't helped things either, which he alternately said was a set-up by the brass to "make the ghosts look good" or "proof that the ghosts don't have what it takes to make tough decisions." Along with Manu, he'd become a focal point of prejudice and downright harassment of the other wyntonan recruits, regularly voicing his overall opinion that "ghosts shouldn't be Marines." Leif just ignored the man as much as he could.

Sometimes, though, that just wasn't possible.

Viking walked up behind him and stood there for a moment. The small hairs on the back of Leif's crest stood up as he kept cleaning. He adjusted his weight, to be ready to jump up if the man attacked.

"This is the only thing you ghosts are good for," Viking said, heaping scorn into his voice. "Cleaning shitters. You sure ain't Marine material."

It took an effort of will to keep from responding. Ferron a'Silverton reminded them at every meeting that they had to rein in aggression, that they could not respond to racial slights. What they were attempting to do was far more important than personal pride. With only the slightest hesitation of his cleaning brush, he kept scrubbing.

"Yeah, I thought so. You'd suck my dick if I told you to. Hell, I bet you're already doing that, you and ghost-lovers like Hernandez. You're doing it, right? That's why that piece of shit likes you guys. So, tell, me, do you like that? Do you like his dick?"

Leif knew that what Viking was saying was the ultimate insult among humans, but it didn't do much for him. It was just ridiculous, a fantasy, like Drill Instructor Wasyk-Templeton's initial attempts at insults on their second day at Camp Navarro, and so it didn't upset him nearly as much as the accusation that he wasn't Marine material.

When that didn't get a rise out of Leif, Viking snorted and stepped up to the urinal next to Leif, unzipped his cammies trou, and just as he started to piss, he stepped back, swinging his dick around and pissing all over the deck—and splashing Leif in the process.

Leif stared at the yellow drops of urine on his arm, not believing what he was seeing. This was outside of his comprehension.

"Oh, sorry, ghost. No matter, you can lick it up," he said, putting his hand on the back of Leif's neck as if to force his head to the deck.

Leif's mind went calm, his thoughts razor-focused in the same way as when he hunted his lion. He slowly stood up, easily forcing back Viking's hand. The human looked startled for a moment before a smile took over his face.

"Oh, so that's the way it's going to be, ghost. OK, I'm going to—"

Whatever Viking was going to do was lost as Leif reached behind Viking's neck and snapped the human forward, his forehead smashing into the urinal so hard that he broke off a piece of the white plasticero. Viking fell to his knees, only being held erect by Leif's grip on his neck. Leif bent over to stare into the unconscious human's face for a moment before letting go, the limp body bouncing on the ground to lie in the urine.

Leif slowly walked over to the sink and carefully washed off every bit of human piss off of him. It took three tries before he thought he was adequately clean.

He came back and stood over Viking, whose red blood was now mixing with the urine, making patterns that were frankly beautiful. Leif reached out with a foot and nudged the human, but he didn't even make a sound. With a humanlike shrug, Leif turned and left the head.

"Hey, Leif! If you're done, can you help—" Jordan said before Leif waved him off. He marched over to the DI shack at the entrance to the squadbay, knocked on the hatch, and announced himself.

"Come in, Recruit," Gunnery Sergeant Richardson scratched with a raspy voice that had spent too many years on the drill field. "What do you want, Hollow?" he asked after Leif came to a position of attention in front of him."

"Senior Drill Instructor, Recruit Nilson is in the head. He fell down."

"And?"

"He's out cold. Maybe he's dead."

The senior erupted from behind his desk and grabbed Leif by the upper arm, dragging him out of the DI shack.

"All 4013 hats, to the head, now," he passed over his lapel mic, then, "Captain, we might have a problem with Nilson. I'm checking now."

"What the hell happened?" he yelled as he bolted down the squadbay as recruits stopped what they were doing and watched.

Leif didn't answer. Jordan caught his eye and gave the People's pursed mouth of an unspoken question. Leif shrugged him off, and Jordan surged forward to join the two.

The senior burst into the head, immediately spotted Viking, and slid to his knees beside him. He reached over and touched the recruit's neck, then gave a visible sigh of relief.

"You, Hottento, get a corpsman here now!" he ordered Jordan before turning to Leif, who was enthralled by how much further the swirls of blood had displaced urine, and asked, "What the hell happened?"

"I was cleaning the heads, Senior, when Recruit Nilson came in. Something happened, and when he started to piss, he pissed all over the deck. Then he went down and hit his head on the pisser, right there," he said, pointing to where the chunk of urinal had broken off."

Not a lie. Just not all of the truth, Leif thought.

The People knew what lying was—all sentient life so far discovered lied—but they weren't particularly good at it. Leif struggled to maintain an innocent expression.

"He pissed on the floor? Was he sick?"

"I don't know, Senior. He just stepped back and let go. That's all I could see."

"And he fell?"

"Fell hard, Senior Drill Instructor."

The senior wasn't buying it, Leif knew. He wasn't going to lie to the gunny, but he wasn't going to volunteer anything that would get him into trouble.

Shit, trouble. Assault's a serious crime, a court martial-offense, he realized. *How's this going to affect all of the other wyntonan recruits?*

He'd reacted out of anger, and by doing so, he may have jeopardized the entire process of integrating the Corps.

"Fell hard, huh?" the senior asked, taking into account the urine and blood. "I just bet. Go to the DI shack and stand there. Don't touch a thing, don't move. Understand?"

"Yes, Senior Drill Instructor, I understand."

Leif bolted for the door, shaking as the realization of what he'd done started to sink in. Jordan and some of the others tried to ask him what was going on, but he ran past and into the DI Shack where he stood at parade rest, his body trembling.

A minute or two later, two corpsmen came running into the squad bay, pulling a gurney. Leif waited alone in the shack, and almost ten minutes later, the corpsmen returned, pushing Viking in the gurney. The human was deathly pale.

It was another five minutes before the senior came back, along with the rest of the DIs. The senior got back on the net with the captain, who had already left for the day.

"The docs think he'll be OK. The guy must have rocks instead of brains in his gourd. Breaking off that chunk of the pisser, that should have snapped his neck." There was a pause, then, "No, I don't think so. Lieutenant Dastarde's got the duty, and she's on her way to get a statement." There was another pause, then, "Yes, ma'am. I'll let you know as soon as the docs get through, and you can update the CO."

The senior sighed and leaned back, closing his eyes and rubbing them.

"All of you, leave me with Hollow here. And close the hatch behind you," he added, almost as if an afterthought.

The DIs filed out of the shack, leaving the two alone, which with the hatch closed, was against drill field regulations.

"So, Hollow. Let me clear some things up. You were cleaning the head when Recruit Nilson came in. While he was taking a piss, he somehow, for some reason, started pissing on the deck. After that, he fell, and in doing so, he hit his head on the pisser and was knocked out."

That's a bare-bones version, not really explaining what happened. I need to come clean.

"Uh . . . Senior, there's more—"

"I asked you if that was what happened. Was anything I said untruthful?"

Leif had to think for a moment before he said, "No."

"OK, then. Lieutenant Dastarde's going to be over in a few minutes. I'm going to repeat what I just said, then she's going to ask you if that is true or not. You will say it is, understand?"

"Yes, Senior Drill Instructor, but—"

"Did I ask you for a 'but,' Recruit?"

"No, Senior Drill Instructor."

"Then shut up and wait."

It was more like 20 minutes before the lieutenant arrived, and it was exactly as the senior had said. He told her the account he recited to Leif before. She asked Leif if that was true, and he told her yes. And that was it.

"I'll go see Nilson a little later and confirm that account, ma'am," the senior said as she left.

Leif knew whatever game the senior was playing would be up as soon as he talked to Viking. The truth—the entire truth, would be out.

The senior pulled out an authorization pass and gave it to Leif, saying, "Go to the chowhall and show them this. They'll get you some food. Come back and stay in the squadbay until lights out."

"Aye aye, Senior Drill Instruction. But Recruit Nilson—"

"I will talk to Nilson. Until then, you talk to nobody. I repeat, nobody!"

Leif barely ate anything in the chow hall, and it wasn't because of the taste of the food. He came back and laid in his rack until the platoon came back from evening classes. Several of the other recruits, wyntonan and human alike, tried to find out what was going on, but he feigned sleep. To his surprise, he actually did fall asleep, not waking up until reveille. For a moment, he was in a good mood, feeling that he'd accomplished something before the memory hit him. He only just managed to get ready and march to chow, where once again, he barely ate. He refused to be drawn into a conversation with anyone else, and they eventually left him alone.

Filing into the squadbay, Leif's heart fell when he saw Viking sitting at the foot of his rack, face bandaged. He told the others he was on a day of bedrest, but he'd be good as new tomorrow, all the time refusing to meet Leif's eyes, which was all the proof he needed to know the human had turned him in.

"Let's go, let's go," Drill Instructor Singh shouted into the barracks. "I want to see asses and elbows!"

There was a mass rush for the front hatch, but Leif slowed down by the DI Shack. He had to get it over with.

"Senior Drill Instructor," Leif started.

"No time, Hollow. You've got close order drill now, and from what Drill Instructor Singh tells me, you need lots more practice," the senior said, not looking up from his work.

"But—"

"I said no time. Get out of here and carry on the training schedule."

Leif stared at him for a second, and just as the senior looked up, mouth opening to yell, he bolted, rushing to join the formation.

Somehow, it looked like he'd dodged a bullet. He didn't know what had happened, what Viking had said, but he was being given a second chance—and he was going to take full advantage of that.

He normally hated close order drill, but for once, he was overjoyed to be doing it.

Chapter 13

With his close escape, Leif kept a low profile over the next few weeks. Jordan had lost his recruit squad leader billet, and both Lark and Johari had stepped up and lost theirs, too. Leif was glad he hadn't been assigned, and he hoped he could escape the task all the way through graduation.

Except for Jordan and Ann in the trail series, no wyntonan had volunteered. There had been some veiled and not-so-veiled requests made by the DIs for them to volunteer, but most of them demurred, only stepping up when assigned. Like Leif, they were more than happy to let the eager humans step into the breach.

Marines were supposed to be aggressive, seizing the day at every opportunity, and in that, the wyntonans did not fit the mold. The DIs and most of the human recruits thought that as a whole, they were not leadership material.

Ironically, this seemed to make things better with their fellow recruits. The wyntonans might outperform the humans from an overall physical standpoint, but they were not a threat for those coveted leadership positions—especially for the chance to be named as a platoon, series, or company honor graduate—which came with an automatic promotion to private first class.

Leif was still neutral about the Corps as a whole. He loved the physical aspects of training, and nothing filled him with pride as with outperforming everyone else in the platoon at the physical tasks. There were quite a few of the humans who could sprint faster in short distances, up to about five klicks or so, but beyond that, it was either Keijo or him who came in first. He was still a weak swimmer, and the heavy-worlders were stronger than any of the rest of them, human or wyntonan alike. To Leif's surprise, he was one of the best shots in the platoon, coming in second in rifle quals the week prior, the last evolution in Phase 2. Swimming aside, Leif was always among the best in anything physical.

He didn't care much one way or the other about the classes, so he didn't perform well on the tests, and he was continually graded low on the DI evals, particularly in leadership. When combined with his physical scores, that put him right in the middle of the pack. There would be no honor graduate for him—and that was OK.

What he didn't like about being a recruit stemmed from the prejudice he and the others still experienced. The DIs exhibited very little of it. They'd seemed to accept the orders of the emperor, regardless of their personal beliefs, and like good Marines, saluted smartly and marched on.

Their fellow recruits were a different story. A few seemed to honestly like them, and more were happy to use their physical abilities to further their own cause. Still more than that simply ignored them, a new aspect of the "ghost" nickname. It was as if they simply weren't there.

The problems were with the "haters," to use the human term. Led by Savea and Nilsen, they seemed to go out of their way to harass the wyntonans, never quite doing enough to draw official attention, but enough to let each of the wyntonans know just where they stood with them.

The image of Sergeant Washburn Gonzales, the Marine who'd rescued him from slavers back in Hope Hollow three tri-years ago, had evolved since then into something almost god-like and had been the driving factor for Leif to enlist. The reality was rather more sobering. His fellow recruits were both good and bad, just like any group of the People back on Home. Leif could work with most of them—he even liked some of them—but the thought of serving a three-year enlistment with haters, even if they were in the minority, did not fill him with enthusiasm. He often wished he hadn't enlisted, and he imagined Ferron a'Silverton calling them all in one day, telling them either the Elder Council or the emperor had decided to curtail the program, and they were all going home.

Absent that, though, Leif was going to keep pushing. He'd never quit anything in his life, and boot camp wasn't hard—just unpleasant at times. The finish line was in sight, though. They'd just entered Phase 3, the final four weeks of training.

They were almost Marines, and despite his somewhat lack of "gung-ho" enthusiasm, the thought still filled him with some pride. Sergeant Gonzales might have fallen a notch or two in the god hierarchy, but he was still someone to look up to.

Chapter 14

Phase 3 turned out to be much more enjoyable than Leif had expected. First, while the DIs hadn't become their best buddies, there had been a subtle shift from out and out harassment to more teaching. They still had punishment runs out to the Stick and back, usually in full battle rattle now. They still were on the receiving end of screaming jags when they messed up, but there were also explanations on what they'd done wrong and advice on how to do those things correctly.

Second, though, was the shift in classes. With the academic foundations laid, the classes were more military-oriented, how to make things go boom, how to take out an enemy soldier. This was more in line with what Leif had imagined, and he reveled in it.

Best of all was the Marine Corps Close Combat Program. The recruits had spent hours in the sawdust pits, learning how to fight with knives, wands, and their bare hands. Leif had developed a somewhat demeaning opinion of the physical capabilities of humans—conveniently ignoring their sprint speeds, swimming abilities, or in the case of the heavy-worlders, their strength—until the MCCCP instructors, referred to as "green shirts" because of the color of their training T's, regularly kicked his ass. For once, Leif was always volunteering to be one of their training dummies, and each time they took him down—often quite painfully—he reveled in the experiences, promising himself that he'd become that skilled someday as well. Some of that hero-worship he'd had for Sergeant Gonzales had begun to make a reappearance, targeting the instructors.

Leif wasn't even the best of the wyntonans: Tessa and Dubois could regularly beat him. But he was the most enthusiastic, human or wyntonan.

And today was a banner day. Today was the pugil stick competition. All morning, they'd been introduced to the pugil stick basics, which essentially boiled down to pure beating on each other. Unlike most of what the MCCCP instructors taught, the stronger and larger recruits—that meant the heavy-worlders—had a distinct advantage.

Leif didn't care. This would be their opportunity to really go at it, to actually fight another recruit. He knew he didn't have much of a chance to win the tournament, but he was going to make whoever did beat him earn the advancement.

After a warm-up bout, the competition became a one and done. If a recruit lost, anytime after that first bout, they were out of the competition, which ended when there was only one recruit left standing.

The competition was one of the five must-pass events for a recruit to graduate. Unlike the O-Course or rifle quals, which had a numeric score or time that had to be met, the pugil stick competition was pass-fail—and the only way to fail was to quit. It seemed the easiest of any of the five to Leif, but in every series, someone did quit, to be dropped from training.

The competition was not just a big deal for the recruits. It was a huge deal for the DIs. They became completely invested in their platoons, and not just for bragging rights. They also bet rather large amounts of BCs on their recruits, which, of course, was patently illegal. But with the officers, supposedly going all the way up to the battalion commanders, doing it as well, it was one of those things that was just ignored.

Leif volunteered to go first, and he was hyped up with energy as Drill Instructor Dream Bear laced up his gloves. He thought he was more excited than he'd been on his a'aden hunt. A lion could be cunning and crafty, but the advantage was with the wyntonan. In this case, Leif was going against someone in Platoon 4042, a sentient being who would be just as eager to knock his brains out.

"Don't be blinded, Hollow," the DI was telling him. "This is just a practice, to get used to being hit."

"Or hitting someone, Drill Instructor!"

The DI laughed, then said, "Yeah, I guess so. But take it easy and feel your opponent out. I want you to be ready when the real competition starts.

"Yes, Drill Instructor!" Leif said, barely aware of what the DI had told him.

He just wanted to start, shifting his feet as his helmet—one of the four specially made for the wyntonans—was put on, the strap tightened around his chin. Feeling like a human samurai of old, he reached out for his stick. He felt a rush as his hands closed around the handles.

The People had combat sports, the most prominent being *listomy*, a stylized wrestling that came in handy for some of the MCCCP classes. What they didn't have, and hadn't had for over 50 tri-years, was anything with a weapon. The pugil stick might be from Earth, but as he hefted it, Leif felt a kinship to the formalized combat of Home, back when wars reigned. It was his *flaak*, like the grandads treasured back in Hope Hollow.

"Shit," the DI said under his breath.

Leif looked up, and his opponent from 4042 stepped up: Recruit Gato Sifuentes. The heavy-worlder looked huge, his armor plates struggling to cover his broad shoulders. Leif might have 25 centimeters of height and a good 10 cm reach advantage, but the heavy-worlder had 30 kg on him.

"Just keep your distance. Use your reach," the DI said.

Sifuentes was one of the nicer heavy-worlders, and Leif had had a few conversations with him, but this was war. Leif did not expect, nor would he give, any quarter.

Drill Instructor Delbert, one of the MCCCP instructors who had regularly dropped Leif with ease, was the umpire for the bout. She looked at both of the combatants, each standing on his side of the ring, then blew her hand siren. Immediately, the crowd of recruits and drill instructors roared.

Leif charged in, stick held high, ready to drop Sifuentes, who stood easily. Leif crossed the pit in two seconds and started to bring his stick down in a knock-out blow, eager to end it.

It ended. With one quick upper-thrust, Sifuentes connected on Leif's chin, dropping him to his knees. The drill instructor stepped in, her hand siren blaring, to keep Sifuentes away, but the recruit knew he'd won, and had turned to the cheers of his platoon.

Leif wasn't sure what had happened until he'd been helped from the ring and his helmet taken off.

"I told you to stay away," Drill Instructor Dream Bear said before he turned to help Bottle—Recruit Glynn Cisnik—get ready.

Leif felt horrible—not from the blow, but from getting beat so easily. He'd let his battle fury take over. This was only a practice bout, but the loss stung. He held back during the remaining bouts, not even evaluating other potential adversaries. He went over and over what he'd done wrong.

The practice bouts were done in about 40 minutes, and MCCCP instructors went over each of them with what the combatants had done right and wrong during the bouts. The series DIs were going crazy trying to hold in their own advice, but this was the green shirts' show, and they had to hold their tongue.

Leif's evaluation was short and sweet: he'd lost his cool and went in without a plan.

I'm not going to do that again, he vowed to himself.

They were all given a break while they waited for the VIPs to show. The pugil stick competition brought out all the brass.

"Hey, you'll do better this time," Jordan said, sitting down beside him.

Jordan had made short work of his opponent, of course. Leif pointedly turned his head away. His friend shrugged and left him alone.

Twenty minutes later, the VIPs showed up. Leif had expected the battalion commander, of course, but he was surprised to see the CG, accompanied by Sept-Minister Iaxi and Ferron a'Silverton. There were several other colonels who Leif didn't recognize, as well as a recording crew who set up their tridee cams around the four rings.

"Green shirts," let's get going!" Drill Instructor McMaster shouted out, not bothering with a throat mic. He as a full master gunnery sergeant, the only one Leif had seen, and combined with his MCCCP skills, thoroughly impressed him.

Even with four rings going at once, this was going to take some time, so the green shirt DIs hurried to their places. Drill Instructor Delbert handed the seniors of 4032 and 4033 the initial pairing.

Drill Instructor Richardson looked at his, then shouted out "Hollow, you're up. LaMont, on deck."

"Shit, we're going to start out with a loss," someone mumbled behind Leif.

He pushed that out of his mind and stepped up where Drill Instructor Dream Bear waited. He helped Leif don his gear, saying nothing.

"We're starting in thirty seconds, with or without you," the green shirt yelled out.

Drill Instructor Dream Bear gave his helmet strap a quick tug—a little too tight—then handed him the stick. "This time, think, Hollow. Don't rush it."

"Now, recruits," the green shirt yelled.

The drill instructor gave him a swat on the ass, then pushed him forward.

Leif didn't even know who he'd be facing, and he looked up to see the smiling face of Deidree Orion. She raised one hand in the Roman salute that many of the recruits liked.

"Hands on your stick, recruit!" Drill Instructor Delbert snapped at her.

Deidree made an exaggerated grimace, keeping the smile on her face. Delbert hit her siren. The two platoons broke out into yells as Leif slowly advanced.

"Fancy meeting you here," Deidree said. "Shall we dance?"

She feinted at his crotch, and Leif jumped back, almost falling. His platoon let out a collective groan.

Concentrate! Leif told himself as he blocked out the crowd, the fights going on in the other rings, everything except for Hawk in front of him.

Leif knew Deidree fairly well, and if not a friend, he considered her close to being one. Right now, however, she was the enemy, an enemy dedicated to taking him down.

He started circling her, his pugil stick in the en garde. She lunged forward, quick as a grazpin, evading his block, and delivering a sharp strike to the shoulder. He barely felt it, and that started to bring back his confidence. He gave a tentative swing, which she easily avoided.

"Come on, let's give them a show!" she shouted, lunging in with a flurry of blows that rained on him.

Many of them landed, but none did much damage. Knocking her stick aside, he hit her in the gut, forcing her back a step. Again and again, he hit her low in the belly, each blow rocking her. On the fourth strike, she folded over and fell to her knees.

Drill Instructor Delbert blew her siren, stepping between them as Leif raised his stick for the killer blow. He almost swung before he regained his senses.

Deidree looked up at him with a smile, saying, "Damn! You're just too strong for me."

Leif dropped his stick, a cardinal offense, to help her to her feet.

"Sorry about that," he said.

"What, for winning? Just keep doing that and take it home for the series!"

Drill Instructor Delbert picked up his pugil stick, handed it to him, and said, "Don't drop that again or you're disqualified.

The universe came back to life, everything registering again, including the cheers of his platoon. He walked back, and as soon as he was divested of his stick and fighting armor, he was mobbed for a moment, recruits slapping him on his back. That immediately quit as Hector LaMont entered the ring, and from being a combatant one moment, a conqueror, he was now a spectator, screaming out his own support.

The first round took over two hours, and when it was over, 42 recruits from 4033 advanced. Their next round was to be against 4035 from the trail series while their erstwhile opponents, 4032 went up against 4034.

Of the 50 wyntonan recruits in both series, 44 had made it through. Leif had been hoping that everyone would make it, but three had faced heavy-worlders and three had been beat by unmodified humans. Guy, from Platoon 4034 had beat one of the heavy-worlders, though.

During the break, word spread like wildfire that one recruit from the trail series broke and ran out of the ring. Leif didn't know if that was true, but while a very few of his fellow recruits expressed some sympathy for the recruit, Leif was more in line with the majority. The Marines could not accept cowards into its ranks.

The next round began, and this time, Leif was one of the latter to fight. He didn't know his opponent, an average-sized male with extremely pale skin, almost as pale as a wyntonan's, but with bright red hair. He moved with an unnatural grace and seemed to be very popular with his platoon. Several of the wyntonans from his platoon cheered him on, which bothered Leif. It shouldn't, he knew, but still, he expected loyalty from his own people.

It didn't matter in the end, because Leif almost immediately knocked the human's pugil stick out of the ring, getting the victory. The recruit stared disbelievingly at his empty hands for a moment before giving Leif a decent approximation of the People's honor bow.

At the end of the round, 57 recruits were left. There was a quick meeting, and fourteen of those who lost were selected for a loser's bracket fight-in. Mark, who had lost his first fight was one of them, but he lost this fight as well and was out once again. Leif's redhead opponent was also selected, and he made quick work in his fight, making Leif wonder if he'd gotten in a lucky shot to disarm him.

With the final 64 recruits set, 28 were wyntonan, 11 were heavy-worlders with eight being from Manapur, one was a chestie, and the rest were regs.

There was another break as Sept-Minster Iaxi, the CG, and the battalion commander and sergeant major came forward to wish the remaining recruits well. The sept-minster shook the hands of each of the wyntonans, and from the looks on the humans, the rest of the fighters noticed their exclusion.

From here on out until a lone survivor was crowned, things would move quickly. Leif was next paired with Gustav Tomagachi from Third Squad. "Tomo" proved to be a tough fight—the two were evenly matched, and twice, Leif almost went down to wicked shots, but Leif's strength and greater reach were the difference, and Tomo was knocked back hard enough that his foot touched the edge of the ring.

His next fight was with Lacey. This was only the third wyntonan-versus-wyntonan, and it attracted quite a bit of attention. He'd sparred with her before, and he knew her style. The fight dragged on, but it had never been in much doubt, and a flurry from Leif, the last one on the back of her head, drove her to her knees.

His number was up right away, so without even removing his gear, he stepped up against a heavy-worlder from the trail series. Wary this time, he kept to the outside, firing shot after shot that connected, all the time staying just out of reach of his opponent. After an unsuccessful lunge by the human that left him off-balance, Leif heard Savea shout out, "Close with that fucking ghost, Arnil!" Leif swung down on the out-of-balance human, connecting hard with a smack that made some of the onlookers gasp, staggering his opponent so that he stepped out.

The recruit turned and grabbed Leif's hand, pulling him in for the chest slam that the heavy-worlders favored, almost knocking his breath away, saying, "Gooda fight dere," in a heavy accent.

Van, the only other remaining wyntonan, was the last fight from the final 16. From some mumbles he caught, he knew Van surprised some of the humans. There had been eight human females in the final 32 and four advanced to the final 16, but Van was the only female left with a chance at the final eight. If this was true hand-to-hand, he knew more females would still be in the mix. If Drill Instructor Delbert were there, the contest would be a done deal, even as small as she was. But the pugil stick was primarily a case of strength and mass, not skill, and most human females were out-massed by the males.

Not so among the People. Wyntonan bodies were quite similar in mass and appearance. Other than the genitalia, which were much like humans', there wasn't much in the way of secondary sexual characteristics to the human eye. The main difference was in facial features. To them, it might be surprising that if any female was to make a run at winning, it wasn't a heavy-worlder but a wyntonan.

Your fault if you underestimate her, he thought, trying not to smile.

As it turned out, she was up first, and she dispatched her opponent, Rance Opua, a heavy-worlder from 3032, in fifteen seconds with a hurricane assault, simply overwhelming him. There were sounds of awe coming from the gathered recruits and Marines alike. From a position of honor right at the edge of the ring, Sept-Minster Iaxi smiled, leaned over to the general, and said something.

The general did not smile back.

And then it was eight. Two wyntonans, Van and him. Four heavy-worlders, one being Savea. Two other were "reg" humans, one being Leif's red-headed opponent from before, to his surprise. The human caught his eye, and Leif nodded his respects.

Leif knew he could beat the red-headed human. He wasn't sure about the rest. Van had a much better chance at getting through to the end

Leif was totally surprised in the first fight of the round when the redheaded human, who was unimaginatively being called "Red" by his fellow recruits, beat his opponent, another heavy-worlder. Leif began to think that maybe he had been lucky to disarm the fighter.

The next fight was a massive clash of muscle mass, two heavy-worlders coming together more like human sumo wrestlers, their pugil sticks merely props in their pushing contest. DI's screamed at them to hit each other, but like animals in rut, they strained against each other until they both went out of the ring. The DIs conferred a moment before giving the win to one of them, who let out a scream of victory, pounding his chest.

Leif was next, drawing the second non-modified human. As with two fights ago, they were evenly matched, and the spectators appreciated the slugfest as both fighters gave it their all. One smash on the kneecap almost felled Leif, but he managed to keep to his feet and laid the human out cold. He felt like screaming out like the last winner had, but he kept it back. There were still two more fights he had to get through.

He stood back to watch Van take down Savea, savoring the thought, picturing the beating she'd give him. There was no doubt in his mind that she was the better fighter, even giving up 20 kg or so.

She lit into him before the green shirt's siren had faded, pounding the troll. He hunched over and advanced, absorbing each blow. He couldn't do it for long, Leif knew, having been at the receiving end of her strikes before. Still, he pushed forward, ineffectually swinging to try and keep her off him.

And Leif suddenly knew what he was doing. He was trying to close in and simply push her out, like the last two heavy-worlders had done to each other.

"Van, don't let him get you to the edge of the ring!" he shouted.

Leif didn't know if she heard him, but as she neared the edge, she shifted to the side, never letting up on her flurry.

And then, a human leg reached out into the ring, right as she was stepping. Her foot hit the leg and slipped, and she went down awkwardly.

"Hey!" Leif shouted as Savea pounced, hitting Van with a shot that broke her pugil stick before smashing into her head. She went limp as Savea leveled another grazing shot before the green shirt called the bout over, putting his body between the two.

Protests sounded from those who'd seen what had happened, and the green shirts looked confused for several moments before declaring Savea the winner.

Leif was incensed, and he started to run forward, only to be restrained by Drill Sergeant Dream Bear.

"Let it go, Hollow!"

"But . . . but he tripped her. It wasn't fair!"

"Just leave it, Recruit!"

He wanted to pull away, to run into the ring, but with a huge effort, he managed to control himself. He pulled his arm out of the DI's grasp.

He wasn't going to ignore what had just happened, however. He couldn't.

Leif marched up to the green shirt acting as umpire and said, "I get Savea, understand?"

The green shirt looked surprised and seemed like he was going to tell Leif to back off, but with a shrug, he wiped out the pairing he had already made, saying, "Your funeral, Recruit."

He paced back to Drill Sergeant Dream Bear and stood there, unmoving as the first semi-final bout started. He barely noticed Red dancing around the heavy-worlder, who was limping heavily. It soon became obvious what the result would be, even to the bigger recruit. Yet, he never gave up, finally being laid low by the quicker recruit. The heavy-worlder got a huge cheer, but Leif barely noticed. His attention was laser-focused on Savea, who was glaring back at him.

He was pushed forward to the middle of the ring as Savea came to meet him. They stood there, no love lost, as they waited for the siren.

Leif sprung into action, swinging low at the bigger recruit's tree-trunk thighs, hitting the right leg just as Savea stepped forward. He might not have been paying close attention to the previous fight, but it was hard to miss how ineffective a crippled fighter was. He wanted to take out Savea's legs, then pound the immobile recruit until he fell.

The only problem was that Savea wasn't cooperating. He seemed willing to take the blows if he could advance, and while trying to keep out of range, Leif had to give way. Then, another thought hit him, and with a smile that he couldn't keep off his face, he adjusted his retreat slightly. He kept flailing at Savea, but he was not as good a fighter as Van was, and where she avoided getting hit by the heavy-worlders, Leif got clipped by the hammer blows several times. Despite the helmet he wore, he could taste the blood flowing into his mouth from a cut on his forehead.

Just centimeters from the edge of the ring, he shifted, making the same movement Van had done. Sure enough, he saw a leg start to snake out. With a huge roundhouse swing, he missed Savea's head, bringing his pugil stick down to connect with the unarmored leg. There was a snap, then a scream. Leif, off-balanced now and vulnerable, jumped back. Savea seemed startled by the scream, and he stopped as soon as he saw the other heavy-worlder on his back, unnaturally bent leg sticking into the ring.

And Leif took advantage. Reversing himself, he lunged forward, connecting with the confused-looking Savea's face. From that moment, the heavy-worlder was on the run as Leif, channeling millennia of warriors, went into full *musapha* mode, what some humans called "running amok." Where it had once been somewhat common, nowadays, not many wyntonans ever experienced it. He'd never felt power surge through him like this, but he immediately knew what it was, and he reveled in the feeling. Five, six, seven times, he struck his fellow-recruit until he stumbled, falling back on his ass, pugil stick held aloft as he attempted to keep his head from getting knocked off his body.

The siren blasted, but that was just an annoyance to him. It took three green shirts to pull him back, and for the musapha to flee his body with a snap that left him empty.

The recruits around the ring were cheering, some hugging each other. A corpsman rushed into the ring to see to the recruit whose leg it looked like Leif had broken.

Leif looked around . . . exhausted. His high had been glorious, but he'd come crashing to the ground. He looked up where Sept-Minister Iaxi was clapping. Even Ferron a'Silverton seemed caught up in the emotions.

It took ten minutes for the green shirts to check on Savea, who seemed to be unhurt and get the other heavy-worlder—who definitely was hurt—off to sickbay. At last, it was time for the last bout.

"That was freaking amazing, Hollow. Now just one more, one more baby," Drill Instructor Dream Bear said. "Just give me this."

All of the platoon DIs, even the senior came to wish him luck. Leif wasn't feeling it, though. *Musapha* was a harsh mistress. It could evoke great feats of strength and heroics, but there was a heavy price to pay. Leif's limbs felt like lead. This was the first time he'd felt the grip of it, something most of the People never felt at all, and if they did, it was after their first breeding cycle and musth. As glorious as it had felt when he was pounding Savea, he now felt empty, a dried-up husk

It wasn't only the absolute lack of energy. He'd taken some heavy punishment, as well. Blood had started flowing into his mouth again, and with his nose swollen, it was hard to breathe. But he had only one more fight, so, he tried to pull himself together. He was so close to bringing honor to his people.

He took several deep breaths as he faced Red. The general was called into the ring for the honors, and after some short speech of which Leif didn't hear a word, she blew the siren.

The fight was on.

Chapter 15

Leif stared up at the sky, confused. He wasn't sure where he was, or why he was there. A rush of bodies surrounded him, humans reaching out to lift a red-headed recruit to their shoulders. Several stepped on him as they shouted, "Regs rule!"

It came back in a rush, and he couldn't keep in the groan. The fight was over, and he'd lost. He'd lost it before the general even blew the siren, he knew. He'd been hurt, and he'd crashed out from the *musapha* rush. He'd been slow and weak.

Without the *musapha*, he started to make an excuse for his loss, but he knew that was not the reason. That only hastened the decision.

The fact of the matter was that Red was damned good. His victory over the human the first time had been a fluke, catching him at just the right moment for him to lose his pugil stick. This time, it had been a joke, and Red had put Leif down within 20 seconds. Even rested and ready to fight, Red would have probably beat him.

A familiar face leaned over him and asked, "*Musapha?*"

"Yeah."

"When you play with the mistress . . ." Jordan said, offering a hand.

Leif took it and let his friend pull him up and out of the way of the chanting humans. Some of his own platoonmates were there, cheering for their hero.

"Regs rule! Regs rule!"

With the heavy-worlders such a power in pugil stick, it wasn't often that a "reg" human won the competition, and with the heavy importance given the contest, they were celebrating "their" win. Leif caught sight of a group of heavy-worlders, staring forlornly at the celebrating regs.

"Let me check you out," a corpsman said, coming up to him.

He gave him a quick survey, then cleaned two cuts, sealing them with plastistitch.

"He'll be fine," he told Drill Instructor Dream Bear.

"You OK, Hollow?" the DI asked.

"Yes, Drill Instructor. I'm sorry."

"Sorry? Hell, yeah, I wish you'd won. But I still made 62 BC," he said with a smile. "And I get to lord it over Frehm until next series, so all's good."

Drill Instructor Frehm focused most of his time on Third Squad, Savea's squad.

"You did good, Recruit. Now, go let the rest of the platoon congratulate you," he said, giving Leif a little push where a good portion of his platoon waited.

To his surprise, his fellow recruits, the ones not running around with Red on their shoulders, at least, seemed sincere as they patted his back and said he'd done good. Even Savea gave him a grudging "Good fight. That guy's one tough son-of-a-bitch."

Leif didn't think they'd ever be friends, but maybe they could have a truce, at least, through next week's Crucible and subsequent graduation. He looked around. Nilsen wasn't there, not that he was surprised. He turned to look at the the mass of still celebrating humans, and of course, Nilsen was in the midst of it all. He'd been knocked out of the competition in the first round, and there he was, acting as if he'd won it all.

"You probably need some sleep, huh?" Jordan said, coming up alongside him.

His body ached, whether from the fight with Red or from the musapha, he wasn't sure. Probably some of both—no, probably a lot of both.

"Yeah, I think I'll be skipping chow. Can you clear that with Dream Bear?"

"Sure thing, buddy," Jordan said, putting Leif's arm around his shoulder.

Together, they pushed past the crowd of humans and made their way back to the barracks.

Chapter 16

Leif stared at his reflection in the mirror. He looked sharp in the Marine dress blues, he had to admit.

Marine. I'm a Marine.

This morning, he'd woken up a recruit, and now, he'd actually been given the title of Imperial Marine. After the pugil stick competition, the last hurdle had been the Crucible, a five-day evolution of constant activity and little sleep. Nothing was that difficult taken on its own, but when combined, they had created a tough test of self-discipline.

Four recruits had been dropped—including Mark. He'd broken a leg on the combat run, a 10-klick run in full packs over a series of real-world-type obstacles. He had a lengthy rehabilitation ahead of him, but he'd be recycled into a follow-on series. Two humans would get recycled as well for injuries, but Recruit Diaz had simply quit—he'd get no second chances.

With the hike up Mount Doom, the Crucible was completed, and a feeling of accomplishment had swept over the recruits. For most, it was because they knew they were going to be Marines. The gung-ho humans seemed to revel in being part of a storied history.

Leif didn't feel quite the same. He was damned proud of what he'd done, but the group-hug that seemed to infect the humans seemed a little corny to him. He understood a part of what the humans felt, but only as a minor factor. For Leif, it was the fact that he'd succeeded. He'd overcome what the DIs had thrown at him. He'd *won*.

He was also proud of the wyntonans as a whole. Fifty had started the class (If Kelli wasn't counted), and 49 had become Marines today. He was sure Mark would make it as well as soon as his leg healed. That was a far better percentage than any human sub-group. Ann was even the trail series honor grad. Leif had heard grumblings that she'd been a token selection, but the recruits who'd said that had to be blind. Ann had kicked ass throughout the 12 weeks.

It was true that the media had focused on her above all the rest of the newly-minted Marines. It was also true that it was with the 49 wyntonan Marines that the emperor posed for the media, not with any of the humans, even Private First Class Angus Zhen, the company honor graduate. If the humans resented that, well, none of that was the fault of the wyntonans.

It had long become obvious that the 50 recruits had been a special project of the emperor. Sept-ministers, an emperor's representative-at-large, did not hang around Camp Navarro, observing the training of a single recruit company.

"Are you going to keep staring at yourself, thinking you're ibent-on-the-hoof?" Jordan asked, "Or are you going to change?"

"Oh, yeah, sure. Give me a second," he said, more than a little embarrassed.

Some of the recruits, mostly those with family attending the graduation ceremony, had left on their first off-base liberty since they arrived on the yellow footsteps in their dress blues. Ann, invited to the reception with the emperor and other VIPs, was still in her uniform. As good as the dress blues looked, though, they were uncomfortable, the high collar pressuring their throats. Leif had thought that it was because they were not designed for wyntonans, but Tolbert and Hawk had assured him they were just as uncomfortable to humans.

For the bulk of the recruits . . . no, *Marines*, he reminded himself, they were going to don civvies for their night out celebrating on the town—the first night of several. They were free until Monday morning, when they would report to their follow-on school. Most of them, including Leif, would stay at Camp Charles and report to the School of Infantry, but others would go to various other schools to learn their operational specialties.

Leif hung up his blues, then unwrapped his single set of civvies, the ones in which he'd reported aboard and had just been returned. They smelled weird, as if they'd been sprayed with something, like a disinfectant.

Can't let the humans catch ghost cooties, I guess.

The shirt seemed small when he put it on, and he checked to make sure it was his. It was, and for a moment, he was confused until he realized that he'd put on some muscle mass during recruit training. He was still slender when compared with humans, but he could see more definition.

"Oh, the Mother. Look, he's posing now," Johari said.

"Yes, you're a stud, but if you want to come with us, finish getting dressed," Jordan told him.

Embarrassed, Leif finished and joined them. Aside from Ann with the emperor, another ten had been 'invited" to join Council Elder Hordun, the elder who had spoken to them back on Home and who'd represented the Home government at the graduation, for a debrief. Leif had breathed a sigh of relief when his name was not called, but a few moments later wondered why. He'd come in second in two of the five prime events, so why wasn't he one of the chosen ones?

He'd asked that of Jordan on the way back to the squadbay, and his friend just told him to thank his lucky stars. Who knows how long it would be before the others could join them? Just enjoy being free.

"If that's everyone, let's go. They've got shuttles leaving every 30 minutes," Ossie said.

Other groups of new Marines were heading to the shuttle stop. Hawk, standing with four other Earthers, gave Leif a smile and nod, but most of the Marines were grouped by home planet or sub-race. Two minutes after they arrived, a full bus pulled up, and all of the waiting Marines managed to crowd aboard. A moment later, the bus was pulling out of the camp, passing underneath the sign that had caught Leif's attention 16 weeks before.

Sic Transit Gloria Stellae: "Thus passes the glory of the stars."

"Hey, you've seen enough of the Pit," Jordan said, elbowing him. "Look ahead to V-town."

"V-town," or Vandermeyer, existed for one reason, and that was to provide services for the Marines of the Camp Puller complex, of which Camp Navarro was only one small part. Whether that was housing for families, clothing, games, or food from home, the citizens in the town prided themselves on providing whatever a young Marine might desire.

The lights were already burning, a kaleidoscope of color, each trying to draw Marines like moths to flames. When they'd arrived at the Pit that first night, the buses had bypassed the main part of the town, but now they were heading right for the center. A starburst shot into the air, sparks forming "2 for 1 House Beer" as they fell back to the ground, to the oohs and aahs of those on the bus.

The bus pulled to a stop in a square, a canned voice telling them they had arrived and running through the departure times back to camp. No one listened as they piled out of the bus to their first taste of freedom.

"Rolex?" a tokit said, coming up to them. "Best wristcomps available, only 25 ID."

Twenty-five Imperial Dollars wouldn't buy a Rolex wristband, much less the comp, but Eva took the proffered comp, saying, "Hey, look at this. Only twenty-five."

"Oh, my sweet, innocent ada," Keijo said, pulling her away. "They're not real."

"I've got Wen Zhous, too. The highest quality!" the tokit said.

"Food?" Jordan asked, ignoring the tokit who kept trying to interest them with more "quality" products.

Most of the humans had immediately bolted for the bars, several trying to track down the one that had advertised the 2-for-1 beer. The wyntonans, however, had discussed trying to find Home food first. Leif was all for that.

"Food," he confirmed.

"Hey, do you know where we can get wyntonan food?" Tessa asked the tokit.

"Ghost food? Yeah, sure. You come with me. I know the best."

Leif was a little suspicious, but with nowhere specific to go, he didn't object as the tokit led them on a meandering hike through the warrens of bars and shops, all the time trying to unload his collection of wristcomps. Finally, they arrived at a small cafe, one that looked exactly like twenty others they'd passed. There wasn't any wyntonan writing on the cafe's sign, which did not bode well.

The cafe was a quarter full, and an actual human came forward.

"What can I get you?" he asked, looking over the group.

"Kabash? Do you have it?" Lark asked

"I don't even know what that is," the man said.

"Grazpin?" Leif asked.

"You got me again."

"Do you have any wyntonan food?" Leif asked, already knowing the answer.

"Ghost food? Not much of a call for it here. This is a Marine town, not a tourist town."

"But that tokit told us you have it," Eva said.

"Banditod? Him? He'll tell you anything if he thinks there's an ID in it for him. Look, I can pull up some recipes from the net and see what my foodjet can make, but that's all I can promise."

The Marines looked at each other, then Tessa asked, "Is there anyplace else that serves our food?"

"Like I said, not much of a call for it here."

Leif had half-expected they wouldn't find real Home food, but he was still disappointed. They conferred for a moment before deciding to just eat here before hitting some of the bars.

The owner hadn't promised much in the way of good food, and in that, he delivered. It was barely edible, even with healthy dosings of spice. They ate quickly before leaving, ready to see the town. Banditod, the tokit, was waiting outside. His eyes lit up when he saw them.

"See, I took care of you. You can trust Banditod."

Another tokit came out of the shadows, and Banditod snarled something at her in their language.

"Come on, let's get out of here," Jordan whispered to Leif as more tokits started arriving. Not just tokits. Two hissers joined the throng of people trying to sell something to the wyntonans.

Jordan, Tessa, and Leif dodged behind the group of tokits, darting ahead. By the time they'd slowed down, they'd lost them, but they'd also lost the rest of their group. The three debated going back for them, but the commercial enclave outside the gate was not as large as the one outside the Camp Puller's main gate, so they figured they'd run into the rest in due time.

"How come none of the street hustlers are human?" Jordan asked as they looked for a likely bar.

Leif looked around. Jordan was right. The cafe owner had been human, and there were humans in some of the shops, but the street hustlers, the ones trying to hustle up a few BCs, were non-human. Most were tokits, but there were alindamirs, hissers, even a couple of sassares, who were not even imperial citizens. Leif wondered how the heck two of that proud race ended up hustling on the streets of Iwo Jima.

"Someone has to do the work humans won't do," Tessa said.

Leif wasn't sure that was the answer. No one *had* to hustle in the street. He thought it might have more to do with a lack of opportunity.

"Leif, J-Dan," a voice called out. "You, too, Tessa."

The three turned to see Hawk, Tolbert, and "Dez" Hernandez. All three had been friendly to the wyntonans— Dez had even gotten into a fight after being accused of being a "ghost-lover."

"We're heading to the Oasis. They're supposed to have the best Lydacaine in V-town," Hawk said.

Lydacaine was a piercing, raucous music—if it even deserved the term—that made Leif's headache, but Tessa looked to the other two and said, "I think we lost the rest. Let's take a look at the Oasis. If we don't like it, we can always leave."

Jordan agreed, so Leif didn't have a choice. He vowed that if the Lydacaine was too discordant, he'd make leaving something they did sooner rather than later.

The three went to join the three humans, and together, they followed Dez, who in turn was following the instructions on his wristcomp. Leif began feeling claustrophobic as they delved deeper into the warrens along narrow alleys. He was a country boy, after all, and more people probably lived in one of the buildings they passed than lived in his entire home village. He imagined he felt eyes on him, and that made him feel uncomfortable. He was relieved when they entered a square, the Oasis on the far side of it, a pink, turquoise, and peach sign welcoming them.

He was even more relieved when they entered, and the music hadn't started yet. A group of humans was setting up on the stage, getting ready to play.

"Live music," Tessa said, sounding too excited for Leif.

At least 40 of their fellow new Marines were already there, and music or not, with the alcohol flowing, they were having a good time.

When the Mother created the various races, she made small differences in them all, but the one constant in every race yet discovered was an affinity for alcohol. Some of the types of booze varied, but another constant was beer. Given cross-pollination of races, beer became even more universal. Here in the empire, the most popular beer, Dynx, was brewed by the sassares, the primary threat/competition to humans. A large, garish sign in back of the bar indicated that they did serve Dynx here. Lief wouldn't admit it to anyone back in Hope Hollow, but he'd rather have a Dynx than a glass of Silver Range aleese.

"Well, maybe we can spend a little time here," Leif muttered.

"What did you say?" Hawk asked him.

"Oh, nothing."

The bar seemed split between regs and trolls, almost all being from their recruit company. One of the regs waved them over, and the six joined them, pulling up chairs from an adjoining table as the others scooted over to make room.

"Keep!" Tintin shouted, already half-drunk. "Get my friends here some liquid!"

From the holovids, Leif thought that all human restaurants, bars, and nightspots were fully automated, but like the cafe, this one had live servers. The woman behind the bar looked up, frowned, and came up to the table.

"Dynx, m'lady, a pitcher for my friends," Tintin said.

She ignored him and said to the newcomers, "You're going to have to leave now."

Hawk and Tolbert exchanged looks, then Hawk asked, "Why? What do you mean?"

"Not you. You're fine. But the caspers, they've got to leave."

Leif heard the woman, heard the scorn when she said "caspers," but he was confused as to what she was saying.

"Why do they have to leave?" Hawk asked, her voice deadly serious.

"They're caspers, that's why? We don't let any of the dung-races in here. Only humans."

There was shocked silence for a moment from the human and wyntonan Marines.

"You can't do that," Hawk managed to get out.

"It's my bar, and I can damned well say who we serve and what we don't, and we don't serve dung-races."

"But, they're Marines," Dez said.

"I don't care if you want to dress them up in your blues, they're still caspers, no better than tokit vermin."

"Now, wait a minute—" Tintin said, standing up. "We're from the same company, and we just graduated today."

"So, you don't know any better. We've got to live with them here and their thieving ways."

Leif started to object—there weren't any wyntonan living in V-town, to the best of his knowledge—but Tessa put her hand on his arm, shutting him up.

"It's OK," she told Hawk. "We'll just leave."

Leif wanted to argue, but he knew Tessa was watching out for them. They were the first wyntonan Marines, and so it was even more important to keep out of trouble than when they were recruits.

"No, it's not OK," Hawk said. "It's not."

"Better pay attention to the casper," the woman said. "If *you* want to stay, that is."

Hawk stood up, stared down the woman, and said, "No, I don't want to stay in this shithole."

The woman shrugged and said, "Suit yourself."

"What's going on, Hawk?" Savea shouted from a nearby table where a dozen heavy-worlders were sitting and drinking.

"This lady here says Leif, J-Dan, and Tessa have to leave."

"I don't serve no caspers here. You trolls, though, you're OK," the women shouted over to him.

Savea leaned back for a moment, staring at the far corner of the bar.

"Come on," Tessa said. "Let's just leave."

Savea slowly stood up, walked over to the woman, and stood too close to her. The woman didn't flinch, staring down a Marine who could tear her into two.

"Like I said, you trolls are OK, but I'll never serve a casper piece of shit."

"So, you're saying no caspers?" Savea asked in a pleasant tone. "You won't let them drink here?" he asked, pointing at the three wyntonans."

"They'll never get a drink in here."

"OK, it's your bar, so you can serve who you want."

"Manu—" Hawk started, only to have him hold up a beefy hand to stop her.

"Well, it's like this, ma'am," Savea said. "When I look around this bar, I see, what, 40 of us here, right?"

She nodded, looking unsure of herself.

"And we've spent maybe four or five ID so far, and in a full night, that might be fifty, sixty ID apiece? Good night, huh?"

"Uh . . . yeah. So?"

"Well, when I look at all of us, do you know what I see? All I see is that we're all Marines. All of us."

"Like I said, all of you are OK. You people too. I'm not prejudiced against you trolls."

"But like *I* said, all I see here are Marines. So, if you don't want to serve us, that's your prerogative. I guess we'll all be going."

"What?"

"We accept that you don't want to serve us, so we're all leaving."

The woman narrowed her eyes, then said, "OK, they can stay for a drink. One drink, until the band starts and the place starts filling up."

"Oh, no, we don't want you to change your principles. We're leaving.

"Hey, everyone listen up," he shouted, getting everyone's attention. "This *lady*," he said, using the same tone for "lady" as she had used to say "casper," "doesn't want to serve Marines. So, we're going someplace else. Now!"

There were some confused looking Marines, but within twenty seconds, every one of them was on their feet, including some of the other Marines who were not from their recruit company.

"You've got to pay for those pitchers," the lady said, pointing at three on Savea's table.

"They look full to me. Take them back."

"Let's go," he shouted out and started leading the pack of Marines out the door.

"Tacis," the woman shouted at one of the older Marines who had joined the exodus. "Tell them."

"Sorry, Kassie," the Marine said. "You kind of blew it. And that heavy-worlder's right. We're all Marines first, and you dis one of us, you dis all of us."

Leif missed whatever else she had to say as he was caught up in the push to the exit. His mind was whirring like a baz-beetle in spring. He would never have thought things would play out like they had.

He'd been angry when the woman had said she wouldn't serve them, but he'd been willing to swallow down his anger and follow Tess out of the bar. He wasn't surprised when Hawk had taken issue—she was a friend, after all. But Savea? Along with Nilsen, he'd been a focal point of their harassment. On top of that, after being embarrassed by Leif in the pugil stick ring, Leif had assumed things had gotten worse. They hadn't exchanged a single word during the Crucible or at graduation.

Of all the humans, Leif wouldn't ever have guessed that Savea would be the one to stand up for wyntonans.

But he hadn't stood up for *wyntonans*, Leif suddenly realized. He'd stuck up for fellow *Marines*. For maybe the first time, Leif understood the esprit the corps, the gung-ho spirit, that made Marines Marines.

"So, where do we want to go?" Savea shouted to the group as they assembled in the square.

There were shouts, too many to make much sense of, and the big Marine shouted, "Quiet!" then, "You guys," he said, pointing at the three wyntonans, "where do you want to go?"

Leif was speechless, still trying to absorb what has just transpired, but Tessa said, "I heard the Rabbit and Fox is pretty good."

"Rabbit and Fox it is, then," Savea shouted as the new Marines, many already half-drunk, shouted a series of ooh-rahs.

As they started out in a mob, Savea stepped up and put a steel arm around Leif's neck, pulling his head down to the heavy-worlder's level.

"I was beating you, you know, until that shithead Will got his leg broke. Without that, even with you running amok, I'd have had you."

Leif didn't say anything, and he didn't try to pull back.

"And I'll admit it, I hated being beat by a fucking ghost. But you know what?" He pulled Leif's head down further and kissed the top of his head before releasing it. "I don't mind being beat by a Marine, if you know what I mean."

Yes, I think I do know what you mean, he thought as he followed the mob for a night of letting off 16 weeks' worth of steam.

BOOK 2

NORTHUMBRIA

Chapter 17

Leif was excited despite telling himself that this was just one more step in the journey, nothing extraordinary. But it was different. He was a fleet Marine now, done with training, and ready to start his service. After their initial check-in—where they'd drawn their fair share of stares from the other Marines, the nineteen of them were in a conference room, waiting for the sergeant major to officially welcome them aboard.

Of the nineteen, twelve of them were wyntonan. Instead of spread-loading them across the Corps, the powers that be decided that only four battalions would receive them. Ferron a'Silverton seemed to think this was a good idea, that in this way, they could "support" each other. On one hand, Leif liked that fact that he did have others of the People with him, but on the other hand, he was afraid that clumping them together would make them stand out, making them "others." Leif didn't think he understood humans well yet, but he'd seen enough so far to know that the human Marines placed their "Marineness" above everything else. That lesson had been drilled into him back on Iwo at the Oasis, where it had worked to his advantage, but now, grouping them together might only highlight that they were different.

He had a pretty good group, however, he had to admit as he looked at the other Marines. From the wyntonans, he was there with Jordan, Tessa, Johari, Moria, Dubois, Carlton, Lim, Katerina, Manuel, Ray, and Alim. Leif knew two of the humans well: Manu Savea, Zhen-man, and he knew Boise Portuno, who'd been in the trail series, but had been quite friendly and open at the School of Infantry. He'd gotten to know the other four during the transit, and they seemed OK. What would be more pertinent, however, was not his fellow newbies but rather the Marines he'd be serving with, from the fire team level on up.

"Attention on deck!" someone shouted, and the group shot to attention, recruit instincts still flowing through their veins.

"Sit down," a gruff voice said as he entered the conference room.

Sergeant Major John Crawford looked every bit the Marine staff non-commissioned officer as he strode to the front, completely confident and in control of himself. His hair was the salt-and-pepper of going grey, something that could be easily controlled, but a full head of black hair was obviously not important to him. Leif was impressed before the human even spoke.

"I'm Sergeant Major Crawford," he said, taking a moment to look each of them in the eye. "I'm here to welcome you to the Third Battalion, Sixth Marines. Lieutenant Colonel Jarvinkus is on leave, but she wanted me to give you her welcome as well.

"If you want to be on the cutting edge, you've come to the right place. We've just gone through workups, and after this final admin stand-down, we're assuming the division's alert battalion mission. That means, as of twenty-two days from today, we can get called out on a mission at a moment's notice."

Leif shared a quick glance with Jordan. He wanted to see some action, but that was a little quick. The School of Infantry had taught them basic tactics and had introduced them to the tools of the trade, but firing weapons on a range did not equate to proficiency as a member of a fire team.

"As you can see, twenty-two days isn't shit, and we're on a port-and-starboard leave right now. I'd rather have had you here during the work-ups, but things don't always work out as we want. I do have to get you snapped in, so for the first week here, Master Sergeant Picolli is going to run you through some extra training before we send you to your companies. As soon as leave ends, you'll join your permanent units."

Leif was pleased to hear that. The more training the better.

The sergeant major kept on for another five minutes, more of an ooh-rah-we're-the-best-unit-in-the-corps and this-is-your-chance-to-make-a-name-for-yourself-type speech before he started to wind down.

Finally, he stopped for a moment, and then said, "OK, you Marines are dismissed. Go out in the passage and wait for Sergeant Wyndam. You wyntonans, remain seated. I want to talk to you."

"Marines" are dismissed, while "wyntonans" are to remain? Leif wondered if the sergeant major even knew what he'd just said.

Zhen-man, who was sitting in front of Leif, turned with a frown on his face. He looked at Leif and raised his eyebrows before filing to the aisle.

He'd heard it, too.

Leif sat quietly, until the humans left and the hatch closed behind them. The sergeant major seemed to be carefully choosing his words.

"Look. I know you're all citizens of the empire, and as such, I'm sworn to protect you and your planet. I've got nothing against you, just like I've got nothing against alindamirs, hissers, or any of you non-humans."

Yeah, and I bet you have wyntonan friends, too, Leif thought sourly.

"But, the one love of my life is the Corps, and I bleed Marine Corps green. All I care about is that we perform our mission with honor, and that we get all our Marines home after its done.

"Now, I know you all did well at Navarro. Hell, you got one of the honor graduates—it was all over the news. But there's a big difference in hitting all the marks during recruit training and serving as part of a Marine unit. You've got to have teamwork, and you've got to trust each other in order to stay alive and complete the mission.

"Now, I'm not saying you aren't good people. Hell, we got plenty of hissers back on Uriah, where I'm from, and they do good work. I'm just not sure you're made out to be Marines. Hell, you don't even have an army back on your home planet—you don't fight wars. That's probably a good thing, more civilized, you know, but we Marines, we're not civilized. We're brawlers, the kind that are needed to keep the empire safe."

He stopped and looked over the 12 of them as if gauging their reaction.

"But, the emperor has decided that you're going to be Marines, and just like you, when I stood on the yellow footprints more years ago than I'd like to remember, I swore my allegiance to the emperor. New emperor or old, that don't matter none. My loyalty is to the Granite Throne, no matter who sits there. So, like all Marines, I'm saluting and marching on, and I'm going to do my best to make sure all of you become the best Marines you can possibly be.

"If you can't cut it, though, then you'll be dropped from the battalion, and I'll let someone else figure out what to do with you. For now, though, all of you are going to be assigned together to Kilo Company. Kilo will be designated the battalion reserve, so unless things go to shit on some mission, you'll have the chance to observe how real Marines get the mission done. Watch and learn, and things will go just fine."

He started to say something else, but then bit it back before saying, "I guess that's about it. If you have any problems with other Marines, I want to know about it. Try to get it resolved within Kilo, but if you can't, or you think the problem is because you're wyntonan, then don't call home, don't go public. You come to me or the chaplain first, and we'll take care if it.

"Any questions."

No one raised a hand. Leif knew they were all stewing over what had just been said.

"OK, then Sergeant Wyndam's waiting for you. You've got a lot of work ahead of you, but I'm confident you'll all do fine."

Leif stood up as the sergeant major left. The last five minutes had been a disjointed mishmash of diametrically opposed statements. The sergeant major liked non-humans, but he didn't want them in his Corps. He'd follow orders to make them good Marines, only if they failed, he'd shitcan them from the battalion. He had full confidence in them, but they were to keep out of the way of "real" Marines.

It was a somber group of Marines who filed out of the conference room to join the others and Sergeant Wyndam. Leif had hoped that after boot camp, he'd be accepted as just another Marine, but it looked like they were wyntonan first, Marines second.

This was shaping up to be a long and miserable tour of duty.

Chapter 18

Lance Corporal Rick Ahlstrom let out a large, obnoxious fart, which was immediately followed by a waterfall of pillows enveloping him while he laughed. Sometimes—well, often—Leif didn't understand humans. Ahlstrom had just emitted a vile gas, one that the humans professed to hate, yet he seemed proud of it, and half of the other humans joined him in laughing.

The People also relieved gas formed by the digestive process, but nothing to the level of the humans, who were worse than some of the grazing animals back on Home. More than that, they didn't make a show of it. Johari had started to refer to the humans as "gassers" when they were speaking Uzboss among themselves.

While the alert battalion, they had all moved out of their normal quarters and into barracks. All of the platoon's non-rates, the lance corporals and below, were in a single cubicle, sleeping in three-level bunks. The company NCO's were berthed together while the SNCO's and officers had their own deck. When they were not training, doing maintenance, at the gym, chapel, or at chow, the entire reinforced battalion of over 1,200 Marines and sailors were in the two side-by-side barracks. While a limited number of Marines could be signed out to go to the exchange or the area clinic, the battalion had to be able to be on the buses and on the way to the spaceport within 15 minutes, if the call came out.

All of their equipment, to include their weapons, were at the port already, staged in deployment containers. Their personal gear was in the packs hanging on hooks in each compartment.

After a flurry of training, both with Top Picolli, then with their units, things had quieted down. Because of the time constraints of being ready to deploy, they could not go out to any of the outlying training areas, and without their weapons, that didn't make much sense anyway. So, for the duration, all of their field training would be in the simulators which were less than 200 meters from the alert barracks. Leif was fine with the simulators—they were total-one, max fun. He loved blowing the enemy apart, even if they were only electrons. He couldn't believe that the Empire was paying him to play like that.

The close quarters, on the other hand, were not as pleasant. Before going on alert status, he'd shared a small room with Jordan. Now, he was in an open squadbay, full of noise—and humans farting. And they complained of how the wyntonan's smelled? At one point, the company gunny had threatened to take away their spice for the duration, but new containers were found that kept any smell from escaping. The humans still complained, however.

I'd rather smell that crap the South Islanders call spice than the humans, Leif thought, looking across the cubical where Ahlstrom was kicking the pillows off his rack and onto the deck.

Ahlstrom seemed to be a pretty good Marine, though, Leif had to admit. As Leif's fire team's AR man, armed with the heavier M55 automatic rifle, he'd taken Leif under his wing, giving him extra instruction to bring him up to speed. They were not in training mode—they could be in combat tomorrow, so it had been vital for Leif, and the rest of the new joins, to mesh with their fellow fire team members.

Corporal Wendy Lawrence was Leif's fire team leader, and she had already made the cutting score for sergeant. Private First Class Donte "Donk" Suharto was the other rifleman. None of them had shown any sign that they resented Leif, unlike with Jordan and Dubois, who both had been at the receiving end of anti-wyntonan statements by Marines in their fire teams.

That was not exactly true, though, with regards to Leif. While none of his fire team members had said anything specific to him, Donk had voiced his dislike of the smell of spice, and everyone seemed to think that Kilo Company was considered inferior to the other companies. And that, mostly by inference, but sometimes explicitly stated, was because of the presence of the wyntonan Marines.

In one area where Leif was exactly like his fellow human Marines was in that he longed to run to the sound of gunfire. He wanted to prove himself in mortal competition, to measure himself against the ultimate opponent. While many Marines enlisted out of patriotism and loyalty to the emperor, and while their true loyalty was to their fellow Marines, it was the desire for action that permeated their thoughts.

It didn't look like that would happen anytime soon, however. There were no flashpoints in their sector, no likely spots for an outbreak of violence. After 48 days as the alert battalion, Leif's hope that something would happen had begun to fade, and the next event on his horizon was looking forward to getting back to their normal two-person quarters.

So, of course, that was when fate struck.

The alarms went off, and red lights filled the squadbay. Marines jumped out of their racks, scrambling to get on their gear.

Sergeant Juniper, the First Squad leader and senior sergeant in the platoon, stuck his head in and asked for a head count.

"What's going on, Sergeant?" Lance Corporal Lori Jankowski asked as she pulled on her boots.

"What's going on? We're getting the call out, that's what's going on," he said, then yelled out, "Fifteen minutes people, fifteen minutes!"

****

The enlisted Marines were ready within ten minutes—then left cooling their heels in the squadbay sitting on their racks. The excitement was palpable as they tried to figure out what was going on.

Nose—Lance Corporal Traci-Ann Hathway—who had an opinion of everything that was going on in the galaxy and was more than happy to share that opinion, thought this might be a show of force, probably to remind a planet like Osis IV, that the empire was still a force to be reckoned with. Chuck

Sylvianstri thought this was a dry run, to test their readiness—something that seemed more likely the longer they sat on their asses.

Leif hoped they'd be taking down slavers.

After forty-five minutes, he'd just about determined that Chuck was right when the gunny came in and gave them a five-minutes warning. If this was a drill, it looked like it was going to take them to the spaceport, at least.

Lhesa field, named for some Navy hero of days gone by, was a bare-bones port, nothing like the civilian spaceport out in Graston City. There was a hangar, in which the battalion sat in their sticks, another maintenance hangar, and the open-air warehouse where the battalion's gear was staged in mount-out crates. When the buses arrived to disgorge the Marines, all eyes were on the steady line of autostevedores that were loading the mount-out boxes on barge-shuttles. If this was a drill, then the Corps was going all out.

When the first of the personnel shuttles landed, a sigh went through the Marines. A few minutes later, a hover came up to the hangar, and the battalion commander and operations officer stepped out. Lieutenant Colonel Jarvincus stepped just inside the hangar and flipped on her throat mic.

"Marines and sailors of the Fighting Third. The government compound on Torayama's World is under siege by a mob of yet undetermined proportions. The planetary secretary, with concurrence by the imperial agent-prime, has asked for military assistance, which as of ten minutes ago, has been approved by the Advisory Council.

"Major Gruenstein and the rest of the staff will be developing our operations order during the transit. We will promulgate that as soon as it has been completed.

"I expect each and every one of you to conduct yourself professionally and with honor to the emperor and Corps.

"Master Sergeant Trendi," she said, turning to the logistics chief and the Marine tasked with getting the battalion up to the waiting ship, "Let's load them up."

Kilo Company would be the last to load, but that didn't dampen Leif's enthusiasm as India started boarding the shuttles.

This was it. He was going to war!

TORAYAMA'S WORLD

Chapter 19

If this was "war," then war is pretty boring, Leif thought for the thousandth time since landing on Torayama's World.

He hated to admit it, but he'd rather be back at Camp Martelle. At least there the rack was real and the food hot. Here, he slept on the ground, ate prepackaged grub, and was getting eaten alive by mosquitos.

Who the hell introduced those demons from hell, he continually wondered, and why were they so fond of the blood of the People?

Pests weren't supposed to cross over to other ecosystem beings, but there they were, biting him at every opportunity. Not even the repellent Doc Jones gave them seemed to deter the buggers.

He slapped at one that landed on his neck, but not before it could bite, then went back to watching out across the low string of memory wire that had created a nominal barrier between the locals and the Marines. This wasn't what he'd imagined he'd be doing after landing on the planet.

It wasn't that there hadn't been a full-out siege when they arrived. Over 8,000 humans had surrounded the government compound, demanding that the planetary secretary resign. Several local police had been killed in the initial confrontation, as had 16 of the besiegers. The battalion arrived outside of the city, then marched in grand fashion to the compound, stopping short so that the CO could demand that the protestors leave. Holding aloft posters of their 16 dead, the protestors were not in the mood to obey, and on the morning after their arrival, India and Lima Companies pushed forward, foregoing any detailed maneuver in lieu of a simple demonstration of brute force.

The besiegers fought back—with very little effect. Disorganized and inexperienced, twenty-three were killed before the rest broke and ran. Only two Marines were slightly hurt.

With the siege broken, Leif had expected the battalion to be recalled, but the situation was in flux at the highest levels, and the battalion set up a very Spartan, and very visible, camp surrounding the compound. Every day, protestors showed up to tell the Marines to go home, and every day, the Marines stood duty, two hours on, two off, standing at a modified parade rest and facing the mob.

Rumor had it that the agent-prime, the emperor's voice on the planet, blamed the planet's secretary for the confrontation and wanted him removed. This was treading on dangerous ground. The emperor could theoretically remove a local or planetary head, but tradition had evolved for a hands-off approach to local politics.

Nose told them rest that the Just Counsellor Sturgis's family owned extensive holdings on Torayama's World, and the secretary was in their pockets. Leif didn't know where she got that information, but if it was true, then the agent-prime wasn't going to prevail. From what he'd learned about human politics, the members of the advisory council held the power in the empire, and if a just counsellor wanted something, then they would get it.

That got Leif to wonder about their deployment on this mission. There had been a siege, true, but was the deployment of a division's alert battalion reasonable, given the expense and the relatively stable situation on the ground?

"Heads up, Leif," Ahlstrom hissed. "The skipper's coming."

Leif tried not to roll his eyes. Captain Ethan Formington was the Kilo Company commander. He'd been the H&S Company commander for the first half of his tour, taking over Kilo a few months ago, and he wasn't a happy camper. It had become evident before even assuming the alert battalion status that he thought the wyntonan Marines were a distraction. He was fond of calling the company together, then giving long speeches on the history of the Corps, on tradition, and how he was going to lead Kilo into glory, cementing their place in Marine Corps legend.

The sergeant major had told the wyntonans that they were going to Kilo, and the company was going to be the battalion reserve, so evidently, the CO was not as enthused about Kilo as the skipper was. After Lima and India were used to break the siege, the skipper must have realized the company's relative position when compared to the other companies, and he blamed the wyntonan Marines.

"If it wasn't for the damned ghosts I've been saddled with, Kilo would have smashed those traitors," he'd said loudly to the first sergeant, but staring at Leif and some of the others, knowing full well they could hear him.

"Did I see you slap your neck, Private?" the skipper asked, coming up behind him.

The captain never, at least within Leif's hearing, called any of the 12 wyntonans "Marine." It was always "Private."

"Yes, sir. A mosquito bit me, sir."

"For the love of all that's holy. Something 'bit' you? And for that, you break? What if while you were crying about a mosquito, a traitor used that distraction to jump the memory wire?"

Leif had no idea how to answer that. The protestors were mostly standing in the shade, out of the afternoon sun, and at least 30 meters away. Slapping his neck had zero effect on his readiness. He looked beyond the skipper's shoulder, a trick he'd learned at Camp Navarro—only in this case, the lieutenant was standing there.

Second Lieutenant Essex McDougal was a young, earnest Marine, someone who thought things out before speaking. Most of the mid and senior enlisted tended to make fun of second lieutenants as a matter of course, but Leif was rather impressed with his platoon commander. Now, though, the lieutenant stared back at him with expressionless eyes.

The skipper snorted and moved on, obviously not expecting an answer. The man was aching for a fight. Leif was, too, he had to admit. But he had no power over others, while the lives of 128 Marines and sailors were in the captain's hands. Leif hoped that his commander understood that.

****

The recall came a week later, but to the surprise of everyone, the brass, in a puzzling example of Marine Corps logic, assigned the battalion to the *IS Cape Town* as a deployed unit. Once a battalion was the alert battalion, the normal progression was to next board a ship for a deployment. This would be after returning to a normal training, however, for a month of admin and prep.

When 3/6 was sent on the current mission, their follow-on battalion, 1/8, assumed the alert status. Instead of sending 3/6 back to re-assume the status, they simply advanced the cruise and sent the *Cape Town* to board the battalion.

Leif didn't have family back at Camp Martelle, so it didn't make that much of a difference to him, with one major exception. They'd deployed to Torayama's World with just their break-out packs. If they were going to be aboard ship for 12 months, they needed a little more than just two changes of skivvies.

IS CAPE TOWN

Chapter 20

"Looks good on you, Manu," Leif said, eyeing the single stripe insignia of a private first class on the human's collar.

"Forty-four extra ID each month!" Manu crowed, making a show of blowing on his knuckles, then buffing the insignia.

"I could use that," Leif said.

"How come you aren't on the list. Shouldn't you be?" Manu asked.

"I don't know. I'm sure I'll be on the next list," Leif said.

But he wasn't so sure. None of the wyntonans had been on the message for promotion to PFC. Normally, promotion was a given after time-in-grade. A Marine had to screw up not to get promoted. Somehow, all 12 of the wyntonans must have screwed up, because none of them were on the list. Of the humans in their recruit group, only Art—Artimus Flaxholder— wasn't on the list, and he'd received Battalion Commanders Office Hours for falling asleep on post.

Leif was not surprised that Captain Fornication, as some of the troops called him, would not approve them for promotion, but certainly someone higher up the chain had to notice that?

Other than this slap in the face, life on the *Cape Town* wasn't bad. To everyone's relief, the ship had returned them to Camp Martelle, where they had nine days to prepare for deployment. Now, in space for four weeks, life was settling down into a routine. The highlight of the cruise so far had been the takedown of the *IS 34*. The *"Three-four"* had been a commercial liner two centuries before, and now it was a Navy trainer. The sailors and Marines had conducted two takedowns with the 34 being defended by a Navy red team.

This had been pure fun, a virt-real game on steroids. The best part was that after only simulations, Leefen a'Hope Hollow, a boy from the nethers had transited the black. He'd "dangled his feet." More than a few of his fellow Marines had hated taking the atlatls on the EVA across to the *Thirty-Four*, but Leif had simply been excited.

As per tradition, he and the rest of the newbies for which this was their first EVA, had the shit kicked out of them. "Kicked" was an accurate term. Crawling on their bellies down the ship's main passage, other "danglers" had poured some evil black concoction over them as they crawled, while still others used their feet to rub it in. Much of the rubbing was done with force—anywhere else, it would be called "kicking."

The Navy was full of these traditions, and while Leif had thought it stupid when he'd first learned about it, it had oddly been fun to participate in it.

"Yeah, probably," Manu said. "Next stop, lance coolie. Another 50 BC, I think."

"So, what's India up to now?"

Manu had been assigned to India Company. He'd already made a name for himself as part of the flying wedge that had pushed through the protestors on Torayama's World where the general consensus was that by using pure muscle mass, the civilian casualty rate had been drastically cut. Leif was a little jealous of him, and he didn't like that he felt that way.

His relationship with Manu was a strange one. The People tended to make both friends and enemies forever, and he and the big heavy-worlder had started out as enemies. They had a grudge match in the pugil stick ring, for goodness' sakes. Yet now, Manu acted as if they were long-lost friends. It had been harder for Leif to come around. He couldn't say that he considered Manu a great friend, but at least they were on good terms.

"Just same old, same old. Lima's got the sims until tomorrow, so it's more make-work for now. I'm heading to the gym at 1630 if you want to meet."

"Can't. We're first sitting. Can't work out and shower by then."

Even on a ship the size of the *Cape Town*, space was limited. Most things, from the gym to meal sittings to when they could visit the ship's store were scheduled.

"Don't shower," Manu said. "Just go to chow all sweaty. It'll make you ghosts smell better," he added, throwing a solid punch to Leif's upper arm.

That was another thing that still confused Leif. Back at Camp Navarro, when Manu used the term "ghost," it was derogatory. Yet right now, Manu had not only used it, but criticized the People's smell *and* punched him in the arm. Logic said that this was a bad thing, but the smile on Manu's face, and prior experience with humans, let Leif know the guy was being *friendly*. It just made no sense.

"But then I'd have to smell you humans' farts and burps," he said a little hesitantly.

Manu opened his mouth and let out a huge burp. He mimed flapping his hands to bring the aroma back to his face, then said with a smile, "Just like roses, my man, just like roses."

There was no doubt about it. Humans were strange creatures.

Chapter 21

The sergeant major stood silently for a long moment, then asked, "I told you when you joined that if you ran into any problems, my door was always open, right?"

The 12 wyntonans all nodded. Leif wondered why they'd been called to meet in the ship's chief's mess. Whatever the reason, it probably wasn't good.

"If that's the case, then why didn't you come talk to me?"

Leif looked around at his fellow privates, and they looked as confused as he was.

"Look, I'm not going to conduct an investigation, but Marines take care of Marines. They do not air their dirty laundry. Is that clear?"

All 12 nodded again.

"I'd like to say all of that's in the past, but I don't know what the fall-out is going to be. I don't think the CO's going to get relieved . . ."

What? The CO is getting fired? And that is connected to us?

The sergeant major shook his head, then said, "Just stand by while I'll let comms know we're ready.

"This does not sound good," Jordan whispered.

They sat in silence for over five minutes before a voice over the speaker said, "He's on now, sergeant major."

"Ah, there you are," a holo image of Sept-Minister Iaxi appeared over the baseplate that had been placed on the table. "It's good to see all of you. Ahem.

"First, I want to give you the emperor's greeting. He is very, very proud of you, and he wants you to know that.

"Second, I want you to understand that you are full Marines now, and the emperor will not tolerate you being treated differently than any other Marine. As such, he has signed an imperial decree, appointing all of you as privates first class, dating back to the first of the month."

Oh, so that's what this is.

On one hand, Leif felt a thrill that what he'd seen was a wrong had been righted. On the other hand, as he looked at the sergeant major's blank face, the cure might turn out to be worse than the disease.

The sept-minister went on about equal rights, and how important this was for the Empire. The next group of wyntonan recruits was getting ready to graduate, and so Leif's class was paving the way for a fully integrated military. He also noted that the emperor would not stand for the wyntonans to be kept out of combat. They were real Marines, not pseudo-Marines only there for photo ops, something Leif was glad to hear.

He finished with, "I've instructed the ship's commanding officer that his communications center maintain a direct line to reach me at all times. If you ever experience another instance of discrimination, then any of you can march up to the center and call me. No one can stop you. I hope I've made that clear. Any time at all, you call me."

Oh, sure, like that will be a good idea.

The sept-minister thanked them all again and assured them that the emperor was watching over them before he signed off. As one, 12 sets of eyes swung to look at the sergeant major, who seemed to be struggling to control himself.

"I told you before, I don't care what kind of creature gave you birth. You're imperial citizens, and I've sworn my very life to protect you. And if the emperor thinks you should be Marines, who am I to naysay it? But, and listen to this 'but,' when you demean the unit, when you put the CO in jeopardy, you cross the line. If I ever find out that one of you goes above my head—without giving me a chance to address the problem first—I will bury you. And yes, you can tell the honorable sept-minister that," he almost spat out.

Leif could see that the sergeant major wanted to say more, but with an extreme effort of will, cut himself off. He understood the sergeant major's point, though. If one of them complained without going to him first, then he had every right to be angry. How can he fix what he doesn't know?

Except he did know. He knew that not one of us was promoted when we should have been, and nothing was done.

Well, nothing that we know off, he conceded.

The sergeant major reached into his cargo pocket and pulled out twelve sets of PFC insignia. With a flick of his hand, he tossed them onto the table.

"You should have had these two weeks ago, I'll admit. And maybe we should go through a ceremony, but I advised the CO against that. So, if you're going to report that, make sure you blame me, not her. All things told, there is going to be fallout, so less fanfare, the better. I'm tempted to ask you to wait until the first to put them on, but they're yours. Do what you wish."

With that, he turned and left the mess. A head poked out of the serving window, spotted the new PFC's, then disappeared back inside the galley.

One by one, they reached over and picked up a set of collar devices. They looked pretty insignificant from outward appearances, just a single strip of black ceroplast.

"I think we should refuse them," Katerina said, reverting to Uzboss. "They're going to cause problems for us when everyone finds out it was because the emperor intervened for us."

"I agree, but not because of problems any of the monkeys have. If Captain Fornication, doesn't want us to be promoted, then screw him. I don't want anything to do with their precious ranks," Ray said.

They fell quiet for a long moment, before Dubois asked, "So what, do we just put these on now or forget them?"

Leif pulled the insignia off the backing and put it on his collar.

"Hell, it's forty-four more ID a month. I'm taking it."

Chapter 22

The next few days marked a significant downturn in the wyntonan's relationship with the rest of the Marines. It was no secret that something was up with the CO, and Captain Formington was on a rampage. During a snap inspection, he focused on the wyntonans, and he tore Katerina's junk-on-the-bunk apart, telling the first sergeant that he wanted her brought up on charges of negligence.

Leif didn't know whether it was the first sergeant or someone from the battalion staff that got to him, but nothing came of it except that Katerina, who advocated against wearing the insignia, worried for days that she was going to get busted back down to private.

Some of the rank and file Marines, and more than a few sailors, actively scorned the wyntonans, with comments like "crying to mommy" being the most common. Their friends supported them, but while most of the rest understood that they had been screwed out of their normal promotion, they did not approve of "squealing." Marines took care of things in-house and did not involve politicians.

Leif wasn't sure that one of them had, in fact, gone past the sergeant major and somehow gotten a message to the sept-minister. He asked each one of them, and all denied it. The People were not good liars, but he also wanted to believe them. If the emperor really was watching them—or more likely the sept-minister—then he would have noted that the twelve of them hadn't been promoted as scheduled.

After beginning to feel accepted as just another Marine, Leif was rapidly getting disenchanted, and being crowded together on a ship, with no way to get away, made matters worse.

Six days later, when the ship was diverted for a possible mission, a wave of relief swept through the ship. With something to focus on, Leif hoped the entire incident of their promotion would be forgotten.

Chapter 23

"Is Kilo up for this?" the CO asked, walking among the troops as they prepared for the drop.

She wasn't specifically asking the wyntonans, but Leif hadn't missed that she'd made sure to address each fire team that included one of them. Even before the mission orders were delivered, the general feeling was that the CO was not getting relieved. It would have been difficult, relieving a commanding officer while her battalion was deployed, but it had happened before. Leif was glad she'd retained her job, and not just because he knew the wyntonans would be blamed for getting the popular CO fired. He respected her, and he thought the battalion would suffer if someone else took over.

Captain Formington was another story, though. The rumor had it that he was going to be transferred to be the assistant operations officer, and the current assistant, Captain Tzama, would take over the company. It was only the mission orders that saved his hide, and he knew it. It was obvious that he thought he could save his job by kicking ass in the mission, and he was everywhere at once, never stopping to even take a breath.

He'd get his chance, too. Leif didn't know if the CO was giving the skipper one last chance to prove himself or if the sept-minister's comments had made a difference, but instead of being the battalion reserve, Kilo was to be the point of main effort.

The CO chatted for a few moments, asking casual questions from both human and wyntonan alike. Leif was sure that her pattern was not random but was rather carefully planned. Instead of reeking of insincerity, he thought she was making some good choices. He was never going to be a Marine battalion commander, but that didn't mean he couldn't take lessons in leadership.

"Ma'am, we're five minutes to launch," Captain Gasert, the S4, said as he came up to her.

"Well, I guess I'd better get in my place," she said, patting Rick Ahlstrom on the back. "I'm counting on Kilo, and I've got full confidence in you."

As soon as she made her way across the hangar bay, the Captain went into overdrive with, "You heard the CO. She's got full confidence in us. I've got confidence in you, Killer Kilo. I know you're going to make yourself proud and make Colonel Jarvincus proud . . ."

Leif tuned the human out. It wasn't that he was doing anything wrong, but it was just too much cheerleading. They had a word for that in *Uzboss: to-otmar.* Jordan had laughed when Leif had used the term. It generally described an ada, full of confidence and excitement, but without consequence, like a Tri-Year Three telling someone about to go on their a'aden hunt that "they" were going to succeed. Aside from his yammering, Leif still hadn't forgiven the human for creating the entire promotion incident in the first place.

Unfortunately, they didn't get a respite when the first wave took off for the planet's surface. India was landing first to secure the LZ, followed by the headquarters element, Weapons, and Lima. As the point of main effort, Kilo would be last off the *Cape Town.* The captain made sure that he was visible, making the rounds of the troops, slapping shoulders and making awkward small talk. It wasn't until Lima was loading that he slowed down. He called the lieutenants over for a last brief, giving the rest of the company a break.

Two hours after India departed, Kilo loaded the shuttles. A few minutes later, they left the *Cape Town* behind for Omeyocan's surface. Within hours, the chances were extremely high that Kilo would be locked in battle.

OMEYOCAN

Chapter 24

Omeyocan was a beautiful planet. The name meant "heaven" in an obscure human language, and Leif could see that the name fit. Lush vegetation with a profundity of flowers and gentle warm breezes, it seemed an unlikely setting for the Marines to face battle.

It was one of the few Mother-seeded planets without a sentient life-form, but unlike other such planets, this one had not been stripped bare upon discovery. Unidawn, a human corporation known for its progressive policies, had obtained the initial charter, but it had left most of the planet pristine, and by doing so, had created a luxury tourist destination for people who enjoyed green vacations. But the corporation was still in the business of making money, and it had built a thriving pharmaceutical empire—all the facilities built with low-impact, of course, but still huge revenue generators. What they had not emplaced was a strong security force. Unidawn did business not only within the empire and other human governments, but with the Sassares Hegemony and various noxes tribes. With little fear of an invasion, spending resources on security seemed like a waste.

Where there is a gap, some sentient beings, no matter their race, will seek to exploit it.

An armed group of over 150 individuals had landed on the planet and taken over one of the campuses, taking more than 3,000 people, mostly human, as hostages. Their demand was simple: Unidawn was to pay them 100,000,000 BC, transferred to more than 100 floating accounts, or they would kill the hostages and destroy the facility. Any attempt to retake the campus would result in the immediate execution of the hostages. By targeting the "progressive" Unidawn, they undoubtedly felt their chance of getting the payment was worth any risk they were taking.

They neglected to take into account two factors, however. The first was that among the hostages were not only other races of the empire, but also 38 sassares, and the sassares were not known for being complacent to threats. The Hegemony had already contacted the Empire and threatened to take military action unless the hostages were rescued. The second factor was that as progressive as their public persona was portrayed, Unidawn was a very rich and powerful company, and it didn't get that way by lacking in resolve.

The result was that Third Battalion, Sixth Marines, was thrust into action.

Intel had determined that the hostage-takers were associated with one of the minor clans. The underworld clans were not driven by religion or creed: they were motivated by profit and power. These were not fanatics, willing to die for a cause. While no one doubted that they would kill the hostages if they could get away with it, they were not willing to die with them.

For a low-to-mid-level clan, if they were successful, this would vault their prestige within the underworld. Even attempting it would prove they were a fearless force, a clan with which to be reckoned. Those actually conducting their operation, however, would want to be alive to take advantage of that improved reputation. They would only suicide as a last-ditch option, if even then.

That was the crux of the matter. The Marines had to take control of the situation quickly enough so that the criminals didn't have that option. Kilo Company would be key to that effort.

The criminals would know they landed, but they wouldn't know what the Marines planned, and they would be weighing their options. They still had the hostages, and they could still blow the facility, so that gave them the upper hand—at least, that was what Intel determined as their most likely frame of mind.

Since they knew the Marines had landed, Kilo boarded commercial buses and openly rode the 15 klicks to the campus, unloading seven hundred meters short of the main gate. This seemed surreal to Leif. This was probably going to be his first taste of combat, and he rode a luxury Yutong bus to the assembly area?

As the initial point of main effort, Kilo's mission during Phase 1 of the operation was to fix the criminals in place. Overhead and orbital surveillance indicated that the criminals had emplaced automatic defenses around the campus. Kilo was to probe those defenses, taking out some, but never making it far enough to enter any of the buildings. Hopefully, this would give the criminals confidence, making them think they could manage to hold off the Marines and still negotiate a settlement.

While this was happening the key element in the operation would take place. Guided by company security, the attached recon and electronic countermeasures team, code-named "Jupiter," would enter the campus though maintenance tunnels. The criminals would probably have them covered. If that was with personnel, the recon Marines would quietly take them out. Anything else would be neutralized by the ECM team.

The ECM team would try to identify the placement and type of explosives emplaced in the campus. Unless the triggers were strictly mechanical, if they could locate and analyze them, between them and the *Cape Town* in orbit overhead, they could block any detonation signal. If the triggers were mechanical, then the recon Marines would take out anyone attempting to set off those explosives.

This is when subterfuge would kick in with Phase 2. Knowing full well that the criminals would have eyes on the spaceport, the ship's XO, dressed in civilian clothing and accompanied by a dozen sailors in civilian clothing as well, would land, making no attempt to hide it. The XO would march to where the colonel had set up her CP in the control tower. A few moments later, Kilo would stop their attack and pull back.

Leif tended to see things in a pretty straight-forward way, so to him, this was genius. The criminals would think that a civilian official had come over to keep the Marines from being, well, Marines.

However, as Nose said, the underworld clans were not noted for being naive, and they could easily suspect such a ruse. They probably had a few tricks up their sleeve as well. When it came down to it, this was going to be a fight.

While the fake official took over communications with the criminals, Kilo would remain in an offensive posture, and Lima would join them. Inside the buildings, recon and ECM would be doing their thing.

Phase 3 would be the assault. With the recon Marines on the inside attempting to remove any of the criminals who were in position to execute the civilians, Kilo and Lima would attack in earnest, hoping a quick assault would overwhelm the enemy. Kilo was to search out and kill the enemy while Lima would rush to the concentrations of civilians and getting them out of the campus as quickly as possible.

With two full rifle companies and the recon team inside, there wasn't much of a chance that the 150 criminals could hope to push the Marines back, but they could proceed with their threat to kill the civilians. This was going to be a rush to get the job done.

A "rush" that was starting with Kilo falling into formation, of all things. The skipper actually fit the scenario, Leif had to admit, with his preening like an Earth peacock as he gave a short speech, one sure to be picked up by the enemy, about glory and dedication. Leif had no idea how much of this was for show and how much of it was real, but it seemed to fit the operations order.

The formation broke up, and the platoons moved forward in a company V, which was a standard formation that gave good firepower to the front. Leif felt his pulse rise in anticipation. This was to where all his training had been leading him, and his one thought was that he hoped he didn't screw up. He could not let his fellow Marines down. He felt fear—not fear of dying, not fear of the enemy, but fear of failure. He was afraid of being a coward once the fighting commenced.

"Keep it steady, nothing to it," Sergeant Roy Holmes passed over the net. "Just watch your dispersion."

Leif gave a quick glance to the others in his fire team to check his position, afraid the comment was aimed at him. He was OK, though, five meters to the right and in front of Corporal Lawrence.

They closed the distance to the front gate, and Leif kept waiting to be taken under fire. They were well within range of the autogun emplacements the enemy had set up, but nothing happened. The campus ahead was quiet except for bird calls that sang back and forth to each other.

Despite expecting it, when the first autogun opened up, he was momentarily confused. The sharp cracka-cracka took him by surprise. It sounded too inconsequential to be much of a weapon. The company shifted into their immediate action drill, rushing forward to push through the kill zone. One of the Weapons Company missilemen, just to Leif's right, deployed her Dagger, the hypervelocity missile streaking forward almost too quickly for the eye to see to take out the autogun—as two more opened up.

The company surged forward, firing as they went, to reach the cover of the campus walls. Leif had his M88 ready, but without a target, he didn't fire, as he sprinted up the last 50 meters.

Third Platoon had been on the company's left flank, and now Lieutenant McDougal was rushing along the wall, organizing his Marines. Second Platoon, which had the company center, had reached the wall as well, and they were firing through the entrance. Leif craned his neck to see what was happening, only to catch sight of a Marine down, 30 meters back. Doc Ponsoby, "Pon," rushed up to him, unmistakable with his heavy-worlder physique, only to be dropped at well.

With a shout, Leif started to get up when Corporal Lawrence said, "Get down, Hollow. Pay attention to what's going on here."

Two more Marines rushed out and managed to pull Doc and the other Marine out of the line of fire.

One of the combat engineers emplaced his charge against the wall, making sure everyone was back ten meters. There was a muffled blast that kicked up a lot of dust, but didn't sound like much, but when the dust had cleared, there was a large opening in the wall. This was supposed to be Third Platoon's entry point, both for now and when the actual assault commenced. It looked pretty small, which would make it a focal point for enemy fire, and the entire platoon was going to go through it in just a few moments.

The platoon had conducted two full weeks of combat in a built-up area training, but that was prior to Leif and the rest joining them. They had gone through walk-throughs in the hangar bay on the ship, and Leif had gone over the manuals in detail, but this was going to be his first time through a breach.

He just followed the rest, mumbling his "Coming through" as he passed into the campus grounds. Second Fire team immediately broke left after entering as fire peppered them.

Rick stumbled, almost going down, but he passed, "I'm OK."

The fire team's objective was a small gazebo alongside a pond. The overhead image didn't do it justice—it was beautiful, something Leif noticed despite the rounds zipping by. It was more artistic than sturdy, so it didn't offer much cover, but it was better than nothing. Using the rails as supports, they fired their M88s, despite not having defined targets. From the heat-signatures, they knew where most of the hostages were being held, so that building was off-limits for the moment. Anything else was fair game. There were four signatures high in another building, and the four Marines focused on them, sticking with the 88s instead of anything heavier. They were trying to fix the enemy force while recon and ECM made their way inside the campus.

Not much changed over the next 15 minutes. Without hard targets, Marine fire diminished. At least five enemy autoguns had been knocked out. Leif did not have access to the company net, so he couldn't see the Marine casualties, but he'd seen three go down, and Rick had been hit. His armor had stopped the round, but he said his shoulder was pretty sore.

Leif didn't really know what combat would be like, but he never imagined it could be so . . . so boring? They were technically in a fire fight, but nothing much was happening. The rush of adrenaline that had coursed through him had been cut off, leaving him feeling flat.

On the pond, two swans paddled regally out of some reeds, followed by a dozen black babies. Rounds were still being fired, but the swans didn't seem to mind. He'd never seen a real swan, and he watched them seemingly float across the water.

The recall ripped him back to reality. It was time to retreat. Leif and the others jumped up, causing the swans to adjust their course away from the gazebo. Following Sergeant Holmes' commands, the squad moved by overwatch, two fire teams covering the third while it moved. Within a minute, they were darting through the breach in the wall again, taking position 30 meters to the right.

"Did it work?" Leif asked Donk. "I mean, did we fool them?"

The other Marine shrugged and said, "I guess we'll find out."

Leif had never warmed to Donte Suharto. There was no animosity, but the team's other private first class seemed lost in his own world much of the time. Leif looked to Corporal Lawrence instead, dying to ask what was happening, but biting his tongue. As Donk said, they'll find out soon enough.

Doc Irrawaddy came over to check Rick, then gave him the go-ahead to stay with the fire team. The lieutenant was next, checking on each Marine.

"How does it look, sir?" Leif asked, unable to restrain himself anymore.

Several other sets of eyes looked up at the question. They wanted to know just as much as he did.

"I'm not on the battalion command net, but Captain Formington told me to stand by. You can read into that as well as I can."

"Did we lose anybody, sir?" Lori Jankowski asked.

"Not in Third. Two hit," he said, nodding at Rick. "Nothing penetrated."

The fact that only two of the platoon were hit was unbelievable. There had been rounds flying all over the place, at least initially, yet only two rounds had found their mark.

"First Platoon lost two, though," the lieutenant said soberly. "Corporal Brock and Doc Ponsoby."

Corporal Lawrence gave a quick intake of breath. She'd been close friends, maybe even more, with Brock, Leif knew.

"KIA?" she asked, her voice catching.

The lieutenant nodded.

"Fuck," she said quietly.

Leif knew who the other two were, even if he didn't know them well. But looking at the tears welling in his corporal's eyes, he began to realize that this was the real deal. Death wasn't just some vague concept. There were consequences, real consequences.

"Well, just . . . just be ready. There're over 3000 imperial citizens in there who are depending on us. Focus on that," the lieutenant said before moving on.

"You heard the lieutenant," Staff Sergeant Saoirse Donovan said as she came around, scanning each Marine's weapon. "Just be ready."

The platoon sergeant had full readouts of everyone's weapons, both in rounds and charge remaining, but she was somewhat of a micromanager, and now she was using her external scanner to re-check. That made Leif second-guess his own weapon, so he checked his display. The charge was at 98%, and he had 1192 rounds in his magazines. He'd thought he'd fired far more than eight rounds total, but the numbers didn't lie.

He checked the magazine he was carrying for Rick. The M55 the other Marine carried was an automatic weapon, the round itself much larger than Leif's M88 2.21 round, so the other three team members helped shoulder the load. Leif was carrying another 200 rounds for him. The M55 had not been cleared for the first feint, so Rick still had his full combat load.

He leaned back against the wall, looking out past a green area so perfectly manicured as to look natural. This really was a beautiful world, and he idly wondered if he was destined to die here. The thought didn't bother him nearly as much as the fear of letting down his team had been before the feint.

To his great surprise, Leif dozed off before the lieutenant's voice came over the comms, telling everyone to get ready. Leif sat up with a start, shaking the cobwebs out of his mind.

"Morning, Hollow," Nose said. "Glad you can join us."

How the hell did I fall asleep? he wondered.

"Jupiter is in position. We kick off in two," the lieutenant passed. "Check the positions of the hostages. These are M88-cleared only. Everywhere else is weapons free."

Leif felt a wave of relief sweep over him. The entire operation had depended on recon and ECM getting in unobserved and finding the hostages and charges. He did a quick check on his helmet display. Nothing had changed about the hostages. They were all grouped on the third floor of Objective A, the administrative building.

"Buddy check," Corporal Lawrence passed.

Leif turned to her while Rick and Donk turned to each other. He gave her the once over, tugging on her combat gear, making sure it was secure, and then she did the same. All the high-tech equipment did a Marine no good if a simple clasp failed and the equipment fell off.

Glancing down the line, he could see the other two platoons stirring, too, getting ready to go. The adrenaline started flowing again, and Leif felt his mind sharpen. Somewhat surprisingly, he felt confident. Today was not going to be the day he died.

. . . which was stupid. Over-confidence had probably killed more soldiers over the millennia than anything else. Still, he couldn't change the way he felt.

"First Squad, in five . . . four . . . three . . . two . . . one . . . go!" the lieutenant ordered.

First Squad poured into the gap in the wall. Immediately, Second followed, a cluster at the opening, then the Marines dispersing out as the space opened up. Second's objective was the machine shop to the right. There were at least four of the enemy inside the shop.

The swans were still out in the pond, but stopped in the middle, the two adults trying to surround the cygnets, as the heavy cracka-cracka of autoguns rang out, the reports from the chemically-propelled rounds louder than the whispers of the mag-ring M88s. Leif looked back at the admin building as they ran, hoping that it wouldn't go up in a blast.

Somewhere above him, the *Cape Town* was blanketing the area with jamming, focusing on the frequencies given to them by the ECM team. Leif couldn't see any of that, but the building remained standing as First and Second Platoon rushed it, forgetting more tactical assault techniques in favor of simply closing the distance as quickly as possible.

Leading the charge, his face display retracted, was Captain Formington, waving his handgun over his head while screaming something Leif couldn't hear. One moment, he was turning as if to yell something to the Marines who were following, and the next, he was down.

Leif couldn't watch any longer. Their objective loomed, and the entire squad reached in intact, backs up against the wall.

"First team!" Sergeant Holmes yelled.

Like clockwork, first team broke down the door with a simple kick, then they disappeared inside.

"Second!"

As the rifleman, Leif was the first to enter, calling out "Coming in right!" He darted inside, then bolted to the right of the small outer office. Within moments, the entire squad was inside. Sergeant Holmes pointed to the stairwell, then to Corporal Fan, the First Team leader. Fan nodded, then took his team up the stairwell. The sergeant pointed at Corporal Lawrence, then at the door into the machine shop.

The four Marines took positions on either side of the door. Rick stepped back, and with a heavy kick, knocked the door half off of its hinges. Leif was the first one through, and something hit him hard in the chest. A flash caught his eyes, and he was hit again.

He swung around, and a human, clad in black body armor, had leveled a weapon at him. Without conscious thought, Leif started firing as fast as he could pull the trigger while rushing the clan soldier. The fighter hesitated a moment, looking like he was going to run as Leif's shots glanced off his armor. The fact that he was still standing seemed to give him a boost of confidence, because he stepped back up into the attack, firing twice more, one round hitting Leif's thigh. Leif had fired at least a dozen rounds before one either defeated the armor or made it through a gap, and the fighter dropped.

Movement to his right caught his eye, but before he could bring his 88 around, Rick took the enemy with a single M55 round that about tore the man in two. Bright red blood and human chunks splattered the clean, white lathe that had given the man cover.

The rest of the fire team entered, followed by Third team. Two bodies were on the floor, but the *Cape Town's* sensors had indicated that there had been a total of four. Sergeant Holmes wasted several minutes trying to get word from the ship on where the other two were, but he gave up, spreading the two fire teams out to sweep the remainder of the machine shop. Leif had to walk past the body of the human he'd killed, and it didn't really bother him any more than killing a grazpin back at Hope Hollow. Maybe less. A grazpin wasn't vermin.

He did note that the killing shot was just above the neck guard. Whatever commercial body armor the criminals wore had the ability to stop his .221 round. Pulling his rifle back, he ratcheted up the mag-rings. Going too fast could make the light rounds slightly unstable, but he'd give up a potential loss of accuracy to gain some more penetration power.

The nine Marines swept the machine shop, finding no one else. There was a door at the back, and Sergeant Holmes thought they must have gone out that way. Chuck Sylvianstri was about to open it when Lori stopped him, pointing to a slight blemish near the handle. No one knew what that signified, but the sergeant said they weren't going through it.

They trooped back to the front, picked up First Team, then sealed the door shut with a bright turquoise zip-tie, signaling it cleared. Leif stared up at the admin building, glad to see it still standing.

Sergeant Holmes checked in with the lieutenant, the the squad was ordered to take a position covering the entrance to a large fabrication factory. They were not to enter the building, but rather keep anyone inside from coming out. From being the point of main effort, they'd moved to a support role, and now they were security.

As they passed the rear of the machine shop, all of them could see the packet of explosives that had been taped up to the door. If Chuck had opened the door, there were enough explosives there to have wreaked havoc on the two fire teams. He caught Lori's eyes and gave her a nod of appreciation.

As they settled into their new position, Leif rubbed his thigh where he'd been shot. There was a small divot where the armor had deformed. This was as it was designed to do, but he'd have to get the thigh-plate replaced once they got back. The round had struck him very close to the armor seam. Another centimeter or so to the left, the enemy round might very well have penetrated. He put it out of his mind, knowing he had to be alert for whatever came next.

But there wasn't a next for the squad. Their battle was essentially over. No one tried to come out of the factory, and while firing broke out several times from within the admin building, it didn't explode into smoke and flames. Five minutes after taking their new position, streams of hostages started pouring out, escorted by Lima Marines off the grounds and into waiting buses. They were to be taken to the fieldball stadium, to where India and the bulk of H & S Company had relocated. The Marines would provide security while the Unidawn security forces, augmented by *Cape Town* crew members, would screen each of them. No one wanted clan personnel to escape by pretending to be hostages.

It wasn't until the lieutenant came to retrieve Second Squad that they found out that eight Marines had been killed, including the captain and Katerina.

Private First Class Kaatrn a'Telltell had become the first wyntonan to be killed in combat as an Imperial Marine.

Chapter 25

Two days later, Katerina's body was loaded onto a shuttle to be transferred to a waiting imperial packet for transport back to Home. The battalion had already conducted a heroes' ceremony the day before, which had been surprisingly moving. Each of the fallen had a small memorial at the front of the makeshift chapel, an M88 stuck barrel first into a pair of combat boots, a helmet mounted on the buttplate of the stock.

The CO gave a brief speech, mentioning some small detail about each one. Leif hadn't known much about the skipper, and for some reason, he was surprised to hear that the captain had been married and had three children.

Everyone knew that the captain had been about to be fired, but it seemed as if all his sins had been forgiven. Leif accepted that to an extent, but the complete 180 seemed odd.

Leif paid more attention to what the CO said about Katerina. She knew quite a bit about her, and Leif appreciated the kind words said. It wouldn't bring his friend back, but her service to the empire and Corps had been appreciated. What he appreciated more, though, was that while the CO mentioned Katerina's home village, family, and other aspects of her life, she never once said the word "wyntonan." Katerina was a Marine, first and foremost.

And now, Katerina was going home. Eight Marines from First Squad, which included Carlton and Moria, acted as pallbearers. The pallbearers might be a human affectation, but the rest of the wyntonans wanted to keep the pallbearers restricted to themselves. It wasn't until Ferron a'Silverton reached them the evening before that they relented, accepting that only two of them would join the human pallbearers. Ferron told them that it was important that humans show their respect. Leif hadn't liked it, but he understood the point.

He stood at attention as her casket was loaded aboard the shuttle, a bugle playing a lonely version of taps. This was a human tradition that felt right to Leif. It sounded as if the bugle was alive, and mourning Katerina's loss.

By all accounts, the mission had been a resounding success. Over a hundred of the criminals had been killed, and another thirty-three captured. The Marines had managed to rescue 2,854 hostages—278 had been killed by the clan fighters. The Marines had lost eight, with ten wounded. The cost to the Marines had been high, as the CO said, but it was a price they would pay again if it meant saving the lives of imperial citizens.

Leif knew she was correct, but that was Katerina's body being loaded up for the long trip back Home. She would have been the first to say her sacrifice was worth it as well, but he felt the loss. Katerina, their moral compass, was gone.

The mission had been a success, another battle streamer for the battalion, but something else happened—maybe something subtle, but a sea change just the same. The wyntonans had shed their blood with the humans, and they'd spilled enemy blood. That transcended a mere proclamation, even one issued by the emperor himself. Even the most ardent critic of wyntonans being Marines had to admit that they now had earned the title.

The price of that acceptance had been high, Leif thought, as he watched Katerina's body being loaded onto the shuttle.

TXX-39

Chapter 26

"Who're you going ashore with?" Lori asked as she pulled on a well-worn tan jacket with unreasonably small buttons running up the front.

"I don't know. Jordan's got the duty, so I figured I'd just go alone and see what's up, then get back to the ship before taps."

"You're here on Tee-Double-X, and you're going to wimp out and sleep on the ship? That's not in keeping with Marine Corps tradition, Leif."

Leif shrugged, but didn't respond. TXX-39 was a well-known resort world, a liberty port par excellence. Most of the Marines and sailors on the ship had been giddy with excitement, but none of that translated to him. With only Jordan and him in the squad, and despite how the battle on Omeyocan had changed the human/wyntonan dynamic, he still felt like an outsider, and no one had asked him to hit the beach with them. He'd go and take a look out of curiosity, but he didn't see any reason to pay to sit in some small hotel room and watch the holovid. He could do that for free up on the ship, and with almost everyone gone, he'd have the place to himself. Besides, Jordan would be off duty tomorrow, and they could do something together then.

"Well, we can't let that happen," she said. "Get out of your shorts and into some liberty gear. You're coming with me."

Leif looked sharply up from the novel he'd been reading, trying to read into her words. While most of the Marines had left in groups, all the better to hit the bars and hot spots, more than a few couples had gone to the planet together, and from the jokes, innuendoes, and downright boasting, Leif knew that they'd planned on romantic liaisons. Council Elder Hordun's words came rushing back to him, about some humans being attracted to the People.

Lori was quite slender and a little taller than most humans, so she better approximated what the People considered attractive. If he squinted and looked at her in low light where he couldn't see her ruddy complexion, she might even pass for one of his race. But Leif wasn't in musth, and he had no desire to explore physical intimacy with a human female.

"I said get up and get ready. As a lance corporal, I can order you to come, PFC."

Can she really . . . he started before he realized she was joking.

She didn't look like the others who were leaving with prospective lovers, all over each other. He looked back at the novel, not even remembering what he'd just read. With a sudden change of heart, he switched off the book and stood, lifting up his rack to access the storage compartment.

"That's a good boy, Leif. You don't want to make mamma unhappy now."

She watched as he changed, but without the predatory look that too many humans had when sex was on their mind. Within a minute, he was ready.

"Let me leave a message for Jordan," he said, tapping it out in his wristcomp.

She tapped her foot impatiently until he was done, then turned and led the way to the hangar, Leif hurrying to keep up with her. The bulk of the crew had already left the ship, but there were still about a hundred or so left waiting for the next shuttle. The two settled in back of the line to wait.

"How come you aren't already ashore?" Leif asked.

"What, when there are a thousand anxious liberty hounds in here? No, thanks. I went to the gym first."

Leif wasn't 100% confident in his ability to read humans, but he was pretty sure she was lying to him. Not that he understood why she would do that, though.

The next shuttle, a bright yellow commercial model, came into the hangar. The line surged forward, but first, three Marines came out, two holding another between them. They let go, and she stumbled to her knees and vomited to the amused roar of those still in line.

"That was quick," Lori said. "Liberty was called, what, two hours ago? And she's already drunk on her ass?"

"Any charges?" a Navy lieutenant asked.

"No, sir. We brought her back. Just drunk."

"Very well," he said before turning to one of the Marines on the watch section. "Corporal, get someone to take her to berthing."

"Can we go back down, sir?" one of the two Marines asked.

"You look fine to me. Get on back down," the lieutenant said before adding, "Good job you two."

They darted back into the shuttle, which caused some of the waiting sailors and Marines to complain, but Leif didn't mind. Both the ship's captain and the colonel had gone on the 1MC before they reached T-Double-X stressing that the Navy and Marines looked out for each other. TXX-39 was the playground of the rich and powerful, and the last thing those worthies wanted was to be bothered by rowdy military men and women. If liberty were going to run the full three days, then there would be no . . . zero . . . nada liberty incidents. So, if anyone was too drunk or about to cause an incident, it was up to their peers to stop them and get them back to the ship. If they hadn't done anything that could have gotten them picked up by the police, then no harm, no foul. No disciplinary would be taken.

Leif had seen newly minted Marines back on Iwo enjoying their liberty a little too much, so the captain's rules made sense. Sure, even as a non-rate, he realized that the rules were somewhat self-serving. The captain wanted to make admiral, and the colonel wanted to make full bird, and having a Marine or sailor do something stupid enough to get thrown into jail and cause a formal incident could put the kibosh on that. Self-serving or not, however, it just made good sense.

The civilian shuttle loaded only 80, but as soon as it took off, one of the ship's shuttles arrived. Five minutes later, the two were on their way to the planet surface. The shuttle had no windows, but a wrap-screen in the front displayed the approach to the tan, almost cloudless planet. TXX-39 had been one of the first big finds by the humans, before they'd discovered other races. Full of mineral wealth, those minerals were long gone, so the planet had made a sea change and switched to being a holovid production center and a tourist destination with a healthy influx of permanent immigrants— all with wealth—attracted by a generous tax situation.

Leif hadn't been too excited to see the surface, but the closer the shuttle got, the more his interest picked up. The T-Double-X was one of the planets well represented in the media, and he'd seen enough holovids, usually holonovas, that were set there. He wondered if there would be a tour to see some of the holovid studios.

As they filed off the shuttle, a chief was waiting at the gate, checking everyone's liberty attire. That made no sense to Leif. If they were going to check, they should have done it back in the hangar where the miscreant could go back and change. One young sailor was stopped by him, and despite loud protests, was ordered back to the ship.

"Sucks to be him," Lori said as they passed and got out into the terminal.

There was a tourist information booth right in the main terminal, and to Leif's surprise, there was a studio tour with a guarantee of watching at least one holovid being recorded. He didn't even have to convince Lori—she'd been all over that as soon as the volunteer handed them the brochure and said military got half-priced tickets.

The next four hours were spent on the tour, going to two of the studios. Leif got a holostill of him standing on the set of "All of Time," Soran's favorite holovid. It wasn't as good as actually seeing the holovid being produced, but Soran would be jealous just the same.

After the tour, Lori declared that she was famished, so the two wandered into the first cafe that didn't look terribly expensive. Leif wasn't hungry . . . until he saw to his amazement that they had grazpin casserole, "A favorite dish of the Wyntonan Ghosts." He immediately ordered it, his mouth watering, while Lori ordered a Todo Beef Sandwich. She kept recounting the tour, and Leif barely managed to nod as if he was listening, so focused he was on his dish. The menu had been full of foods from various races, both human and non-human, but the People rarely travelled, so he couldn't believe this little cafe actually had Home food.

He should have trusted his instincts. When the food arrived down the chute to plop on the table, it didn't look like grazpin casserole, it didn't smell like grazpin casserole . . . and it tasted nothing like grazpin casserole. As far as he could tell, it was the normal protein base shoved through a fabricator and covered with a cloying human sauce.

Lori enthusiastically dug into her sandwich, but with a resigned sigh, Leif took out his vial of spice and sprinkled it on top of the fake Home food.

"Do you guys really like that stuff?" Lori asked between mouthfuls of sandwich. "I mean, you put it on everything."

"And you humans put ketchup or hot sauce on everything," he said sourly.

She shrugged, then opened up her sandwich, holding the top half of it to him. It didn't look horrible—the mustard helped—but he wasn't about to take it.

"Come on, your spice stuff," she said. "Give me some."

The People tended to be a little reticent about sharing their spice mix with others from outside their village or neighborhood, but that wasn't the only reason Leif hesitated. From the looks most humans gave when they got too close to any of their spice mixes, he really doubted she'd like it. She didn't waver, holding out the top of her sandwich, eyes boring into him. With a mental sigh, he took out his vial and sprinkled a little on the bread.

Lori nodded her thanks, closed the sandwich, and keeping her eyes locked on his, took a big bite. Those same eyes watered, and her throat convulsed. She managed to swallow with an evident force of will.

"It's not . . . not bad," she managed to get out, the rictus of what she must have thought was a smile on her face.

Leif stared at her for a moment before bursting out into laughter, saying, "The Mother, Lori. You hate it!"

People at the surrounding tables turned to look at them disapprovingly at his outburst.

Lori rolled her eyes, gave a half-chuckle, and dropped the half-eaten sandwich to her plate. "I'm sorry, it's . . . it's horrible!"

Leif reached over, picked up the sandwich, and took a bite.

"Not too bad, if I say so myself. Just needs more spice," he said, opening it up and sprinkling some more on.

"I swear, how do you eat that? I mean, I know people say it's nasty, but I didn't think it would be that nasty!"

"What about some of your cheese? What's it called? Roquefort? Now, that's nasty!"

"Oh, you don't know what you're talking about, Leif. Roquefort's great," she said, leaning back.

They both looked at each other for a moment before simultaneously bursting out into laughter again. More of the humans in the cafe looked at them disapprovingly, but Leif didn't care. He'd gotten used to humans and their prejudices.

Yet, here I am with a human, and having a good time.

He realized that he, along with the others, had been keeping to themselves, not just at Camp Navarro, but here in the fleet as well. Maybe it was up them to reach out as well, to forge bonds with their fellow human Marines.

"I think I need to order something else to try and get the taste out of my mouth, OK?" Lori asked.

"I don't have a schedule to keep, so go ahead."

She ordered a bowl of soup, but instead of leaving when she finished, the two sat for almost three hours, just talking. Lori was heartily disappointed to learn that most of the People no longer went on a'aden hunts as depicted on the holovids, but she was very impressed that he had. She had him go over his hunt in great detail, her eyes alight with interest.

On his part, he was equally enraptured with her tales of surfing Propenta III, with its southern seas' 30-meter waves. She seemed to think it a matter of course, but to Leif, still a weak swimmer, a wave that big was far more dangerous than a lion—and she surfed it for fun!

Leif was surprised when their tabletress chimed, informing them that the cafe was closing in 15 minutes. The street outside was well-lit, but the day had turned to night while they chatted.

"Wow! I didn't know it had gotten so late. I guess we should get going," Lori said.

"Yeah, I guess we should. But, I've had a great time, Lori. Thanks for inviting me."

"Are you going back to the ship now?" she asked, sounding disappointed.

"I guess so," he said with a shrug of his shoulders, one of the many gestures in which humans and the People had in common.

"Well, you could go back to the ship and waste another hour getting up there and an hour coming back with J-Dan tomorrow," she said. "Or, you can just stay with me here on the planet tonight."

Oh, fuck.

Leif had been having a good—no wonderful—afternoon, and now this. He respected Lori as a Marine, and he liked her now as a friend, but he was not interested in her on a physical level, and that wasn't even taking into account Council Elder Hordun's warning.

"Uh, Lori . . . I . . ." *Just say it!* "I like you, but do you think it's a good idea if you and me, you know, have sex together?"

Lori's eyes widened, then she sat back, her posture going limp.

"Hell, Leif. You wyntonans are just like the rest of the guys. I was hoping you'd be different, you being another race and all," she said quietly.

"I'm sorry, what are you saying?"

"I'm saying that not every girl is excited about what's in your pants."

The levity and degree of comfort that had surrounded the two had vanished like a puff of smoke. Leif was confused.

He knew he'd said something wrong but wasn't quite sure what. Was she upset that he turned her down?

"But I thought—"

"I know, I know. Just like every other guy or gal, you thought that if I invited you to stay with me here on the surface tonight, I had to be suggesting a night of wild and rollicking sex. I was just hoping you wyntonans were different. I mean, we're not even the same race. My fault for assuming, I guess."

"So, you weren't . . ." he started, now embarrassed to continue that train of thought.

"Look, I'm ace. Do you know what that is?"

Leif shook his head.

"It means I'm asexual. I'm not interested in sex. It just doesn't do anything for me."

"You don't like to be with other people?"

"Of course, I like people. And yes, before you ask, I can love people. I just don't particularly like others pawing at me."

Leif hadn't heard anything like that. From the People's perspective, humans were desperate creatures, slaves to their hormones. It was right there in almost every holovid ever made. The council elder had even warned them about this.

"So, you can't have sex?" he asked, curious now.

"Of course, we can have sex. I've got all the parts like anyone else. And some aces do have sex."

"I don't understand."

"We can have sex, and if we are in love and our partner needs it, we will do it to make them happy. It is just that people like me, we don't pursue it and would just as soon skip it."

This was new to Leif. Nowhere in their briefings on humans was this "ace" thing mentioned.

"I asked you to stay with me because you're good company, and we could split the cost of a room, that's all," she said, looking down and not meeting his eyes. "I'm sorry I gave you the wrong impression.

There was something more there, but Leif couldn't quite put his finger on it.

"It's OK. I don't want sex, either," he said.

She looked up at him quickly. He knew he'd taken her by surprise, then she seemed to consider what he'd just said.

"Oh, because of the race thing. I understand."

"No. Not a race thing. Look, I find you attractive, for a human," he said, immediately regretting the "for a human" phrasing. "But we wyntonans, we're sort of asexual ourselves. For the most part, we don't have much sex."

Now she was surprised, he could tell.

"For the most part?"

"Yeah. We . . . our females come into estrous every three years, 'tri-years,' we call them, and when they do that, the males come into musth. Then, we have an overwhelming desire to mate. At other times, we're really not that much into it."

"Wow! I didn't know that. So, you only have sex once every three years?"

"I haven't been through musth yet. It will come up with my tri-year next year for the first time."

"So, you're a virgin?"

"No, I've had sex. There isn't a prohibition against it, after all. How can anyone object to something like that? Call it curiosity, but we don't have a strong desire like you humans do. I mean, like most humans do," he quickly added.

"But when you are *mus*?"

"Musth. When that overtakes me, I think it'll be different. But for now, I guess I'm 'ace,' too."

"No, not really. More like a Gray-A, I'd say. You don't want it sometimes, but you do sometimes. Huh. I never would have thought it.

"The Progenitors work in strange ways, I guess."

He knew what she meant. All of the intelligent races in the galaxy were very closely related, but there were always some seemingly unnatural differences. The noxes could see in almost pitch darkness. The little-known qiincer could fly with their spindly bodies and huge wings. The tost'el'tzy lived their short and rapid lives in just a handful of wyntonan tri-years. The general consensus was that the Mother/Progenitor/whoever varied all the races in some important ways to ensure variety, to ensure survival. Estrous was not a rare trait among the mammalian species in the galaxy, but Leif had never wondered why only the People, of all the prime races, followed that pattern as well. To him, it just was how things were.

As he looked across the table at her, he realized what else had been tickling his mind, just out of reach. He'd seen more than a few men and women hit on Lori, something she'd brushed aside with a laugh or joke.

"So, Lori, if you're ace, and I'm not a guy on the prowl, then I'm camouflage, right? I can keep the horndogs at bay."

"No, it's not like that. I like you. Really."

She was blushing a bright red, a sure sign among humans of embarrassment. Leif believed her that she liked him, but he was also pretty sure he was right. He was a shield against unwanted advances.

Not that he cared.

"It's OK if it is," he said. "I might need a little cover, too."

She seemed deep in thought for a moment before looking up, a smile on her face, and asked, "So, if I'm not going to rape you in the middle of the night, are you up with splitting the cost of a room? It'll save you the trip up to the ship and back."

Leif wouldn't have minded going back to the ship, and it would save his meager ID account, but she was right, it would save him a couple of wasted hours. And he liked her.

"Well, when you put it that way, how could I refuse?"

"I found a place a couple of blocks from here. Twenty-two ID for the night, so that's eleven apiece. Is that OK with you?"

Leif would have rather kept the eleven BCs in his account, but it really wasn't that much, so he agreed, and the two left the cafe while Lori led the way, following the directions on her wristcomp. Within a few minutes, they were walking up to a small hostel. A local standing on the street outside nudged his friend and pointed at the two as they entered the door.

"Ignore them," Lori told Leif, then as she swiped her comp on the autovet, added, "I've got this for now. You can pay me back on the ship."

The two made their way to the fourth floor, down the hall, and to Room 406. Lori swiped her wristcomp again, then leaned in for a retinal scan.

"You do it, too, in case we get separated," she said, pointing at the scanner. After he was registered, she threw her backpack on the right bed, pointing at the left for Leif to take. "We can get you a toothbrush and some clean skivvies, if you want."

Leif sat down on the bed and bounced. Even in a hostel, the bed was more comfortable than his rack back on the ship. He began to think this was a better idea than going back up.

"What now?" he asked.

"What now?" We're on T-Double-X. It's Saturday, and the night's still young. We're going out on the town, that's what. Just give me a sec."

She reached into her backpack and took out a shimmering blouse of some high-tech cloth Leif had never seen. Colors, almost looking like images, but not quite, slowly shifted across it.

"Well?" she asked, doing a pirouette after she slipped it on.

"Hurts my eyes," he said.

It actually looked intriguing, but Marines did not compliment their buddies, as a rule.

"What do you know?" she said, punching him in the shoulder—hard. "You sure the hell aren't going to wear something like this out spearing a lion-thing."

Insults completed, the two left the room. Outside the hostel, the civilian who had pointed at them was waiting, but now there were seven of them. As soon as the two appeared, the civilians postured up. All of Leif's alarms went off, and he stopped dead on the steps to face them.

"Come on, forget them," Lori said, taking his arm in hers and pulling him along.

That act seemed to trigger the group. The first human, the one who pointed, stepped up and blocked their path, backed by the other six.

The human was average height for the race, but broad across the shoulders with the look of a gym rat, muscles evident with the sleeveless shirt he was wearing. His hair was buzz-cut short and dyed purple, and while he looked nonchalant, he reeked of tension.

"Come on, guys, we don't want any trouble," Lori said, trying to pull Leif to the side and around the human.

"Then what the merde you doing with a fucking casper, huh, sista?"

Lori's mouth dropped open in shock before she managed to get out, "He's a Marine" as if that answered all the questions.

"Hell, boys, this is one of them we seen on the holovid. A real life Marine. Only I don't care if he's the emperor himself, he's still a fucking casper."

Lori had stepped between the human and him, but now Leif moved forward, noting where each of them were standing. His MCCCP training kicked in as he analyzed the seven, trying to see a weakness.

The only weakness went the other way; he and Lori made two, and there were seven of them.

"Oh, lookee, this skinny-ass casper wants to protect his girl," the man said, turning back to his buddies.

"I'm not his--" Lori started only to be cut off by the human's, "*Ferme ta guele, pute*! We'll take care of you, later, just as a little reminder of you who you are."

He took a step forward, chest thrust out, and said, "Look casper, you think you can come here, fuck our women. You might be hiding behind your uniform, but we all know that's political merde. You're still a casper, and you don't touch human women!"

He reached out and grabbed Lori's arm, yanking her toward him.

"Get your hands off of her!" Leif said, stepping up.

The human shoved Lori to the side, his fist already moving forward, ready to connect with Leif's chin—but Leif didn't just stand there, waiting to be hit. He ducked to the side as his left arm, all 98 centimeters of it, snaked out with lightening quick speed, impacting on the human's nose and rocking his head back. The man went over backward, his legs buckling underneath him.

Leif stared at the man for a moment, savoring his victory—a big mistake. There were six more of them, six guys angry that their leader had been dropped by a casper. One of them hit Leif low, shoulder in his gut, which was probably fortuitous because the heavy metal belt buckle being swung by another just grazed his cheek as he was pushed back. Leif brought down elbows, one after the other on the human trying to tackle him, driving each one down into his neck with all the strength he could muster. The man took six shots before he let go, dropping to his hands and knees.

Beside him, Lori was whirling like a human dervish, the heel of her leg connecting on the chin of the man rushing her. Leif didn't have time to see much more than that—the guy with the belt was back, and as he swung, Leif stepped in, closing the distance. The buckle went past him, the belt itself wrapping around the side of his face so that the buckle hit him in the back of the head. It still hurt, but it didn't cut him open. The man's eyes opened wide as Leif cupped his hands in back of the man's head, forcing it down with a jerk to meet the knee he was bringing up. He felt bone crush as his knee drove through the human's nose.

Lori let out a moan behind him. He spun to see her hit the street, face-first and motionless.

"*Fyastya!*" he screamed, charging the man with the collapsible baton standing over her as the first stirrings of musapha flickered inside of him.

Something hit him in the side, but he ignored it, so intent was he on the man who'd dropped Lori. The human waited, a smile on his face, and just as Leif reached for him, the man, with cat-like reflexes, whipped the baton around, connecting with Leif's temple. The world went fuzzy, the tiny ember of musapha snuffed out, and he fell to his knees, right at the man's feet. Tunnel vision constricted his view so that all he could see was a pair of heavy brown work boots. Time slowed down, and one of those boots rose up, seemingly in slow motion, to connect with his chin. Leif fell over as two humans moved up and started kicking him in the side, one stomping on his chest.

Get up!

He tried to rise, but the humans were relentless, screaming impossibly loud. But then they were not kicking him any longer, but the screams continued. Blood dripped out of his mouth as he slowly got up, the sirens, as he now recognized the "screams," got louder.

"Freeze," a mechanical sounding voice said. "Tourist police!"

As far as Leif could tell, he was the only one standing. Lori was motionless a few meters from him. Four of the human thugs were down as well, one still on his hands and knees, moaning. There was no sign of the other three, but humans had started gathering to watch as the police drone trundled up.

"You are ordered to freeze until police personnel arrive in approximately forty-eight seconds."

"She needs help," Leif said, spitting out blood and reaching for her.

He turned to Lori, reaching out to her, ignoring the second, "Freeze, under the authority of the TXX-39 Tourist Police."

"I am just trying to—" was all he got out until a blue halo enveloped him and shut him down cold.

Chapter 27

"There, that's bringing him around," a voice registered.

Leif slowly opened his eyes and groaned. His heart was racing, and his body hurt. A man in physician whites was standing over him, a drug pen in his hand.

The doctor turned to say over his shoulder, "The medipedia wasn't clear as to the dosage, but he looks to be doing OK. I'll hang around for a few minutes to make sure, though."

"Where am I?" Leif croaked out.

The doctor stepped back, and as a featureless white room came into focus, he could see three humans standing by, staring down at him: a woman in a police uniform, a man in civilian clothes, and a . . . a Navy lieutenant!

"Sir, what's happening?" he asked the lieutenant.

"Stand up," the police officer ordered him.

Leif didn't know what was going on, but he felt vulnerable, so he struggled to his feet, swaying a moment before he caught his balance.

The police officer looked to the doctor, and when the doc nodded, turned to Leif and said, "Leif Hollow, you are under arrest for assault resulting in grievous bodily harm and disorderly conduct. More charges may be filed upon completion of the investigation. You are being held here at Central Holding Facility until brought before a magistrate to hear your plea at which time legal representation may be requested. So, you understand what I've said?"

"What? Assault? *We* were attacked! They assaulted *us!*"

"I asked you if you understand what I've said."

"But—"

"Private First Class Hollow, just answer the officer," the Navy lieutenant said in a calm voice. "You are not admitting to guilt, just that you understand the charges."

Leif stood there, mouth hanging open while he tried to process what he'd just heard.

They are charging me?

"Do you understand what I've said?" the officer asked again.

"Uh . . . yeah. Yes, ma'am. I understand it. But—"

"Noted. The prisoner has acknowledged the charges. Beltran, Lysle. Four-eight-six-six-three, TXX-39 Police." she said in an even voice before turning to the lieutenant and saying, "OK, Lieutenant Terzi, he's yours."

She and the other civilian turned away, and part of the wall recessed into a door. They left, and the door closed again, the wall featureless.

"Sir, what's going on?" Leif asked.

"What's going on, PFC, is that you're being held on charges of assault."

"But they attacked us, Lori and me. Where's Lori? I saw her go down."

"Lance Corporal Jankowski is back on the ship in sickbay. She's in a medically induced coma," he said, holding up a hand to stop Leif, who had started to interrupt him. "She's been put into a coma, but she should have a full recovery. She was to be charged as well, but due to her injuries, the booking magistrate authorized her release to the Navy for humanitarian reasons."

"Her injuries, sir?"

"Broken jaw, broken orbital bones. Concussion, too. She'll be fine in a couple of weeks."

Leif let out a sigh of relief. She'd gone down hard during the fight, and he knew it could have turned out worse. That didn't explain though, what he was doing here in a human jail.

"Sir, why have I been arrested?"

"Really? You're asking me that? You and Jankowski start a fight on the planet, and you almost kill one and put two others in the hospital with serious injuries."

"Sir?" was all he could say in his shock.

"What, you think jumping four civilians, breaking one of their necks and smashing another's face into bits isn't grounds for arrest?" he asked, a scowl on his face. "Not to mention the third guy with a broken clavicle."

"That's not what happened, sir. They jumped us, and there were seven of them. They didn't like seeing Lori and me together."

"And that's not what the report says. It says that the two of you jumped them, taking two down before they had a chance to try and defend themselves."

"But the recordings, did you see them?"

For the first time, a look of doubt crossed the lieutenant's face, and he said, "No, they haven't released any yet."

"But, you're the Imperial Navy, sir!"

"Yes, we are the Imperial Navy, but we have to tread lightly with the planetary officials. Especially here where the bonds to the emperor are . . . well, not the best. We came here to show the imperial flag, to show why it behooves T-Double - X to remain in the Empire, but then you and Jankowski have to go caveman.

"Didn't we brief you over and over about getting into trouble?" he asked.

"Yes, sir, and we were careful."

"Not careful enough. And then there's the other little factor . . ."

"Of me being a wyntonan," Leif said.

"Yes, that. You are an imperial project, and your little escapade is going to give the humanists more ammunition."

Leif didn't know this Lieutenant Terzi from a grazpin, and he didn't know what the officer thought about wyntonans, but from his tone, he thought the lieutenant might be in the humanist camp himself. Leif knew that many in the military were, but their marching orders had been issued, so it was time to salute smartly and march on.

"So, what happens now?" Leif asked.

"Now? Well, you sit here in jail, for one, until your hearing, and then probably for your trial. After that, it depends on the outcome of the trial now, doesn't it?

"We will get you a lawyer to represent you, so don't worry about that."

"And Lance Corporal Jankowski?"

"Her? That's up to the captain. Or maybe the commodore—that's beyond my pay-grade."

Leif was feeling defeated. He knew what had happened, but if he was being played as a pawn, then there wasn't much he could do about it. It's not like he wasn't already a pawn just by being a Marine. He hoped Lori, at least, could escape punishment.

"Well, that's about all I have. Do you have any questions?"

"Not now, sir. But how can I contact you if I need you?"

"You can't, PFC. We've cut the port visit short, and we're leaving orbit tonight. Someone will contact you once a JAG arrives."

If Leif had been feeling defeated before, he felt a huge emptiness now. He was being abandoned by the Navy, by the Corps, on a hostile planet that wanted to use him for political gain. He'd never felt so alone in his life.

"Do you believe we really attacked seven civilians, sir?" he asked.

The lieutenant started to say something, then paused as he tried to formulate his words before saying, "I don't know, PFC. Maybe yes, maybe no. OK, maybe no. But what I think doesn't matter much now, right? We're leaving tonight, and you'll be transferred to your division's legal-hold platoon. Who you have to convince is the magistrate."

"Who is going to be fair? Really, sir?" he said, unable to hide the bitterness in his voice.

"I don't know. Maybe you're just caught up in something bigger than you are, but that's the way it goes, sometimes."

A random memory surfaced in Leif's mind, from back in one of the innumerable and terribly boring classes at the Pit.

"Sir, I thought that the Status of Forces agreement gives *primacy*, they called it," he said, stumbling over the word, "to military jurisdiction. We are subject to military confinement and trial."

"Well, yes, in most cases. But that doesn't mean the military is required to take over all cases. I mean, you get a littering ticket from out in the ville, and we're not going to take over that."

"But if someone was accused of breaking a civilian's neck?"

"Well, it looks like it was Lance Corporal Jankowski who broke the civilian's neck—you did the broken collarbone and the face re-arrangement—but yes."

"So, you can take me," he said hopefully. "I can go to a court-martial. Can you ask the captain, sir?"

The lieutenant's eyes deflated before he said, "The captain has already decided. Look, you broke the law here. Hell, you put three guys in the hospital."

So much for you believing me.

"The captain isn't going risk an international incident to pull a criminal back to the ship because of SOFA. He can abrogate that option."

And he wants to make admiral, so nothing that can be hung on him.

"And the colonel?"

"I don't know, son, but it's not her call. Look, I shouldn't tell you this, but she did request custody over you, and the local authorities refused. Given that situation, what's she supposed to do? Threaten T-Double-X with bombardment? Send in your Marines? No way. She's going to let things play out in the local legal system.

"It's not that bad, Hollow," he added, calming down. "We'll get you a competent JAG, so we are not abandoning you."

Leif didn't say a word.

"Well, I've got to get back to the ship. Someone from the imperial service will come tomorrow and check up on you." He stood there awkwardly for a moment, then said, "Good luck, PFC. I hope things work out for you."

He turned to face the wall of the jail cell, and the door whispered open. He didn't look back as he stepped out, the door sliding close behind him.

Leif was more alone than he'd ever been in his life.

Chapter 28

Leif sat on the bench, a plate of untouched food beside him. He'd been sitting on the floor for five hours before he found the wall-release for the bench and he could sit normally. The food was some sort of mystery meat, and his jailers must have relieved him of his vial of spice when they brought him in, so it was pretty much inedible for him. Not that it mattered; he wasn't hungry.

He couldn't believe he was sitting here, rotting in a jail while his so-called family was abandoning him. Marines never left a Marine behind—unless that Marine was a ghost, he guessed.

Leif had always known he and his fellow wyntonans were outsiders, but after the battle on Omeyocan, he'd thought things were getting better. If not friends, then at least he'd made compatriots, and he was considered a Marine first, a wyntonan second. Now he knew he was sadly mistaken.

If what the lieutenant had said was true, the Marines or Navy would be sending a lawyer, but he could read between the lines just as well as anyone else. He meant nothing in the big scheme of things, no matter what the emperor had said to them. He was going to be sacrificed to political expediency. That sacrifice might make sense on the grand scale of galaxy-wide gamesmanship, but Leif looked at things from a much smaller scale, and from his perspective, it sucked.

Don't feel sorry for yourself, Leefen.

It didn't work. He *was* feeling sorry for himself, and he regretted ever leaving Hope Hollow.

He heard the muffle sounds of talking outside of the cell's door, and he stood up. He hadn't been physically abused since he'd been in the cell, but he'd seen enough holovids to be expecting it. If they were going to come in and "soften him up," then he was going to make them pay the price.

He didn't have a weapon, nor anything he could fashion as one. The only other thing in the cell was the plate of food.

Better than nothing.

Maybe he could throw it and distract a guard for the moment it took for him to knock him out cold.

The door whispered open, and Leif held the plate up, ready to throw it . . . and Sergeant Holmes stuck his head into the cell.

"Sorry, Hollow, I've already eaten."

Leif let the plate tip over to fall on the floor.

"Well, you ready to punch out of this place?"

"Uh . . . yes, Sergeant. Sure!"

"Well, then, let's go."

Leif was confused, but his feet were moving before he realized what was happening. Outside the cell, the entire squad, minus Lori, and the lieutenant were waiting, weapons slung over their backs.

"Got him," the lieutenant said into his throat mic, then "Aye-aye, sir.

"Let's move it," he added to the squad, pointing down the hallway.

"What's going on?" Leif asked as he was hustled between Corporal Lawrence and Rick.

"Damned, you're a dumb one, aren't you?" Rick asked. "We're breaking you out. What does it look like we're doing?"

Leif wanted to ask more, but the thought of freedom suddenly became overwhelming. Get out of here first, then ask questions later.

They entered a common room, where First Squad was standing ever so casually around a civilian in a uniform, probably a jail guard. The man was sweating heavily, and he looked scared.

"Let's go," the lieutenant told First Squad. "Fall in behind us."

"Now, Gregori, like I told you, you just sit tight here for fifteen minutes." Sergeant Juniper said. "The mine will deactivate then. So, no hero stuff, OK?"

"No. I won't do anything. I promise," the guard spit out.

First joined Second as they swept through. As soon as they entered the next hallway, the sergeant reached up as if emplacing something on the ceiling, then nodded through the window back into the common area. Leif glanced up—there was nothing there. Despite the situation, Leif laughed aloud.

"I'm glad you think this is funny," Corporal Lawrence said, but without any rancor evident in her voice.

The lieutenant reached a closed, high-security door, and for a moment, Leif thought they'd been trapped. Something close to panic started to well up inside of him, but the lieutenant rapped on the window, and a moment later, the door recessed into the wall. In a rush, both squads ran into a processing center. Four Third Squad Marines stood too casually over what had to be the night's influx of prisoners. Their weapons were slung, but their hands were hovering where they could employ the weapons in a split-second if need be. A few of the new prisoners looked worried, but most looked to be enjoying the spectacle.

In the middle of the room were three police and five guards huddled together. The rest of Third Squad surrounded them, along with Staff Sergeant Donovan.

What surprised the living heck out of Leif, was that not only was the skipper waiting for them, but the CO herself, along with the sergeant major.

"Let's head on out," the CO said as the two squads poured into the room.

"You heard him," Captain Tzama said. "Now!"

"That's us," Corporal Lawrence said, hand still on Leif's upper arm and he pulled him toward the entrance where two Marines stood ready.

They rushed out into the night air to the most beautiful sight Leif had ever seen: one of the ship's tac-skiffs. The moment they came out, the skiff powered up, rising a few centimeters off the ground.

Fifteen seconds later, Leif was taking his seat and buckling in. His mind was still whirling as the rest of the Marines entered in echelons. The CO was the last in, and the minute her foot hit the ramp, the pilot was lifting off. As the ramp closed, Leif watched through the back of the bird as the jail disappeared from view. Only then did he feel safe. Several eyes were on him, but in the dim lights of the compartment, he couldn't tell if they were angry or not. He settled back and closed his eyes while trying to take in what had just happened.

Beside him, Corporal Lawrence elbowed him in the ribs, and he opened his eyes to see the CO standing in front of him, helmet off and under the crook of her elbow.

"You OK, Hollow?" she asked leaning in close to overcome the noise of the skiff's engines as it shot up to escape the planet's grip.

"Yes, ma'am," Leif shouted back.

"OK, good. We'll talk later after we get back to the ship."

Leif reached out and grabbed the CO by the arm and pulled her close. If the human took offense at his impudence, she didn't show it.

"Ma'am, why did you come?" Leif asked. He had to know.

"You're a Marine, son. We're not going to leave you to rot on some ball of sand."

"But the lieutenant, the Navy lawyer—"

"Had to purvey the fact that we were not going to fight the police, that we were leaving."

It took a moment for that to sink in, and then he asked, "But the fight? Those civilians? They all said Lori and . . . Lance Corporal Jankowski and I jumped them first."

"Well, good thing one of the ship's sailors saw the whole thing and told the ship's captain, huh? Made it easier for me to come down with his blessing, don't you think?"

Leif wasn't trying to argue, and he wasn't trying to talk the battalion commander out of rescuing him, but he didn't understand. What the lawyer has said was true about the grand politics of the situation, as much as Leif had not wanted to listen.

"But your career, ma'am. If you've caused an interplanetary—"

The colonel put up a hand to stop him and said, "Fuck them. Marines don't leave Marines behind . . . period!"

IS CAPE TOWN

Chapter 29

Without a helmet and its internal comms, Leif had sat in silence once the colonel had taken her seat. The skiff did not have artificial gravity, so, once out of the planet's gravity well, everyone remained strapped into their seats. He'd gotten more than a few thumbs ups and nods, but he wasn't sure what his fellow Marines were thinking, and despite the CO's comments, he wasn't sure if he was going to be subject to Marine Corps disciplinary action.

Not that he was too upset about that. He'd much rather be facing Marine non-judicial punishment than face whatever would have happened back at TXX-39.

When gravity took ahold of him again, he knew they were back on the *Cape Town*. The ramp lowered to the brightly lit hangar. From the front of the skiff, Leif couldn't see much through the Marines exiting the craft, but he was surprised when he got to the back to see hundreds of sailors and Marines gathered in the hangar, seemingly filling every square centimeter of free space.

As Leif stepped off the ramp, those hundreds erupted into cheers.

Leif stopped dead in his tracks. Marines and sailors crowded forward, congratulating everyone in the platoon who'd come to rescue him, but also reaching forward to slap him on the shoulder and back. In a daze, Leif followed Sergeant Juniper's broad back as the Marine cleared a path. Tried to clear a path, that is. The going was tough, and both of them had to return high-fives and fist bumps.

Chief Tsumi was waiting at the hatch into the ship proper, and he snatched Leif, closing the hatch and cutting off the noise.

"Let's get you checked out," the battalion's senior corpsman said. "Doc Indigo is waiting."

"I'm fine," Leif said.

The chief laughed, then said, "You don't look it. Besides, captain's orders."

Out of the crush of the mob in the hangar, each of the Marines in the platoon gathered around to welcome him back. Even one of the sailors who had only last week made a snide comment to him about "caspers" said a gruff, "Good job, Hollow," as he shook his hand.

"OK, you'll get him back, but I've really got to get him to sick bay," the chief said after a couple of minutes. "Let him go."

There were a few more handshakes, but Leif broke free of his platoon and followed the chief to the ship's sick bay.

"How's Lance Corporal Jankowski?" he asked.

"She'll be fine. Thanks to you, of course."

Leif wasn't quite sure what the chief meant. They'd been attacked and gotten the shit kicked out of them. He certainly hadn't been able to keep Lori from getting knocked unconscious.

He entered sick bay . . . and immediately came to attention.

Captain Worchester was waiting there. Lieutenant Colonel Jarvincus, as the battalion commander, was a god, the entire battalion subject to her commands. But the ship's captain transcended mere godhood. Leif had never been this close to him, and now he wasn't sure how to act.

"Relax, son," the captain said in what was a surprisingly low-key voice. "Glad you got back OK."

Silence was always the best bet when dealing with the brass, so Leif didn't say a word.

"And you are OK, right?"

Silence worked only when not asked a direct question.

"Yes, sir."

"Well, we'll get you checked out," he said, nodding at the two doctors—Doc Indigo, the battalion surgeon, and the ship's own doctor, a lieutenant commander whose name Leif didn't know.

The captain's lapel speaker hissed to life with, "Captain, we're ready to break orbit."

"Very well. Proceed."

He turned back to Leif and said, "I just wanted to be here to welcome you back. It's not every day that we conduct a jail break. It's not in the SOP, after all, so you made us create the entire mission from scratch."

"I'm sorry, sir, for causing you trouble."

"Hell, son, relax. Don't you wyntonans have a sense of humor? I'm joking. No one's mad at you. You two defended yourselves, as you should have. Kicked some ass, too, from what Seaman Yancy told me. I'd sure like to see an undoctored recording of that, not that I think the planetary cops are going to ever release one now."

"Sir, what's going to happen now? I mean, with the government?"

"Now? Not much. At least that is what I'm hoping. The imperial agent-prime has registered an unofficial complaint that a kidnapping was thwarted—"

"A kidnapping?" Leif interrupted, then caught himself and shut up.

"According to witnesses, two of the assailants were attempting to drag Lance Corporal Jankowski away, and that looks like kidnapping to me. Between the two of you fighting back, though, that didn't happen." He paused a moment, then said in a more subdued tone, "If they really were trying to kidnap your friend, then the repercussions . . ."

Leif wasn't an expert on human politics, but even he could see the ramifications. A street brawl was one thing—a kidnapping of an Imperial Marine upped the ante. He wasn't sure the humans were trying to kidnap Lori, but the thought was sobering.

Still, Lori had almost killed one of them, so they'd paid the price for their actions.

"Well, I've got to get back to the bridge. You'll get debriefed as soon as you get cleared by the good docs. I want that done tonight while things are fresh in your mind." He held his hand out to shake and said, "Welcome back, son."

As soon as the captain left sick bay, Leif turned to the two doctors, asking, "How's Lance Corporal Jankowski? She's in a coma?"

The ship's doctor turned to Doc Indigo, then shrugged his shoulders and said, "I think we can delay our exam for a few minutes so you can see for yourself."

He pointed to the ward, and one of the ship's corpsman opened the hatch. Leif hurried through, expecting the worse, but Lori was sitting up on a rack, eyes on a scanscreen. She looked up, then threw down the screen, hands extended.

"Come here, Leif!"

Leif rushed over to her hug.

"I thought . . . the lawyer, he said—"

"That Lance Corporal Jankowski was on her death bed, and the Navy should take responsibility for saving her if we could. And the blame for losing her," Doc Indigo said from the front of the ward.

"Oh, Jankowski does have fractures and a concussion, but it seemed like a good thing to tell them in order to get her to the ship."

"I'm kind of messed up, but the docs don't want to keep me awake for now," Lori said. "I guess I forgot to duck that guy with the baton."

"He got me, too," Leif said. "But you almost killed one of them, Devil Dog."

"Lucky kick. Surprised the shit out of me when it connected. I just freaked out when they tried to pull me away from you."

"That was no lucky kick, and you sure as hell didn't learn that at MCCCP. Where did you learn how to do that?"

"OK, Hollow, you can see she's alive and well, so can we get to you now?" Doc Indigo asked before Lori could answer.

"Yes, sir," Leif said, starting to pull away.

"Hey," Lori said, grabbing his arm to stop him. "Sorry for getting you into this shit."

"Not your fault."

"No, I mean it. If I hadn't insisted on you staying with me, none of this would have happened. I was so freaking worried when they told me you were still down there."

"Well, I'm here now, so all's good, right?"

"Yeah, I guess."

As Leif turned to let the docs do their checkup, he realized that he was right. It all *was* good.

Chapter 30

The hangar was dark, the doors open to the black with the light of a million stars shining above them. It was as if the battalion was sitting in open space. A blast sounded filling with hangar with a series of notes. A single light flashed on, shining on the Marine blowing the carnyx, an ancient human horn. The bell of the Celtic instrument was in the shape of a mythological creature called a dragon, mounted high on an extended leadpipe. Once known only from archeological digs and images, the Marine Corps had adopted it as their symbolic instrument. The bugler played the call to colors, and another spotlight flashed on, illuminating the color guard. Three of the guard were human: the two with weapons and Sergeant Roy from Lima, who was carrying the Marine Corps colors. Johari was carrying the imperial flag, standing tall and proud. Leif got a lump in his throat, and he felt so proud as well as the Marines all rose to their feet and stood at attention.

This was the 689th Marine Corps Birthday, and the battalion was gathered in celebration.

The four Marines marched forward, all the way to the curtain, until it looked like they would step through the curtain and out into the black. At the last second, they conducted a counter-march and were marching back to the head table. Leif had always hated drill, but they looked sharp. They stopped before the head table, then turned and faced the hangar as the imperial anthem played. Leif had never given the Empire much thought. It was bloated, and sometimes corrupt, but he was caught up in the moment, and his oath of loyalty to the emperor took on a greater weight. The general hangar lights came on, illuminating the space, and it was time for the Marine Corps Hymn.

Leif sang along with the rest as the words and music moved him. This was what the humans did well, using tradition and effects to garner emotional responses. He knew this, but that didn't matter. He felt good, and that was the bottom line.

"Battalion, take your seats," the adjutant shouted.

"Damn, I'm hungry," Donk whispered.

But there was one more ceremony before the massed Marines could eat. Major Gruenstein, the president of the mess for the ceremony, stood up, and in a loud voice of authority, ordered "Parade the beef!"

Two Navy mess attendants servers pushed a large silver tray on wheels. The top was opened up to reveal a huge prime rib roast, harvested from a real animal. There were oohs-and-ahs from the humans around him.

The Navy senior chief who ran the galley made a show of cutting a slice of the beef, then placing it on the plate of the major, who took a tiny bite, then loudly announced, "I find this beef fit for human consumption!"

There were cheers of ooh-rah, and mess attendants appeared in a rush, all carrying plates of food. Leif and the others at the table were served first, but as according to tradition, they waited before eating until everyone was served.

This is pretty amazing, he told himself.

A Navy man-of-war was not a cruise ship, but along with a healthy number of volunteers from the ship's crew, they sure made a valiant effort to give the Marines a good birthday.

Once everyone was served, the president of the mess shouted out, "Ladies and gentlemen, you may now eat."

Around him, the Marines dove into their food like a swarm of jostons stripping a field bare. Leif was happy to just sit a moment, taking in the scene.

"You're not going to put your spice on that?" Lori quietly asked Leif looking at the plate the mess attendants placed in front of him.

"I . . . *we* decided that for this, we'll go naked," Leif said.

"Hey, everyone. Jordan and Leif are doing without their spice tonight because they think it'll bother us. What say they have at it?" she asked the rest of the Marines at the table

"Hell, if they want that shit, let them," Rick said, raising a glass of wine. "If you're going to put ketchup on your prime rib, they can put their shit on theirs."

"No, it's OK," Leif said.

"Bullshit. It's the Marine Corps birthday, Marine, so don't hold back."

Leif looked across the table to Jordan, who shrugged.

OK, then. I guess I will.

He grunted as he tried to reach into his pocket. He was still pretty beat up from TXX-39, and his arm didn't have full range of motion.

"Let me help," Lori said, reaching into his pocket for him with her unbandaged hand, removing a small vial of spice and handing it to him.

He was embarrassed, feeling like an invalid. He really wasn't hurt that badly, but the dress blues were difficult even in normal times. As the other Marines said, there was a price to pay for looking so good.

The eleven wyntonans had only decided to forego the spice an hour ago, while waiting for the hangar to be set up for the Marines. They were on a new offensive to integrate, which was why, when offered their own table, they declined, choosing to sit with their squads.

He was glad Lori had interceded for him, however. He was almost out of spice, and because of that, he'd gotten used to eating some of the food "naked." He wasn't too sure about this beef stuff, though. Leif didn't shy from meat—he hunted back at Hope Hollow, after all. But he'd seen holos of Earth cows, and they looked pretty disgusting. With the spice, he hoped he could hide the taste and choke the meat down. This was going to be his first birthday while in the fleet, and he didn't want food to spoil the experience.

He took a small bite of the prime rib . . . and to his surprise, it wasn't bad at all. He just had to forget this came from a cow, imaging a nice ibent steak instead. The others were giving Lori a ration of shit as she spooned the "human spice," as the wyntonans called ketchup, all over her meat. She gave them all a group finger, then started in on her meal.

The easy camaraderie around the table was beginning to feel like the new norm. Leif was still riding a hero high after Tee-Double-Ex, but the others said they'd been experiencing the same thing. They were still wyntonans, but that seemed to be accepted, just one more difference like the heavy-worlders or chesties, humans from low O2 worlds who were modified at birth for higher capacity lungs. They were different, yes, but not worse.

Leif had second-guessed his enlistment many times, but now he was sure he'd finish it up without a problem. He also realized he'd always cherish his service as a Marine. No matter what he was going to do for the rest of his life, the Corps had made him a better person.

"Hey, you with us?" Lori asked, snapping her fingers in front of his face.

"Oh, sorry. I was just thinking."

"Dangerous that. You know, thinking," Rick said.

Leif quickly finished the last of his meal just before one of the sailors he recognized from the ship's store took his plate. There weren't enough mess attendants to wait on the Marines, but there were always numerous volunteers among the crew to help out. Even with the extra help, it took ten minutes to clear away the tables and prepare for the ceremony.

The carnyx bugler blasted out another call, and Lori said, "At last, cake!"

It took six sailors to guide out the cake. It was immense, and if this was like other cakes he'd eaten, he didn't need spice on it. Cake had to be one of humanity's finest contributions to life in the galaxy.

The CO, followed by the sergeant major and Private Hector Olivia from H & S Company, stepped up to the cake. With her sword, she cut a piece and gave it to the sergeant major, the oldest Marine in the battalion. The second piece was given to Private Olivia, the youngest Marine. The chief motioned to the side, and six cooks descended on the cake, and in a surprisingly short amount of time, the cake was cut up and being delivered to each of the tables.

It tasted as good as it looked, and Leif had to restrain himself from licking his plate clean. He looked back up to the cake. There was more left, and he started wondering about his chances of scoring another piece.

He'd have to try that later, as the mess attendants started clearing the plates until there were only the port decanters and the glasses left on the table.

"Mr. President, the port is placed," intoned the adjutant.

This was the cue for the pouring of the port. On each table, the decanter was poured, then passed to the left, sliding the decanter along the table, never lifting it off.

"Mr. President, the port is passed," the adjutant announced once he saw that every table had finished pouring.

With the port passed, the toasts started. First was to the emperor, then the empress in waiting. This was followed by toasts to the empire, the Corps, the Navy, the families of the battalion's Marines and sailors . . . pretty much everyone received a toast. Leif dutifully sipped after each toast, but while he liked many of the human alcoholic drinks, port was not one of them. It tasted like tree tar to him.

After the last toast, it was time for the speeches. First up was the ship's captain, welcoming the Marines aboard, then the CO, who before she finished, had the battalion stand and applaud the sailors who'd volunteered their time to pull off the birthday celebration. The adjutant then read the commandant's message to the fleet, which covered the history of the Corps, recounting battles of days gone by and expressing confidence that today's Marines would carry on the proud traditions of the past.

That reading marked the end of the formalities of the celebration The colors were marched off, and the officers and staff NCOs made their rounds, shaking hands, before leaving. Not everyone was anxious to leave. For a shore birthday ball, groups would be heading off for private parties or to meet up with others, but on the *Cape Town*, it wasn't as if there was anyplace pressing to go. Marines lounged around at their tables or went to say hello to others, simply enjoying the company of each other, sharing the bonds of the Corps.

Leif was enjoying it, too. He didn't say much, but he listened to the give and take of the others. Lori left, and he was considering heading off as well when she returned, balancing six more pieces of cake on her arms.

"I saw you eyeing these," she said, putting two of the small plates in front of them. "Happy birthday, Marine."

"You, too, Lori. Happy birthday."

Chapter 31

The battalion was already in short-timer mode, deployment calendars almost filled out, when the call came in. One moment, Marines were planning their first few days back at Martelle, and the next, they were rushing back into warrior mode. This time, Leif felt particularly vested.

Slavers usually relied on speed to kidnap their victims, getting in and out before a response could be mounted. This was no longer the old days when it took months or years to reach other planets, but space was still vast.

But even slavers can screw up. They hit a manufacturing station in an asteroid belt in an otherwise unpopulated system, overcoming the company security force and kidnapping over 500 of the tokit work force. A skilled work force like that would be worth a lot of money to the right buyers. What they hadn't done was to thoroughly investigate the Navy's ship schedules. It was their bad luck that the *Cape Town* was in transit within reaction range—their bad luck, but hopefully good luck for the victims.

It was going to be a close thing, however. Without a gravity well to overcome, the transfer of victims to the slaver ship was proceeding quickly. If the slavers finished and left the system, then hauling them in would be problematic. They had to get there before the slaver attempted to flee.

Leif sat in the hangar with the rest of the Marines, praying that the ship's navigator could take them through the microjumps quickly enough to get there in time. The entire physics of ship navigation was beyond his comprehension. He didn't understand how a ship could travel as such high speeds, hitting microjumps, but then arrive at a destination ready to debark Marines. He liked to think of it as magic, something he'd never admitted to any of the humans for risk of being branded as uncivilized—but that was before he found out that none of his fellow Marines, even Nose, who could yammer on convincingly about almost anything else, understood it either. It just had to be accepted as a fact of life and leave it at that.

That didn't mean he couldn't mentally urge the navigator and the huge navcomp to hurry up and get them there in time. It was almost like praying to the Mother for good weather or a successful a'aden hunt. Conflating the Mother with a human navigator made him feel uncomfortable, but he still kept sending positive thoughts at the human.

Sitting lined up in sticks with nothing to do was bad on the nerves. There had been a flurry of activity drawing weapons and EVA suits, and they'd been given a quick frag order, but nothing much over the next hour. The officers were huddled together, creating a more detailed operations order, one that was probably changing with each additional piece of intel being sent their way. The EVA suits precluded casual chatting. He could bring up individuals on the net, but being enclosed in the suits also created a sense of isolation, and it was just easier to sit there with only his thoughts for company.

He knew what was going on with the slavers. He'd been on the other side and had felt the panic, he'd felt the despair. Hope Hollow had been lucky when the Marines got there in time, and that was why Leif was a Marine today. Now, sitting there on the hangar deck of the *Cape Town*, he'd come a full circle.

Leif had secretly hoped to test himself in a real battle, against a real military force, during his enlistment. With the deployment almost over, it didn't look like that was going to happen sans a major war between now and his EOE, his End of Enlistment. But this would be even better. He could be part of something positive. He could free people from a lifetime of misery—and hopefully send some slavers to the depths of hell.

The ready lights in the bay had been lit red, but they turned to amber.

"Listen up, Third," Staff Sergeant Donovan passed. "We're in the final progression. The lieutenant's still getting the final order, but we're part of the breaching team. Lima's hitting the station, while India and Kilo are to breach the slaver ship. We've done this before, so just listen up and follow orders."

They had done breaching exercises, but each time, they'd had ship diagrams, and every Marine knew exactly what was going to happen. This time, they'd be going in blind. Leif liked to be able to improvise during training, but with 500 or more lives on the line, he'd feel a lot more comfortable with a detailed operations order, not to mention a few days of rehearsals.

Well, it is what it is. Just listen to Corporal Lawrence, he told himself.

The platoon sergeant cut off this comms for a second and turned to one of the Navy green shirts. A moment later, he came back on and said, "OK, they're ready for us to mount up. First Squad, you're up."

Since the Marines were already in their EVAs, they could simply walk through the curtain, then fly to the target. However, when speed was of essence, the Marines would lock into an atlatl, which was a frame with its own propulsion system. Combined with skijoring behind a Navy sled, they'd be able to cross the expected 1500 meters between the *Cape Town* and the slaver ship in 30 seconds instead of minutes. Leif had only skijored once—it had been a training highlight, but the stakes were much higher now.

Success relied on surprise. The *Cape Town* did not look like a merchantman, but she had a very robust spoofing system. At distance, she could simulate any number of smaller vessels—in this case, a common Case-Havoc supply drone. As a supposedly unmanned vessel, the hope was that the slaver ship would not pull away the second the *Cape Town* came out of its final jump. Visually, however, there wasn't a way to make the man-of-war look like anything else than what she was. At some point, she would be identified as she maneuvered in to the Station's gate.

Lima Company would board the station through the gate, but Kilo and India would EVA as the ship approached, breaching the slaver before they knew they were under attack—hopefully.

Across the hangar, Marines from the two companies, along with the ship's SEAL detachment, were moving into their atlatls, which were already in skijoring position behind the sleds. It took a few minutes, but then it was Second Squad's turn. Leif walked up to his designated atlatl, then stepped in the boots, feeling them clamp around his ankles. He leaned back, and the side arms clamped around him. A green shirt came up, ran down the checklist, finishing with releasing and reapplying the clamps that would hold Leif in the atlatl.

"All systems check," the sailor said.

"Roger, all systems check."

"Kick some ass out there," he said before going to check Donk.

A Navy coxswain, in his grey EVA, stepped up the sled. This would take the entire squad to the slaver even quicker than the atlatls and while saving their power for the deceleration. He ran a check over his sled before turning to the squad, holding up three fingers. Leif switched to Hangar Circuit 3.

"OK, I'm Petty Officer Two Jasper Orinkiny. I'll be your friendly taxi for today. Just a few things first. Do not touch the tow line until I give the OK, but when I do that, I want you to lock in with your inboard hand, then raise your outboard with a thumbs up so I know you're good to go.

"The transit is going to be quick. As soon as I release, reverse vector your atlatls, or you're going to splat yourself all over the slaver ship. This will be at combat specs, so you'll need to be at 6Gs."

The atlatls did not have G compensators like ships, so the Marines would feel every G. Leif had done the training maximum of 3Gs, but this would be much heavier, and the wyntonans were not as G-tolerant as humans. He hoped that the pressure cells in his EVA suit would do their job and keep him from G-lock.

"You've all got your breakout angles, so just let your atlatls take over. If you all understand what I've said, give me a thumbs up."

The twelve Marines all gave a thumbs up, then he said, "Good. God's speed, all of you."

The lieutenant returned and gave them the operations order, bare bones as it was. Kilo Company was to hit the aft end of the ship, securing the main hold where most of the victims would probably be. India would focus on the bow, eliminating any slavers, and taking over the bridge. The SEALs would breach the engine room to disable the ship and keep it from leaving, with Kilo backing them up if needed.

A generic ship's diagram popped up on Leif's faceshield, delineating egress routes and areas of responsibility for each squad. Third Squad, with the attached engineers from the ship's company, would conduct the actual breach. This wasn't a matter of simply blowing a hole in the ship. Hundreds of Imperial citizens were inside, and if the ship lost atmosphere, they would die. The engineers had to emplace a space bore that would pierce the ship's skin, but with a curtain that would keep the atmosphere from escaping. The curtain was just a mini-version of the huge hangar curtain that allowed for shuttles and personnel to pass while keeping the ship's atmosphere inside.

The civilians were also the reason why the *Cape Town* didn't cripple the ship with any of its weapons. Slavers used civilians as shields around vital functions precisely for that reason. Knocking out the engine room with kinetics or beam weapons would kill untold innocents.

The lieutenant went into more detail, more than Leif would have thought given the short time since the mission had been assigned to the battalion, but no matter how it was cut, the plan was very basic, leaving much to relying on the Marines' training.

They're slavers, though, not Marines. This is what we do.

The amber light flashed ten times, then went to blue. The *Cape Town* had just completed the final jump into the system. Immediately, the hangar doors started to open.

The coxswain jumped off his sled, then brought his two fists together, the signal for the Marines to lock into their tow line. A green shirt ran down giving each Marine's gauntleted hand a tug. He gave the coxswain a thumbs up, then ran back out of the way.

The hangar doors were almost open, and Leif craned his head to catch a glimpse of the station, but there was nothing in sight except the system's sun, a harsh white globe that his faceshield filtered to something manageable. The blue alert lights started flashing, and Leif instinctively braced himself. At ten, the lights changed to green, and the artificial gravity was cut, while at the same time, the ship started rotating. Leif watched through the curtain until the station slowly came into view, so close that he could almost reach out and touch it. The station was a hodgepodge of components probably added over centuries, all showing different degrees of wear, affixed to the edge of a vast array of gossamer solar fabric which stretched out for kilometers. There, at the end of an extended gate, the slaver hung like a ripe *wotti* on a branch. Leif had expected an evil-looking ship as depicted in the holovids, but it looked like a normal, well-maintained freighter.

He was so caught up in the view that he almost missed the first nine sticks taking off, nine sleds with twelve Marines each hanging on the tow lines, "dopes on a rope," as the Navy sailors referred to them.

Ten seconds after the last of them cleared the curtain, the next rank of nine, which included Leif's squad, took off. They passed through the curtain, and the coxswain adjusted the sled to take them to their breach point.

Two of the ship's shuttles flashed into view as they took off out of the adjacent Hangar C. The shuttles were not fighters—the *Cape Town*, as a troop transport, did not have any small combat craft in her complement. They were military craft, however, so they were armed, and they would provide covering fire if needed.

"Energize, weapons," Sergeant Holmes passed.

His M88 was clamped in its holster. Leif reached with his outboard hand and activated the mag rings. He was ready to rock and roll.

The tow line automatically rotated each Marine slightly so as to keep them from contact with each other. It was slightly disorienting to look "up" and see Corporal Lawrence, head towards him, feet pointing away at an angle. She saw him looking at her and gave him a thumbs up.

"Nothing to it, Hollow. Just like training," she passed.

He gave her a thumbs up in return just as something flashed by, almost too quickly for his mind to comprehend, and a wash of light so bright he thought he could see the corporal's bones through her EVA suit lit up the black.

The Cape Town!

He managed to turn his head far enough to see the ship . . . which was thankfully still there. Little fingers of lightening danced across her hull.

"They know we're here," the lieutenant passed. "That doesn't change anything. Just keep to the plan."

Leif turned his attention back to the slaver. She might look like an ordinary freighter, but she packed a punch. Luckily, the *Cape Town* was not defenseless. If the slaver had targeted one of the shuttles or a squad of Marines, that would have had a different outcome.

"Releasing in five . . . four . . . three . . . two . . . one!" the coxswain passed, and suddenly, Leif's gauntlet was no longer attached. His atlatl, as it had been programmed to do, nudged him further away from the others while, at the same time, initiated deceleration.

The ship was huge now, looming before him, and as the G's kicked in, he was sure he wouldn't stop in time. He kept his thumb on the jet control, ready to divert his course to miss the slaver itself if he had to.

The G's were brutal, and his peripheral vision grayed out. The atlatl was constantly pinging the ship, not caring about his condition. If he went into G-lock, it wouldn't matter to its single-focused silicate brain. Leif was aware of his EVA suit pressuring up, but he wasn't sure it would be enough. Someone passed something on one of the comms circuits, but he didn't understand a word as he struggled to stay conscious.

And then, with a rush, he was back, stationary, 30 meters from the slaver. His atlatl automatically detached and slowly moved back out of the way.

"On me," he realized Sergeant Holmes was passing.

Each EVA had a small transponder, and Leif's Battle-I translated those responder frequencies into colors. The Second Squad Marines all had a light lilac tint through his faceshield. Leif touched his EVA suit control and formed up on his squad leader, ready to enter the ship.

Jonathan P. Brazee

The Navy engineer team with Third Squad had already employed their bore, which had pierced the slavers' hull, half of it sticking out like a thorn in a foot. This thorn was hollow, though, and it was their passage in. The first fire team had already disappeared when the slaver started to back away from the gate.

"Now, now, now!" the lieutenant shouted. "She's running!"

That had been the ongoing fear. The Marines had hoped that the slavers would react too slowly at best, but at worse, that the two companies would be onboard before the slavers would run.

The Marines outside the ship crowded to their respective bores, keeping in relative position as the ship maneuvered. This far astern, Leif couldn't see the gate, but he hoped civilians hadn't been caught past the emergency vacuum doors there when the slaver broke free. A few of the slavers themselves now breathing vacuum? Screw them.

There were two modes of breaching: a deliberate breach, as when a ship had been disabled, and a hasty breach. The deliberate breach was conducted much as with MOUT operations, with each compartment cleared before the next. A hasty breach was a matter of rushing, overwhelming any resistance by numbers and force of will. With the slaver ship breaking off, this was now a hasty breach.

A ship this size has a tremendous amount of mass, and it couldn't just scoot out of the gate and away from the station like a sportshover. It looked as if it was barely moving, but that was an optical illusion. Leif's little EVA suit was pushing at the max to keep even with the bore as he watched the two sailors who were hanging onto the end of the bore and directing traffic. He goosed his suit forward the second they pointed at Sergeant Holmes, so tight on Corporal Lawrence that he hit her feet as he dove into the bore.

Halfway through, the ships gravity kicked in, and he fell from what had been his "up" to the ship's "down," landing on the corporal's legs. He got kicked several times as they scrambled forward and fell into one of the ship's

204

compartments. Two Marines were standing there, hauling them up to their feet, and yelling at them to move forward.

There was a log jam at the hatch, but Leif pushed through and turned right, moving forward until Sergeant Holmes stopped him, telling him to provide security. He held his M88 at the ready, thumb on the safety, staring down a featureless passage.

"That's the last of us," the sergeant passed. "We got everyone aboard. Drop your Level Twos."

Every EVA had two components. Level One was a simple helmet and undersuit over which they wore their battle rattle. This was enough to keep a Marine alive in a vacuum, but not much else. The Level Two was the bulkier suit that gave long-term protection as well as mobility in space. The Twos were not conducive to effective fighting, however. Within fifteen seconds, each Marine had dropped their Level Twos and were ready to engage the slavers.

"Second Team, move out," the sergeant ordered.

As point man, Leif led the squad down the corridor, following a route highlighted on his faceshield. He needed it to show the way, but it was a little distracting, and he had to be laser-focused on spotting any slavers before they spotted him. A ship passage did not leave much room for a firefight, and the advantage would be to whoever got off the first round.

"Third Platoon, listen up," the lieutenant passed. "We didn't get all of Third Squad aboard in time, and First Platoon is at 50%. The ship is building speed for a jump, but we still have time. Continue with your assigned missions, but be ready for a frag."

He then switched his circuit to isolate Second Squad and passed, "The SEALs are aboard and heading to the engine room. Be ready, though, to divert to them if needed."

"You heard him," Sergeant Holmes said. "Be ready for anything."

They went up two levels to an inner deck, then continued around, seeing no sign of the slavers. It was as if the ship was deserted—which they knew it wasn't.

The one advantage to this mission when compared to some other hostage situations was that this time, the hostages had value. Other terrorist groups, whether race, national, or religion-based, wanted to make a statement, and killing hostages was the most impactful way of doing that. The more dead, the better. Slavers needed the hostages alive. They may kill some, but only when necessary when they thought they might succeed in their operation. They might—probably would—kill hostages if it was evident that they were going to be caught and executed, but short of that, they would want to keep their "product" alive.

Just as the presence of the hostages limited what the Navy and Marines could do, it also limited the slavers' options. Leif hoped that since the ship was underway, they might feel more confident in being able to overcome the Marines who'd made it onboard.

Faulty thinking, but I sure hope you're that overconfident.

They reached the hatch to their objective, which was a large space, possibly berthing. The hatch was closed. If there were armed pirates inside, they would probably have booby-trapped the hatch and almost assuredly had it covered by fire. Leif didn't stop there but continued another six meters before coming to a halt and kneeling, weapon pointing down the passage.

Donk stepped up and placed a small black box on the bulkhead. Leif was dying to see the reading, but he kept his eyes forward. Evidently, the scanner indicated that the immediate area on the other side was clear, because Rick stepped forward and took a tube of cutting paste and applied the paste to the bulkhead, tracing a large, 2-meter by 2-meters square. Leif stood and turned to the square as the squad crowded forward. At Sergeant Holmes' nod, Rick touched the paste with his detonator and stepped back. The entire square flashed into a white-hot, one-second-long flare, and Leif kicked it in.

They caught the slavers by surprise. There were six of them, with a mass of tokits huddled fearfully in the back of the berthing space who started their typical undulating trill of fear.

Right in front of Leif, one of the slavers had been kneeling behind one of the racks, his rifle resting on the bunk and aimed at the hatch. He looked up in surprise and started to swing his weapon around to engage Leif, but the barrel hit one of the bunk supports, giving Leif just the time he needed to fire his M88 in a three-round burst—which was two more than were needed. The first round hit the slaver just below his nose, taking out the back of his head and an explosion of blood, brains, and skull.

Leif shifted his aim to take another slaver under fire. She fell to one knee, a look of surprise on her face before the Marine's combined fire laid her flat. Five seconds after Leif fired the first round, all six slavers were down. One was on his back, moving a single leg in vain as if trying to push himself out of the line of fire, his heel slipping in the blood on the deck. The other five were motionless.

"Clear the compartment!" Sergeant Holmes shouted.

Leif rushed towards the tokits who were trying to sink into the back bulkhead, their undulating cries filling the space.

"Don't worry, you're safe now! I'm Private First Class Leif Hollow, Imperial Marines!"

He had a flashback, almost strong enough to make him stumble. His mind raced to Hope Hollow, over three tri-years ago, when Sergeant Washburn Gonzales had said almost the same words to a young wyntonan ada.

The trilling faded in spurts, and a tokit female reached out, taking Leif's left hand and pulling it to her forehead.

"Thank you, oh, thank you," she said quietly.

"Secure them, Hollow!" Corporal Lawrence shouted out. "You don't have time for that."

She was right. The tokits had to be searched to make sure there were no human slavers using them for cover. For that matter, there could be tokits slavers, hoping to use the others as camouflage. Evil was not limited to humans, after all.

Leif slowly pulled his hand off her forehead and out of her grasp.

"I'm sorry, ma'am," but I need to make sure there aren't any more slavers in here."

Most of the tokits were nervous as the Marines started separating them into groups, but they readily cooperated. No other human was found, and the tokits would have to be interviewed, but not by the squad.

"Third Team, stay here and provide security. Doc, you check out the hostages," Sergeant Holmes suddenly passed. "First and Second, we're moving out. First, you've got point."

A route appeared on their faceshields. It led to the engine room.

"The SEALs have casualties and are pinned down. There's a force of slavers in the engine room with over forty tokit hostages. The lieutenant and First Squad are heading there now, and we're to meet them there," he passed as the two teams took off past the hole they'd made in the bulkhead and continued at a controlled jog.

After only 15 seconds, there was the sound of firing from the front, but they didn't stop, and a moment later, Leif ran past a slaver body, dead eyes staring at the overhead. Blood was pooling from underneath him. Leif felt nothing, only reminding himself not to step in the slaver's blood and possibly slip, just the same as if someone had spilled a glass of bug juice in the galley.

They went two decks deeper, and the lieutenant and First Squad had arrived just before Second. Sergeant Holmes moved forward to confer while Corporal St. Jules put the two fire teams in a defensive posture, oriented to the aft end of the ship. Leif tried to focus on the empty passage, but he kept stealing glances back to where the lieutenant, the staff sergeant, and the two squad leaders were trying to come up with a quick plan of action. Time was of an essence, however, and Leif knew that any action was better than no action.

"Why don't we just cut another hole in the bulkhead, like what we did back there?" he asked Rick on the 1P.

"Can't. The engine room is shielded. My little cutting paste won't do much to that."

"Well, we've got pyroplast," Leif said, knowing it wouldn't be used because of the risk it would create for the hostages inside.

He "knew" wrong, however. The lieutenant called the Marines together and told them they would be blowing two breaches into the engine room with a charge 3 on the pyroplast.

Pyroplast was an incremental explosive, carried in strips by all the members of a squad. They could be stuck together, from two strips to a hundred, and detonated with a simple mechanical fuze. They were almost never used inside a ship as with enough strips, they could blow out the hull of even the strongest military vessel, something the slaver most certainly was not.

"We've got two SEALs down, and the other four are trapped. There are between eight to ten slavers with over 40 tokits hostages inside," he said, pausing for a moment. "And we don't have time. We are approaching jump speed, and the *Cape Town* is tracking us. The CO won't let us jump."

"How long do we have?" Corporal Lawrence asked.

"Eight minutes, so you see what I mean about the time. The skipper and the other two platoons are heavily engaged, and he doesn't think he can get here before that, so it's up to us. We've got to stop the ship."

Or the Cape Town will do it for us, taking out the hostages, the SEALs, and probably us as well as collateral damage.

Even if the *Cape Town* didn't take out the engines, no one knew who would be on the other side of the jump, but if he had to guess, Leif would say more slavers, enough to overcome the Marines who'd managed to make it aboard the ship. A quick death on the other side might be preferable to whatever degree of life they'd have as a slave if they were captured.

"Gunny Salinas says that a charge 3 should breach the inner bulkheads but leave the hull intact, so that's what we're going to do. Vacuum up, though."

Marines had a habit of cracking their helmets when in an atmosphere. Upon the lieutenant's word, at least five hands reached up to re-seal their helmets. The fact that the lieutenant ordered that meant that breaching the hull was a very real probability, unfortunately for the tokits being held as shields. If they were given the choice, Leif wondered for a moment if they would prefer to burble out their lives in a vacuum right now or live a life as a slave. He was glad this wasn't his choice to make.

"Second, go down to G-3-44. That's your marker. Place the charge at waist level a meter-and-a-half to the right of the marker. First, your marker is G-3-22. This will put us inside with the length of the acceleration tubes in front of us. Your primary mission is to stop the ship." Six images of the engine room popped up on his faceshield. "Any two of these should do it. Your secondary mission is to save as many hostages as possible.

"The SEALs will be to your left, in back of a control panel. Keep that in mind. That's all we've got time for now, so move it. I want synchronized charges for a minute from now, no longer. Go!"

The Marines from Second Squad immediately wheeled and ran down the passage, looking up at the space markings as they ran. Leif spotted the G-3-44 stencil up against the overhead and pointed—as if the others really needed him to see it for themselves.

Lori stepped off a meter-and-a-half, then pulled out her pyroplast, hand out for two more. She slapped them together and up against the bulkhead, the main blast aimed inwards. Sliding the timer in one of the receiving slots, she waited while the rest of the Marines moved away.

The pyroplast strips were designed to focus the blast wave in one direction, but there still would be blast waves radiating back, and the confines of the passage would funnel the pressure wave for quite some distance. The squad turned into a connecting passage 10 meters from the charge.

As soon as they reached their position, the lieutenant passed, "Set charge timer for fifteen . . . fourteen . . ."

At "three," Lori came barreling down the passage at a dead sprint, almost failing to make the turn if not for helping hands pulling her to safety. At "zero," a blast of fire shot down the #3 passage, followed almost immediately by a pressure wave that pushed on Leif's chest.

The Marines were up immediately, bolting back down the passage to where the pyroplast had opened a jagged hole in the bulkhead. It wasn't very big, barely enough for the larger

Marines to squeeze through. Donk was first through the hole, then Jordan. Chuck Sylvianstri was next, and just as he was half-way through, he slumped, blocking the entrance. Corporal Lawrence pulled his limp body back out of the way, then jumped through. When Leif squeezed through, smoke obscured much of the engine room. Bodies, mostly tokits, were on the deck, some motionless, some crawling to get out of the line of fire. Leif was surprised that anyone inside was still functioning, but at least some of the slavers were. He was hit in the chest, but his armor held true.

Rick stepped up beside him, his M55 at his shoulder as he took aim. With the heavier weapons, he and Lori were given the task of destroying the key points in the room. He let out a string of heavy fire.

"Got it!" he said, turning to Leif, just as a heavy round of some sort smashed through his faceshield.

"Rick!' Leif shouted, taking a step to him before he got control of himself. His friend was gone, and he had to get that out of his mind. He scooped up Rick's M55, then looked for another of the targets.

With his normal combat gear, he could program his battle-I to spot one of them, but the EVA helmets were not as sophisticated. He had to spot a target on his own. He kept the images up on his display, ignoring the firefight raging around him. Time was running out, and the *Cape Town* could open up at any moment. Movement caught his eye, drawing his attention, and then he saw it. He had no idea what "it" was, but it matched the image. He brought the M55 up and fired ten rounds at it, reducing it to a hunk of junk and what he hoped to be inoperable.

Another round skipped off of his helmet, and as if remembering where he was, he rushed to a control panel, out of the line of fire. Nose was behind it as well, popping up to fire a burst before dropping back down. She looked over at him, then with a crazy smile visible through her faceshield, gave him a thumbs up.

Leif hoped the primary mission had been completed and they weren't waiting for the *Cape Town* to reach out with her cannon's kiss. There was still the secondary mission, though, and if the slavers knew they weren't getting through the jump, they would probably start taking out the tokits. It was up to the Marines to eliminate the slavers before they realized what had happened.

He peered around the edge of the console and fired off a few quick rounds of the M55 at a fleeting silhouette.

"Fuck this," he muttered, placing the M55 on the deck and pulling the M88 out of the holster.

The M55 was overkill, especially in such close quarters. His M88 was a better weapon for the circumstances. He leaned around, then jumped back when he saw a slaver aiming at him. Rounds skipped off the side of the console where his head had been a moment before. One round went right through the corner of the console. Leif didn't know what had fired it, but if it went through the console like so much tissue paper, it could blast through his helmet without much effort as well.

He was actually amazed that he was still in one piece. Thousands of rounds were being fired, yet only a few slavers or humans were down that he could see. More tokits were, and their modulating trilling cut through the snaps of mag rifles and the louder reports of chemical rounds being fired.

He fired another burst of his M88 before ducking back again. This wasn't doing anything, he thought. Something had to break.

And it did.

"They're killing the tokits!" someone shouted over the net.

Leif spun around, and he spotted a slaver, holding a tokit in front of him as a shield as he shot at prone figures. Another tokit rose up, hands clasped as he pleaded for his life, and the slaver shot him in the face.

Leif had been holding his emotions in check. He knew he'd mourn Rick later, but seeing the human murder the tokits put him over the edge, and a rage roiled from deep inside of him, consuming him like a wildfire. He stood up as the musapha took over, not even trying to fight it. With a wordless shout, he charged forward, mindless of his safety, his entire attention focused on the evil face in front of him. The slaver shot a young female who was huddled on the ground before he seemed to sense the fury bearing down on him. He swung his shield around to face Leif and fired around her.

He might have realized that the ship was not going to make the jump. He might have realized that he was going to be executed. He didn't look like someone who accepted the immediacy of his death, however, as he back-peddled, his face in a panic as he fired shot after shot at Leif.

Leif closed the distance in five strides, vaulting over the plasma pipes. He didn't fire his M88—it would have been too easy to hit the tokit shield. Besides, it was too impersonal, and that wouldn't do. He thrust his M88 forward like a Roman gladius, just clearing the tokit's neck and smashing through the slavers cheek bones, shattering them as it drove just under the orbit and into his brain.

The slaver dropped the tokit, who fell sobbing to the deck, but he was held aloft, pinned by Leif's rifle. Lief shook the rifle twice, then had to lower the muzzle, and putting his foot against the slaver's neck, he pushed the body free.

Another slaver saw what had happened and fired at him. Leif tried to fire back, but his rifle had been ruined, the magrings knocked out of position. He took the rifle by the barrel and advanced, swinging it like a human baseball bat, connecting on the side of the slaver's head, taking half of it off off in a spray of bloody gray matter that splattered tokits who were trying to crawl away from this apparition from *Loscan*, the tokit hell.

He looked around, his fury fed by the violence. Another slaver scuttled back on her ass, eyes looking in horror at him, but before he could go after her, she was cut down by Marine fire.

He looked around, wanting—no *needing*—another victim. Everything, from watching Kollun killed on Hope Hollow, to the abuse he'd suffered as a wyntonan in a human corps, to these scum that wanted to enslave free beings, emerged to fill every molecule of his being. He didn't just hate the slavers; he hated *humans*. All humans.

And there was another slaver, laying there, staring at him. He had his hands over his belly, blood covering the ground. Leif stepped over dead tokits to reach him. With a resigned expression on his face, the slaver watched, raising his hands in surrender as Leif stood over him.

Leif didn't care. They were animals, vermin to be exterminated. He hefted the rifle in one hand and brought it back for the death blow, but as he commenced the swing, something held him back. Angry, he shrugged off the obstacle.

"Leif, Leif, it's over. Stop!"

He didn't want to listen to the annoying voice. What did he care what a human was saying? But the voice grabbed him, not relenting until it had snagged his soul and pulled him back to reality.

"Leif, calm down. It's over," Lori said from where he'd tossed her. "Calm down."

Leif lowered his rifle, and the musapha started to flow from him.

"You back with me, big boy?"

"Yeah, I think so."

"Thank goodness for that. You were . . . where the hell were you?"

"Fucking A, Leif, you were amazing! I've never seen anything like that!" Donk came running up and pounded him on the back. "I mean look at that," he said, pointing at the dead slaver Leif had hit with the stock of his M88. "Fucking awesome!"

"He's still alive," Leif said matter-of-factly and pointed at the prone slaver.

"Not for long. He'll get a trial, then he's done for. But wow, he won't go like these two," he said, toeing the body of the dead woman.

"Check every body," Corporal Lawrence said. "If they're alive, zip-tie them."

"Hey, are you OK?" Lori asked, coming up alongside him. "Let me . . . shit, you're hit."

Leif looked at his arm, where two holes were leaking blood. Only after he saw them did they begin to hurt.

"Not there, here," she said, pressing on his side.

His musapha gone, all the pain came rushing in, and he stumbled. He looked down to where Lori was applying pressure, noting that her hands were *inside* of him and only vaguely aware that she was calling for a corpsman.

He was confused. A person should not be able to put her hands inside of him. It didn't make sense.

And that was all he remembered.

NORTHUMBRIA

Chapter 32

"And this will be your new kidney," the Navy regen surgeon said, holding up what looked like a dried piece of lace.

It sure doesn't look like a kidney.

Leif had awoken to find out he was back at the Naval Hospital at Camp Martelle to where he'd been CASEVAC'd. He'd been put in a medically induced coma on the *Cape Town* and his metabolism was slowed to a crawl before being sent back, so he'd been out of it since the fight back on the slaver. Shortly after being brought back to full consciousness and given his first extensive medical survey, he'd received a group call from the squad and others. More than a little drunk, they were in a bar on Waterhouse Station, their final liberty port on their way back. They'd given him shit for wimping out on the liberty, told him they missed him, and raised more than a few glasses of sundry typess of alcohol in his honor.

Lori and Donk called him again a few hours later to bring him up to speed. By all standards, the mission had been a success. Lima Company had managed to capture 23 slavers and free a couple of hundred tokits without a single casualty on any side. The fight on the slaver ship had been far more costly. Six Marines and a corpsman had been killed, including Rick and Lieutenant Tanaka-Stevens from Kilo. Fifteen other Marines had been wounded, with two others being CASEVAC'd back to Northumbria and Camp Martelle along with Leif. Two SEALs had been killed as well.

Fifty-three tokits hostages had been killed, but four-hundred-and-sixty-one had been rescued. The cost would have been higher if the slaver had not been stopped. The Cape

Town had been 43 seconds from firing its cannons when the ship was finally disabled.

Six slavers on the ship had surrendered, and fifty-nine were killed. This was the largest kill of slavers in over fifteen years, and the media was trumpeting the success as a sign that the slavers' days were numbered. Leif wasn't so sure about that. Slavers seemed to cross all races, and as long as there was a demand for slaves, more would arise from the cesspit of evil. Leif thought it would take a single government across all the races and a concerted will to eradicate them.

That call had been two days ago, and the ship should be on its way back to offload the battalion. During those two days, Leif had been tested to within a centimeter of his life, all leading to the beaming Navy captain and his staff standing before him, his kidney in his hand.

"We'll implant this in you tomorrow," he said to Leif, but turning to look at the others crowded in his room.

This is feeding his ego, he realized.

He'd told Leif far more than once that this would be the first time Navy medicine had regenerated a wyntonan kidney. Now, he was preening in front of his colleagues.

Leif didn't like the fact that he was a test case. Back on Home, the technique had been refined, even if only in the capital, and even there, it wasn't commonly done. Here, at Camp Martelle, this was a new procedure, and the captain couldn't hold back from his enthusiasm. Leif felt like a shiny new sports hover, something to be salivated over.

"The matrix itself wasn't the problem. We had full surveys of wyntonan physiology, and when compared to the patient's remaining kidney, we were sure of the construct. The question was whether the patient would tolerate the same matrix material as what we use in human regeneration. We printed out matrix material and ran tests, and I'm pleased to say that the subject tolerated it well.

"No, the issue was to make sure that the conversion to stem cells, then the nudge to kidney cells, was successful. We tested cells harvested from bone marrow, the heart, the kidney, and the stomach lining. To our surprise, the cells from the lining tolerated the transformation to stem cells the best, and as of this morning, they are reproducing as kidney cells.

"As I said, we'll implant the matrix tomorrow. If everything goes well, and I expect it shall, we'll transfer the new kidney cells to the matrix next week. Within three months, the subject should be walking out of here with a fully functioning kidney.

Three months? No one told me I'd be in here that long!

"All of this will be written up for submission to the *Imperial Journal of Medical Science*, and you'll be able to read the details there."

The captain turned back to Leif, and said, "Don't worry son, you're in good hands."

He faced back to the group, and a holographer stepped up, recording the event.

Leif just wished they'd leave. He knew he should be grateful, and he was, but he'd never felt like he was in any danger, he hadn't come to grips with how close of a call he'd had. One moment, he was standing there confused while Lori tried to stop the bleeding, part of her hand inside his wound. The next moment, he was waking up at the Naval Hospital with doctors assuring him he was going to be fine.

Just getting back to the *Cape Town's* sickbay had been a close thing, something where he very easily could have died, but he'd been unconscious at the time, and it hadn't really sunk in.

Now, it looked like he was going to be stuck in the hospital for at least three months. With only nine months left on his enlistment, that probably meant he was about done with doing anything exciting.

Instead of going out of his enlistment with a bang, he would be going out with a whimper.

Chapter 33

"Can you feel it growing?" Donk asked, his face twisted in disgust.

"Feel it? No. Could you feel yourself growing when you were a child?" Leif asked.

"No, but this is different."

"It's his own cells, asshole," Nose said. "Get real."

Donk shuddered, then said, "No, it's different. I sure the hell hope I never have to get an organ regenerated."

Lori laughed, then said, "When you're a hundred-and-twenty, and your heart starts to give out, I expect you'll want a new heart then."

"That's then. This is now."

"Wait until his dick gives out. He'll be the first one in line," Nose said as the others burst into laughter.

Leif listened to their bickering, and he felt . . . good. Yes, good.

Every day since the ship had returned, Marines had come in to see him. The commanding general himself had come in to see him that first day, and the battalion CO, the sergeant major, and company staff had all come in, but it was the daily visits from his . . . his friends that meant the most to him. They didn't have to come, and they certainly didn't have to hang out for an hour or two, yet they did.

Leif had not been on the ship for Rick's heroes' ceremony, so the day after the battalion's return, they had held a second one, right there in Leif's room. To his surprise, Leif had cried. Rick had been a fellow Marine, a friend, but he was human, and Leif had never thought he'd become that close to a human, to actually think of him as he did Jordan or any of the other wyntonans. It hurt when he thought of Rick, and the fact that it hurt made Leif happy, which was weird. But he was happy that he cared enough to grieve, if that made any sense at all.

"Hey, Jordan," Lori called out over the bed. "I thought you had something for him."

"Not for *him*. For me, but yeah, I should tell him." He pulled out a packet from his cargo pocket and said, "My spice mix came in."

That perked Leif up, and he asked, "What about mine?"

"Just this one. I'll let you smell it, though."

Leif almost said no, he'd wait, but he'd been out of spice since arriving at the hospital. Some customs geek had probably tossed it when his personal effects had arrived. Jordan made a show of unwrapping it, then leaned over the bed, holding it out for Leif, who took a deep whiff.

It was heavenly, and his mouth started watering. He couldn't admit that to Jordan, however. Village pride ran deep.

"Do you want me to leave some for you?"

Yes, I do!

"No, I'll wait for mine to arrive. Yours seems OK, but it's not really to my taste."

"Are you sure? It really wouldn't be a bother."

"I'm sure. It's probably OK for you, but I want the Hope Hollow mix," he said, getting a little annoyed that Jordan was pushing it.

"Hell, you haven't learned anything from our human brothers and sisters. You still can't lie worth shit," he said, tossing the packet on the bed.

"I told you—"

"Because this one is mine," he said, pulling out another packet and giving it a long sniff. "That crap I just threw to you is yours."

The rest of the Marines broke out in laughter.

It took a moment for that to register, and he snatched up the packet, breathing in the aromas. It really was a good mix, and he could almost smell Granny Oriono's hands in it.

"You fucking *minta*," he said, using the wyntonan equivalent of the human "asshole."

"Hey, he was just going to give it to you, but just because you're slacking off here in the hospital doesn't give you any breaks," Nose said.

"You're a *minta*, too," Leif said, trying not to smile.

"I don't know what that is, but I'll wear the title with pride."

Lori leaned in and took a tentative sniff, then sneezed.

"I still don't know how you eat that stuff, but I guess with hospital food, anything's better."

The door to the room opened, but instead of a nurse, Sept-Minister Iaxi stepped into the room. Jordan and Leif recognized the man, of course, and the others recognized the easy composure of a a man of power. Even if they hadn't, the hospital's commanding officer hovering at the door would have been a dead giveaway.

"Private First Class Hollow, it's good to see you again. Well, not good in this condition, but good to see you're on your way to a full recovery." He looked at the others, then said, "And these are your friends? Good. And Private First Class Hottento, good to see you again. I trust you're OK?"

"Yes, Vice-Minister," Jordan said, as the others, hearing his title, exchanged worried looks.

"Well . . . yes," he said before turning to the Leif's friends. "If you don't mind, I'd like a little time alone with Leif."

"We'll catch you tomorrow," Lori said as they filed out of the room.

"Well, then," the vice-minister said, pulling one of the chairs close to the bed. I've talked with Doctor deVan. He said your regeneration is going along well, and you should make a full recovery. Good, good."

"Yes, sir."

"And I've got some more good news. I spoke with Lieutenant Colonel Jarvincus before coming in to see you. It seems as if you've been nominated for the Golden Lion for your action in saving those poor tokits. The emperor is very, very proud of you, young man."

That hit Leif hard. He'd never expected to hear something like that. The Golden Lion was the second highest award for valor, and he'd done nothing to deserve that.

"I can assure you that the award will sail through the process."

Leif was still in shock, but the cynical part of him wondered on why that specific award. Did it have anything to do with a wyntonan a'aden hunt and the fact that he'd proven himself against the wyntonan version of a lion? And if the vice-minister had just seen the CO now, then how did the emperor already know to be "proud" of him?

"I can't stress how important having you wyntonans in the Marines is to the emperor. He is following your progress, yours and the next two classes that have joined the fleet. And you aren't the the only ones. The other races will be up next, until we have not just a Marine Corps, but an Army, an Imperial Security force, the imperial bureaucracy—all branches that serve the empire—that reflects the broad array of imperial citizens."

The vice-minister was talking to him, a lowly Marine private first class, but Leif knew the man had made this speech before. This was something in which he believed. All wyntonans looked at other governments with a grain of suspicion, but he couldn't fault what the man was saying. It made sense. He just wasn't sure if the real powers in the empire were willing to accept the subjugated races as equals.

"I know that some consider the Empire a relic of the past, something that has outlived its usefulness. Yes, there is corruption, stagnation. Yes, there have been planets and confederations that have withdrawn from the Empire. Yes, for too long, we've looked inward towards Earth and Wayfare, but don't you see, that is why you are so important. We need new blood, new perspectives if we are going to grow into what the emperor so wants us to be."

He stopped for a moment, then gave a soft chuckle. "Excuse my enthusiasm, Leif. I know I can get carried away, but I wanted to talk to you. What are your plans after your enlistment is up?"

The change in tack took Leif by surprise. He hadn't really thought about it much.

"I'm not sure, sir. That will take place just before my tri-year, and . . . well, with my earnings, I can start a family. Something like that."

"Well, what if I can promise you better earnings. What do you make now? A little over two hundred a month?"

"I'll be a lance corporal next month, so, two-hundred-twenty-four BC."

"OK, two-hundred-twenty-four. What if I can get you fifteen-hundred?"

The number shocked Leif, and he lay there dumbfounded.

"I'm serious. As I said, the emperor has his eye on you, and he wants you to be part of the new empire, one dedicated to all of his subjects. I can get your enlistment cut, as soon as you're healed, in fact. And then you can come to Wayfare and learn the trade."

"The trade, sir?"

"Of statecraft, son. Of statecraft. The empire is vast, and we need talented people to help run it. Give us two or three years under the tutelage of one of us, and you'll be ready to step up. Who knows how far you can go, a wyntonan who not only proved he is loyal to the empire, but who was proven fearless in battle, protecting another race from a horrible fate."

The breath caught in his throat. He was sure the sept-minister was sincere, but he was suspicious about his award. It just made things too convenient, to have a "hero" wyntonan who then could be used to reflect how united this vision of the Empire was, and the visuals of a Golden *Lion* were pretty coincidental. But could the entire slaver mission have been set up? Had he been set up to succeed?

No, that just doesn't make sense, he told himself a moment later.

He could have been killed just as easily as not. He realized that if it wasn't him, it could have been any of the others, but to bet that one of them would have been in the right place and lucky enough to survive was just taking it too far. No, the sept-minister, and maybe the emperor himself, would not have set it up, but they were probably waiting for the first opportunity to fall into their laps.

"You can cut short my enlistment?" he asked, just to push the darker thoughts out of his mind.

"That isn't a problem," he said with a laugh. "You Marines serve at the pleasure of the emperor."

Leif had been looking forward to his EOE, to get back home, and maybe see where Soran was with her life. Speeding that up sounded interesting, but it also touched something he hadn't realized was there. He wasn't sure if he wanted to leave early. He'd like to get back with his squad for awhile, back to normal. He'd be a lance corporal in a month, and even if he couldn't drink while in regen, he'd like to celebrate with the others. More than that, it was his duty, and he didn't want to shirk that. Doing so would somehow negate all he'd done so far.

No, I don't want to get out early. I want to enjoy my last few months with my friends, and I want to finish what I started.

"Sir, I'm not sure that's a good idea . . ." he started before trailing off.

The sept-minister looked puzzled for a moment, then a knowing smile came over his face, and he said, "Ah, good thinking. It would serve you better later on if you complete your full enlistment. We don't want anyone to think you're getting special treatment. Perhaps I let my enthusiasm get the better of me.

"You know, maybe you won't need much seasoning. I think you have an inherent understanding of politics."

That hadn't been Leif's thinking at all, but he wasn't going to naysay what the sept-minister had said. If it meant he could stay until his EOE, then than was what mattered.

"What did you say about your tri-year?" he asked.

"My tri-year. This will be my first breeding cycle. I know you don't have—"

"Yes, I know about your cycles. You're the only sentient race to have them, you know. I'm just thinking aloud. What if I follow you to your planet. You can appear with me while we do a goodwill tour. Seeing how successful you are, maybe that will get more of your kind to enlist. I can easily arrange a media train . . ."

He seemed lost in his thoughts, and Leif tried to withhold a grimace. While some would welcome the sept-minister's presence, others would take offense, and that could get ugly.

"Uh . . . sir? There are still people who don't appreciate the Empire and don't approve of wyntonans getting involved with wars—"

The sept-minister waved him off, saying, "I know not all of you are loyal to the emperor. If we can convince some to enlist, great, but I'm thinking of the human audience. We need to show them a wyntonan hero, a hero to the empire. This tour can extend your celebrity."

Leif still didn't think that was a good idea, but there was plenty of time to think of a way out of it.

The door opened, and a nurse came in. He saw the sept-minister and stopped dead, saying, "Sorry sir. I didn't know you were in here. I can come back later."

"No, stay. We can't delay medical treatment for our young hero, now, can we?"

"Really, sir, I can come back."

"No, I think the private first class and I are done. You do what you need to do."

He looked back at Leif and said, "Think about our discussion. I know you have a great future ahead of you."

He shook Leif's hand and said to the nurse, "OK, he's all yours. Take good care of him."

"I will, sir," the nurse said as the sept-minister left the room. "What was that all about, you having a great future?"

"I wish I knew. I really wish I knew."

Chapter 34

"Grazpin, too. Grilled, stewed, and don't forget the dorca flowers," Leif said.

The gathered family—and Soran—laughed together.

"Yes, yes, you've told me a hundred times," his mother said. "I'll make everything on your list."

He had sent her at least a dozen messages over the last month, detailing what he wanted to eat first, but that was a shifting target. Every time he remembered something different, that moved up the schedule to being first, and he had to send that to her.

It was good seeing them together, all gathered for his call. It wasn't as easy as just dialing them up whenever he wanted. There were no cloned comms in Hope Hollow, or anywhere in the Silver Range, for that matter. His family had to schedule a relay from the capital, and Leif had to get a slot at the ISO that matched their schedule. This was his first vidchat for almost two months, and it would probably be the last before he returned.

Soran had joined his family for the call. She hadn't said much, but just the sight of her made him feel . . . different. This was nothing like how musth had been described to him. It wasn't overwhelming, but there was something there, a tingle of *potential*. Not that childhood friends always bonded. They usually didn't in fact. When estrous and musth took over, no one knew what would happen. But with the tingle, he wondered if there might be something there.

I wonder if she feels anything as well?

But that wasn't something he could ask now, and not only because of the family there. What if she said no?

"I miss all of you," he said, and he meant it.

He felt at home in the Corps, and it had been a great experience, but seeing them all there made him homesick.

"One minute, Lance Corporal," the attendant said.

"OK, my time's almost up. Thanks for getting everyone together, and I'll see you for real soon."

There were some hurried goodbyes and well wishes, and just before the call was cut, Soran made a quick mouth circle, the wyntonan equivalent of a human wink, from behind the rest so no one could see.

She does feel something! he thought.

He was feeling good as he left the booth. Another Marine was already moving forward to take her turn.

"Thanks," he told the attendant, who was probably a retired Marine.

"Anytime, Lance Corporal. That's what we're here for."

The Imperial Serviceman's Organization was all volunteer and relied on donations to operate. The emperor was a patron, but most of the money was raised through smaller donations. Leif hadn't even been to the base ISO for the first year-and-a-half of his enlistment until he found out they offered free calls to the Marines and sailors, but now he liked to come and just hang out, to decompress. It was also here that Leif had discovered reading.

Like most Marines—like most people, no matter the race—Leif watched holovids. With thousands being made on a daily basis, is was easy to find something that interested him. The ISO, however, had an unlimited selection of the written word. Simply curious as first, he'd read a novel on his scanscreen, and he found that he enjoyed it. Reading seemed more intimate, and he could invest himself deeper into the tale.

He stepped out of the ISO and stood there for a moment, simply soaking in the morning sun.

"Leif!" a deep, familiar voice called out.

Manu, Hack Portnoy, and a new Marine Leif didn't recognize jogged by in their PT gear, heading to the gym.

"Manu!" Leif returned the call, waving.

Two words, one by the human, and one by him. Neither meant much taken on their own, just their names, merely identification. Back in Hope Hollow, if someone called out his name, he'd ask "What?" expecting a question or statement. Here, with the humans, the mere fact of stating the name *was* the message. It was branding, an affirmation of tribal identity.

I see you and recognize you as one of us.

He watched the three as they jogged on. It was hard to believe that not too long ago, he and Manu were almost sworn enemies. Now, they were bonded brothers of a sort.

I'm going to miss this, he realized as he hopped down the steps of the ISO and started back to the barracks.

The last several months had been good. He felt fine—his new kidney was working better than his old—despite the fact that his buddies had snuck in a beer to his hospital room for the unofficial wetting down for his promotion to lance corporal. His doctor had gone on a rampage when he'd found out, demanding to know who had brought him the forbidden alcohol, threatening charges until the sergeant major himself had come to calm him down.

He appreciated the extra pay—all the more to set him up back on Hope Hollow—but to his surprise, he was more appreciative of the crossed rifles in his collar device. The first time he walked out of the hospital, he felt that every eye was on them. It was hard not to point at his collar every time he passed someone.

Unlike his promotion (and the make-up wetting down at the Golden Goose out in the ville, which was epic) his awards ceremony had been a mixed experience. He felt like a pawn, from being briefed by a public affairs major on what to say to the media, to sitting in an excruciating meeting with the sept-minister and the CG, to standing there at attention during the ceremony with the entire battalion in formation behind him while the emperor, through a live holo, spoke for 21 minutes, expressing many of the same political ideas the sept-minister had revealed to Leif in his hospital bed.

Leif had expected blowback from his fellow Marines at having to be backdrops for what turned into a political dog-and-pony show, but they seemed to revel in the fact that "one of our own" had been awarded a Golden Lion. He sensed no resentment, but rather a feeling of group pride, one more piece of evidence of the tribalism that helped make the Corps what it was.

And in a way, that simply buttressed the emperor's plan. Leif knew that there were still human Marines who did not like the influx of wyntonans into the Corps, even more so the news that qiincers were being recruited next, but the overarching parameter was the Corps itself. Leif and the others may be "fucking ghosts," but they were "our fucking ghosts."

Not perfect, but better than he'd hoped for after enlisting. There had been progress.

He hadn't been in a dress or class B uniform since the award ceremony, so he hadn't worn the medal or ribbon since, but he'd taken it out of his locker a few times and looked at it. He still wondered if he'd earned it, or if it had been part of a grander plan. He'd finally expressed his worries to Lori, who'd turned out to be his closest confident—human or wyntonan alike. She scoffed at his concern, pointing out that no one made up what he'd done. He still wasn't sure, but he appreciated her support.

Getting out of the hospital, getting promoted, and the award ceremony might have been the highlights of the last nine months, but Leif had enjoyed the daily life. The battalion had been issued the new M88-A5, which was a significant improvement over the A4, and the Corps had issued a shitload of ammo for re-orientation. The CO, in her infinite wisdom, had used that as an excuse for a two-week FAMEX, a "familiarization fire exercise," where all the Marines and sailors had a chance to fire most of the weapons in the Marine Corps inventory. Marines loved to make things go boom, so there wasn't a single Marine reporting to sickbay during the exercise. Leif knew that even on their deathbed, a Marine would drag themselves to the range in order to shoot something.

It had been a tight fit, but Leif had even fired the M-66 Patras tank's main gun, which had been a thrill. What impressed him most, however, was firing the M550 Sniper Engagement System, the SES. Firing at 1500 meters, Leif had hit all ten of his targets. The Sniper School gunny even clapped him on the shoulder, telling him he'd done well, and that simple comment filled his heart with pride.

And now, that is all coming to an end, he told himself, not just a little wistfully.

He was ready for the future, though. He hadn't told his family about the sept-minister's offer, but the more he thought about it, the better it sounded. He'd like to take some time back in Hope Hollow first, not just to take care of biology, but he believed in the human's sincerity, and something told him that the emperor was sincere as well. It might be commonly accepted that the young human was a figurehead, but Leif was not so sure, and he had a feeling that there were going to be some surprised humans before the emperor was finished.

If Leif were right, then this would be good for the Empire and good for the People. If he could help achieve that, then his duty was clear.

As he stepped into the barracks, the duty told him the sergeant major wanted to see him.

"Why didn't he call me?"

The duty shrugged, clearly not interested in the ways of sergeants major.

Leif turned around and left the barracks, walking across the quad to the battalion headquarters. Sunday mornings were generally taken off, but it didn't surprise him that Sergeant Major Crawford was working. It seemed that the man never took any time off.

He rapped on the side of the open hatch, and the sergeant major called out "Enter."

"Ah, Lance Corporal Hollow," he said. "Thank you for coming in. Please, take a seat."

Leif sat down in the chair in front of the sergeant major's desk, wondering what was going on.

"I've been meaning to talk to you since your Golden Lion ceremony, but it seems there's always one thing or the other."

Since the ceremony? What's up, he wondered, his internal alert sounding off.

The sergeant major seemed to be considering his words, his hands clasped in an upside-down 'V," the tips against his mouth.

"I don't know if you remember my first talk with you. With all of you wytonans."

Yes, I do. And you called us ghosts.

"I told you that I have nothing against you people, in fact, that I swore my oath to the emperor to protect all imperial citizens, and that included you," he said, pausing again. "I also said my loyalty was to the Corps, and I'd do anything to protect it. I was going to give you wyntonans a chance, but I thought this was a mistake, that having you gh . . . wyntonans would be a distraction, that it would weaken the Corps."

Just say it, Leif thought disappointed, but not really surprised. *Get it over with.*

The human had not mistreated any of them, and Leif had to give him credit for that. But it had been obvious from the get-go that he had never wanted any of them in his battalion.

"I was wrong . . ."

What?

". . . and I'm sorry about that. Of all people, I should have realized what matters, and it isn't race or planet of origin."

There was a story in there somewhere, but Leif was still gobsmacked at the direction this had taken, and he was speechless.

"Yes, there were some teething pains, but you know what? Fuck the others if they can't see straight. Fuck me for even considering it.

"And from what I've observed, you wyntonans are just like anyone else. You've got your fuck-ups like Smith . . ."

Leif almost winced at the mention of Carlton. He hadn't adjusted well and had acted out. Pulled from the company, he'd been assigned to the battalion supply shed for the duration and had not made the cutting score for lance corporal. If he'd been a human, he would probably have been discharged, but politics must have weighed in and he was going to serve until his EOE.

". . . and hard-chargers like you. And, of course, there's Katerina Tell, making the ultimate sacrifice."

That still hurt. Katerina had been the moral compass of the group.

"But that brings me to you. Forget about your Golden Lion . . . I mean, don't forget about it. That came out wrong. But without considering it, you've done well. Staff Sergeant Donovan has nothing but good to say about you."

Really? She's never said anything to me about that.

"And I've watched you. You're a good Marine."

"Thank you, Sergeant Major. I've tried to be."

"Let me ask you this. Have you enjoyed your tour with the battalion?"

Leif had to think for a moment. He didn't enjoy losing Katerina. He didn't enjoy standing firewatch, the crappy food, parades . . . a whole host of things. But overall, taking everything into account?

"Yes, Sergeant Major, I did," he said, and he realized that was the truth.

"Then, for all that is holy, why haven't you reenlisted?"

The shock of the sergeant major apologizing had been enough, but now this question had totally taken him off guard.

"I . . ."

"Look, we know Sept-Minister Iaxi' has taken a special interest in you, and I'm betting he made you an offer for some cushy job somewhere, probably with a big raise—forgetting the fact that almost anything pays more than a Marine lance corporal. But let me ask you this. Are you willing to be a figurehead, a toy wyntonan who can be trotted out when needed to be shown off? I've watched you, Hollow, and I don't think that's you."

He stopped and looked at Leif as if trying to judge his response. The problem was that Leif didn't know how to respond. Oh, he'd briefly considered reenlisting, especially when Jordan had announced that he was. But it was only a brief flirtation. He'd enlisted to prove himself worthy and as payback from being rescued so many years before. He'd accomplished both, and now it was time to move on with the rest of his life.

As far as the sept-minister, he'd not actually accepted anything yet. The sergeant major made a good point, but if being a toy doll that could be used for a cause could benefit the people, then wouldn't that be worth it?

"Look, I'm not asking you to make a decision right now, but I do want you to consider it. Weigh the pros and cons, then make a decision.

"But, considering the big picture, think of this. Only three of you from the battalion are reenlisting. I'm not sure how many of the rest are, but what message does that convey? What does that say about the place of the wyntonans, and all the races, for that matter, in the Marines? And what does that reflect on your position in the Empire itself?

"Look, I'll let you go now, son, but promise me you'll consider it, OK?"

I already did consider it, he thought, but he said, "Yes, I'll consider it."

"That's all I can ask," the sergeant major said, standing up and offering his hand across his desk. Leif shook it, then the human added, "No matter what you decide, it's been an honor serving with you."

As Leif left the CP, he considered the sergeant major's words. If this was a matter of simple numbers, that not enough wyntonans had reenlisted to make some quota, then how did that differ from him being a "toy wyntonan," to use the man's words, for the emperor? If he was going to be a toy, a token, then why not where it would have the most impact?

The call back home should have made for a calm morning, but that was before the sergeant major had interjected himself into Leif's day. Now, stress had reared its ugly head.

Ah, it's probably just my breeding cycle approaching. That's supposed to cause stress sometimes, he told himself, but not exactly convincingly.

Chapter 35

"Another damned pitcher!" Donk yelled out

"Sit, Donk. Don't be an ass," Lori said. "She'll be here."

"Yes, ma'am, Corporal Jankowski, ma'am!" he said, coming to a sloppy position of attention and saluting.

A waterfall of napkins and a spoon flew through the air, hitting him. He flopped back into his seat and drained his glass.

"It's sad to be young and drunk," Lori said. "What about you? You need a refill?"

"Sure do, ma'am, Corporal, ma'am," Leif said, holding out his glass.

"Fuck you, too," she said, filling it from one of the half-empty pitchers.

Lori had only been a corporal for two weeks, and Leif wasn't above teasing her about it. It sure would have been nice to make E4 himself before getting out, though. Jordan, sitting across from him, had made the cutting score, and since he'd already reenlisted, he'd be a corporal in a couple of months. He'd share the honor of being the second wytnonan Marine NCO along with several others from the first class of wyntonan Marines. Ann, no surprise to anyone, had already been meritoriously promoted over in 2/19.

Leif had missed most of the post-deployment hail and farewells due to being in the hospital, but he'd made half-a-dozen since then. This one, however, was different. This was *his* farewell, his and the other wyntonans, along with three of the humans who'd joined Kilo at the same time. The wyntonans had gotten together the weekend before for a private party, but this was the main event, and Leif was feeling a little melancholy. In four days, he had a ticket back home, and in a month or so, he'd be in the midst of his first cycle, so he was excited about that, but this could very well be the last time he'd be together with the group.

He'd see some of them again. Lori had promised to come visit, and some of the the wyntonan Marines had promised to have a reunion after the cycle, but even that would not include all of them. From the original 48 surviving wyntonan Marines, twelve had reenlisted, and all of them had chosen not to return for now, continuing to take the inhibitors that had kept both genders from the older tri-years from entering their cycles. That included Jordan, who insisted that he felt fine, unlike Leif who could almost feel his musth stirring deep inside of him, ready to make its presence known.

"I'm going to miss you," Lori said quietly, and they watched Addison get on her chair and demonstrate her wawa, a new dance that . . . well, it was surprising that her hips joints remained attached through the entire performance.

"I'm going to miss you, too. But we'll see each other when you come visit."

Of all the humans, he knew he was going to miss her the most, and while he wouldn't admit it to any of the wyntonans, except for Jordan—and maybe even including him—he'd miss her more than any of them. If someone had told him he would ever care for a human more than any of the People, he would have laughed, but he couldn't deny the facts.

She leaned up against him, her head on his shoulder for a long moment before squeezing his biceps and sitting back up. Their relationship had not gone unnoticed, and there had been rumors of something a little more intimate between them, but Leif didn't care. The councilman's warning about horny humans waiting to pounce on wyntonans turned out to be more rumor than fact, but there was still curiosity about inter-racial liaisons, and if some humans thought the two were having an affair, that gave both of them cover.

The tokit waitress walked up, balancing five pitchers on her tray. She placed them on the table, then said, "This rounds on us," pointing back to where three more tokits in their whites had stuck their heads out the door of the kitchen and waved at them.

Everyone protested, even Donk, but she insisted. This wasn't the first time this had happened. The battalion had attracted quite a following among the tokits, and their gratitude had yet to diminish.

"It's OK, we'll just add it to the tip," Sergeant Juniper said, after the waitress left.

Their almost fawning adulation was embarrassing, but it still made Leif feel appreciated. They didn't make enough, though, to be subsidizing the Marine's night out on the town, so he agreed with the sergeant's tip solution.

The first sergeant stood up, tapping his spoon against the glass to quiet everyone down, and after he got a slight reduction in the noise, said, "Let's do this before you're all too drunk to care."

Hoots greeted him. This was only one of four hail and farewells for the first sergeant tonight. He had to make the rounds of each platoon. Second Platoon was upstairs, but the others had their own bars staked out.

"We are gathered here for an honored tradition, that of welcoming new blood into the platoon, and kicking out the old bastards before they fuck up even more."

Glasses were raised and a few ooh-rahs sounded amongst the laughter.

"We've got, what, three new joins, Staff Sergeant Donovan?" When she nodded, he said, "Corporal Winston Lek-Pottis, stand up. Corporal Lek-Pottis is coming to us from One-Nine."

The new corporal, who seemed like a good enough guy, stood up and waved.

"Then we've got two brand-new recruits, direct out of SOI, Privates Deshandra Oliphant and Writ Supanata . . . uh . . . . *tatatwana*," he said, royally screwing up Suphantarida's name to everyone's delight. "You two, welcome to the asylum.

"But the main reason we are here is to share a moment of camaraderie to those who are leaving us. This will be the last chance to give them a ration of shit. Hell, next time you see them, one of these hard-chargers will have gone over to the dark side and come back a lieutenant, so you better take your shots now!

"So, will you three reprobates come here and join me?"

Leif, Jordan, and Sergeant Juniper made their way to stand beside the first sergeant while the catcalls already started. The first sergeant started with Juniper, giving her the company plaque, then said a few words, surprisingly tame words at that. Sergeant Holmes was not nearly so kind, he detailed an extremely embarrassing story concerning Juniper and a certain young man she'd smuggled into the barracks and had to play a game of hide the boy when someone had turned her in. Holmes was a masterful story-teller, and Leif was laughing so hard his sides hurt.

This had to be a "this is a no shitter" story perhaps based in fact, but highly exaggerated. If only half of what he'd said had actually gone down, Juniper would never have made sergeant. She accepted the company parting gift, an inflatable sex doll, with good grace, remarking that at least that one could be deflated and hidden in a drawer.

Jordan was up next, and the story about him, told by Corporal Lin, was not as funny, something to do with him getting drunk on the liberty call that Leif had missed after the slaver mission. Leif never had gotten the full story on that, and Corporal Lin's version didn't shed any light on it. He was given a stein that had been fitted with a baby nipple over the top, something that made those who had been there erupt into laughter and repeatedly call out, "The orange one!" Leif made a note to trap Jordan later and beat an explanation out of him if he had to.

Leif was handed his plaque, and he waited to see what else was going to be said. He wasn't surprised when Lori stood up. Her Leif story was of a different tone. She spoke with a light-hearted voice, but she gave a somewhat accurate account of the fight aboard the slaver. Several of the tokit staff stopped work to listen, and the laughter died down as everyone, especially the new joins since then, listened in silence.

Leif was embarrassed. When she was done, he didn't have a snappy comeback. She handed him his going away gift, and he opened it, to see a child's toy, a comical version of a small yellow lion. Attached to its pink bow was a note that said, "My Hero."

Leif held it up, and the gathered Marines laughed, but not the raucous laugh of before.

Donk came to his rescue, though, shouting out, "If we're done with the mushy shit, then more beer!"

The wait staff laughed and scurried to refill the pitchers, and Leif gratefully took his seat.

"That wasn't a funny story," he told Lori.

She just smiled and said, "But it was the story I wanted to tell."

She grabbed the toy lion out of his hand and gave it a kiss.

The first sergeant left, and the drinks continued to flow. At one point, a group of India Marines, including Manu, came in from another bar, and there was a mutual buying of drinks. Leif was trying to pace himself, but with all the drinks, all the toasts, things were getting a little fuzzy around the edges. He remembered posing for holos with the entire pub staff, then with each of the tokits separately. The owner, a human, also half into his cups, swore he'd put the holo with the entire staff up on the wall, joining those of colonels, sergeants major, and two generals.

That was pretty heady for a simple lance corporal.

He also remembered leaving with Lori, Jordan, and Sergeant Holmes, ready to go to a little hole-in-the-wall that the sergeant knew, but somehow, just Lori and he ended up at the local high school pitchball field, lying together in the middle, and watching the sun rise.

They sat silently as the darkness started to edge to a pastel pink on the horizon, Leif's arm around Lori, her snuggling up against him and holding his stuffed lion on his chest. He didn't know where his plaque was—hopefully back at the pub so he could pick it up later.

And he was content.

They lay together, the sky getting lighter and lighter. Birds started to wake up and great the sun with their songs.

"I love you, Leif," Lori said, breaking the silence.

And he knew exactly what she meant. She loved him not as a potential mate, not as a romance, not simply as a fellow Marine. She, Lauren Mary Jankowski, loved Leffen a'Hope Hollow, a fellow sentient being, not for what he could offer her, but simply for who he was.

"I love you, too, Lori."

And he did. He loved his family, he loved Soran—well, with her, that was probably a little different. The idea of mating with her put that on another level. He loved Jordan and the rest, and he loved his People. But he also loved Lori, a human, just because of who she was as a *person*.

And that was a revelation. Leif always thought of himself as self-focused, always wanting to prove himself, not worrying about what others thought of him. Even the plan to serve the empire was out of a sense of duty, and that to prove himself a worthy being, he *had* to embrace that duty. To do anything less would be to diminish who he was.

That realization, maybe fueled by still being drunk, made him feel good. He wasn't concerned with success alone. If he could lay here on a sports field with a human woman, loving her for no reason that advanced his cause but simply because she was a good person, well, he rather liked that image of him. Maybe there was more to him than he'd thought.

The sun made its appearance, climbing higher into the sky until finally, Lori sat up and said, "I've really enjoyed tonight, Leif, but I've got the duty at zero-eight-hundred, so, I think I've got to get back."

"Oh, sucks to be you."

"No problem. I'll take a Sober-up, jump into the shower, and be as good as new."

The two walked back to the main gate, then took the shuttle to the battalion area. Lori made him promise to see her for lunch, then left to go back to her room.

Manu and four other Marines stumbled in, gave him a wave, then retreated to the India Company wing.

"Rough night?" Lance Corporal George, from Lima Company, asked from where he was leaning on the duty station.

"No, not really. It was good."

"Well, you've got grass on your ass."

Leif bent around, and yes, it was true. He gave a laugh and walked up to his room. Jordan was in the rack, already asleep, but Leif wasn't tired. His mind was working on something, but he didn't quite know what it was. He walked over to the window and stood there, looking out over the quad. A lone figure in uniform walked toward the CP. Leif smiled, watching the sergeant major. Leave it to him to work on a Sunday morning.

And then Leif knew what was bothering him.

He took off his civvies and jumped into the shower, letting the hot jets shock his mind clear. He could take a Sober-up like Lori, but he was afraid of that. He didn't want to change the way he was thinking.

He pulled a set of utilities out of his locker and got dressed, giving himself a quick look-over in the mirror-screen.

Good enough.

Lori, looking clean and sharp, saw him as he hurried down the passage, and yelled out, "I thought you'd be crashed out by now. Where're you going?"

He waved her off and started across the quad, wondering what he was doing. One of the new privates was on duty in the CP, and Leif simply said, "I'm going to see the sergeant major," as he almost ran past.

He stopped at the sergeant major's office, took a couple of deep breaths, and knocked on the edge of the hatch.

"Enter," the sergeant major said.

Leif stepped inside. The sergeant major was standing up by a small table against the far bulkhead, a coffee cup in his hand.

"Lance Corporal Hollow, this is a surprise. I didn't expect to see any of you up and about so early after all the partying last night. To what do I owe this honor?"

"I've got a question, Sergeant Major."

"Shoot."

"It's about leave. Lance Corporal Hottento, he's not going on leave, but could he?"

"Could he? Sure. He's got 30 days, just like anyone else."

"Even if he reenlisted?"

"*Because* he reenlisted. He's between units, so getting the leave approved would be routine. But I understand he didn't want leave. Has that changed?" he asked, then added, "But why isn't he asking me that instead of you?"

"You know, Sergeant Major, that I haven't taken any inhibitors for the last six months."

"Inhibitors?"

"Yes, you know, to block our breeding cycle."

"No, I didn't specifically know that. But sure, it makes sense. You told me before your time was coming up."

"Do you know that we never know for sure when our tri-year females will enter estrous, so we don't know when the males will enter musth. It could be a month after Spice Day; it could be two months."

"Um, OK. But why are you telling me this?" he asked, coming over to his desk and sitting down. "From what I understand, Lance Corporal Hottento is still taking his inhibitors."

"This is biology, Sergeant Major, not something we can control."

"Yes, Lance Corporal, I do understand biology," he said, sounding a little annoyed. "Look, I don't know what you're getting at. If Lance Corporal Hottento has a problem, I'd suggest he come to talk to me about it personally, not sending you."

"Like I said, Sergeant Major, I've stopped taking the inhibitors, and they take months to start taking effect, so I don't know if 30 days leave is enough. I might need more time."

"Leave? You're being discharged as of zero-eight-hundred Wednesday morning. You've got all the time in the world. You won't be on leave."

"And that discharge is official?"

"It will be as soon as you sign them on Wednesday."

Leif closed his eyes and took a deep breath.

"That's the thing. I want to reenlist, if you'll have me. But, I can't fight biology now. I've got to go back home."

The sergeant major went still, then he said, "I think we can work something out. TAD for some reason. Yes, we can accommodate you. It's biology, as you say."

A wave of relief washed over him.

The sergeant major stood up and came from around the desk to shake his hand.

241

"Good choice, Leif, good choice. I'm very pleased."

His grip almost crushed Leif's, but he didn't care. A huge weight had been lifted off his shoulders, a weight he hadn't realized wasn't there.

"Go get some chow. I'm going to get Top Morrison to figure out how we can work this and then draw up the orders for the CO's signature. Can you get back here, say, at 1400 to sign them?"

"No problem. I'll be here."

Leif thanked the sergeant major, then turned to leave. He had a few people—human and wyntonan, that he had to tell.

As he was leaving, the the sergeant major's voice reached him, "Hey Top, it's John. Can you come in today? We've got to figure out how to cut some orders so a Marine can go home to get laid."

Thank you for reading *Integration*. I hope you enjoyed this book, and I welcome a review on Amazon, Goodreads, or any other outlet.

If you would like updates on new books releases, news, or special offers, please consider signing up for my mailing list. Your email will not be sold, rented, or in any other way disseminated. If you are interested, please sign up at the link below:

http://eepurl.com/bnFSHH

Two books were extremely helpful for me in my research for *Integration*:

The Marines of Montford Point: America's First Black Marines, by Melton A. McLaurin

White Man's Tears Conquer My Pains: My WWII Service Story, by Henry Badgett

Other Books by Jonathan Brazee

Ghost Marines
Integration
Unification
Fusion

The Navy of Humankind: Wasp Squadron
Fire Ant
Crystals
Ace

The United Federation Marine Corps
Recruit
Sergeant

Lieutenant
Captain
Major
Lieutenant Colonel
Colonel
Commandant

Rebel
(Set in the UFMC universe.)

Behind Enemy Lines
(A UFMC Prequel)

The Accidental War (A Ryck Lysander Short Story
Published in BOB's Bar: Tales from the Multiverse)

The United Federation Marine Corps' Lysander Twins
Legacy Marines
Esther's Story: Recon Marine
Noah's Story: Marine Tanker
Esther's Story: Special Duty
Blood United

Coda

Women of the United Federation Marine Corps
Gladiator
Sniper
Corpsman

High Value Target (A Gracie Medicine Crow Short Story)
BOLO Mission (A Gracie Medicine Crow Short Story)

Weaponized Math (A Gracie Medicine Crow Novelette, Published in The Expanding Universe 3. Nebula Award Finalist)

The United Federation Marine Corps' Grub Wars
Alliance
The Price of Honor
Division of Power

The Return of the Marines Trilogy
The Few
The Proud
The Marines

The Al Anbar Chronicles: First Marine Expeditionary Force--Iraq
Prisoner of Fallujah
Combat Corpsman
Sniper

Werewolf of Marines
Werewolf of Marines: Semper Lycanus
Werewolf of Marines: Patria Lycanus
Werewolf of Marines: Pax Lycanus

Soldier

Animal Soldier: Hannibal

To the Shores of Tripoli

Wererat

Darwin's Quest: The Search for the Ultimate Survivor

Venus: A Paleolithic Short Story

Secession

Duty

Semper Fidelis

Checkmate (Published in The Expanding Universe 4)

Seeds of War (With Lawrence Schoen)
Invasion
Scorched Earth
Bitter Harvest

Non-Fiction

Exercise for a Longer Life

The Effects of Environmental Activism on the Yellowfin
Tuna Industry

Author Website

http://www.jonathanbrazee.com

Twitter

https://twitter.com/jonathanbrazee

Made in the USA
Coppell, TX
19 February 2022

73781957R00138